HIS HIGHLAND HEART

HIS HIGHLAND HEART SERIES BOOK 1

WILLA BLAIR

OLIVER HEBER BOOKS

"This story is action-packed and full of twists and turns that will keep readers on their toes. It is fast-paced and has a sweet romance that will warm your heart. Well written and full of imagination, this story is a must read for historical romance fans!"

— THE ROMANCE REVIEWS

"...a rich, enjoyable read."

— SATIN SHEETS ROMANCE

THE HEALER'S GIFT

"A Highland romance with a truly great hero...the story is compelling..."

— IND'TALE MAGAZINE

"A story of mystery, regret, hope, danger and trust... The characters are endearing, the story is fulfilling, and the set up for the remainder of the series presents an open invitation to dive right in. THE HEALER'S GIFT is a highly recommended read."

— FRESH FICTION

HIGHLAND SEER

"...this is different enough from other Highland romances to stand out from the pack. Ms. Blair's writing style is natural and evocative..."

— ROMANTIC HISTORICAL REVIEWS

"16th-century intrigue, muscled men with claymores and a doomed romance — is it any wonder I was reluctant to leave the rich, riveting world of HIGHLAND SEER?"

— USATODAY HEA

WHEN HIGHLAND LIGHTNING STRIKES

"Ms. Blair is a consummate storyteller...Can't wait for more from this magical author."

— MY BOOK ADDICTION AND MORE

"Ms. Blair has an easy to read talent for bringing a story to life."

— LONG AND SHORT REVIEWS

HIGHLAND TROTH

"Scottish romance at its best!"

— IND'TALE MAGAZINE

"...an exciting, romantic, historical tale full of angst, action and searing hot passion...With plenty of adventure and the twist of an old murder, HIGHLAND TROTH by Willa Blair, kept me hooked from beginning to end. A wonderful Highland romance."

— FRESH FICTION

HIS HIGHLAND HEART SERIES
HIS HIGHLAND ROSE

HIS HIGHLAND BRIDE

"Ms. Blair has delivered a wonderful and captivating read in this book where the chemistry between this couple was strong; the romance hot..."

— BOOK MAGIC, UNDER A SPELL WITH EVERY PAGE

"This is a very enjoyable and well-written book to satisfy any historical romance lover, especially one who enjoys forbidden love!"

— IND'TALEMAGAZINE

CONTEMPORARY ROMANCE
WAITING FOR THE LAIRD

"Willa Blair spins a beautiful romance set in the Scottish Highlands full of suspense, history and mystery... I highly suggests you pick it up and enjoy."

— NIGHT OWL ROMANCE

"About 3:00 am I finally had to force myself to stop... yes, it was that good. Give yourself a treat and grab this book..."

— THE READING CAFE

"A contemporary romantic tale with a touch of history—and ghosts...Waiting for the Laird by Willa Blair is a delightful romance and unexpected adventure set in Scotland."

— BOOKS AND BENCHES

WHEN YOU FIND LOVE

"When You Find Love is a beautiful romance filled with combative personalities, a family curse and a love that can't be quenched. Character-driven plot with supernatural undertones make this a must-read. The ending was so fantastic, I didn't want it to end. If you love fantasy romance, you'll be smitten with When You Find Love."

— N.N. LIGHT'S BOOK HEAVEN

SWEETIE PIE

"Willa Blair is known for her Scottish historical paranormal romance. She' changes genres with a modern Scottish lass who escapes to the Big Island of Hawaii. SWEETIE PIE is a delicious pupu - Hawaiian word for appetizer. Blair delivers a sweet novella that captures the Aloha spirit of the island."

— K. LOWE

A man knelt beside her, pounding on her back and muttering, "Spit it out, lass. Breathe. Ye are well." She thought she'd met all of her captors, but she didn't recognize his voice. She didn't want to owe any of the Ross men her life. That would seal her fate to his. Donas would give her to this man.

Grit clung to her face as she pushed up onto her hands and knees, still coughing up seawater. Her hair hung in damp tendrils to the sand, blocking her view of her savior, and his of her. At least he had ceased pounding on her when she'd moved. Her coughing eased.

Her wet cloak clung to her back and draped down her sides like a tent, but her shift, now soaked, was nearly transparent where it stuck to her skin. She sank onto her heels, gathered her sopping cloak around her for cover, if not for warmth, then scooped her hair out of her face and took her first clear breath.

The man sat back and regarded her with sea green eyes under russet brows. A stranger!

Muireall's gasp set her to coughing again, but she held up a hand to stop him when he reached for her back. "Nay!" she hissed, then got her breath back. "Give me a minute afore ye pound me back into the sand." She thought she'd seen every man in the Ross village. She hadn't seen this one. She would have noticed him. Even features, broad shoulders, and kindness in the glinting green depths of his eyes. He looked at her with care, not as if he wanted to rend her sopping garments and take her here on the beach.

A grin split his face, revealing even white teeth. "Arguing with yer leech so soon after he saves ye? Ye are well, then."

The man was possessed of a sense of humor, too.

She glanced around while she heaved another

breath. *Ach, nay!* She was still trapped in the far cove with a rising tide. And a stranger. "Who are ye?"

The grin fled his face.

In that instant, she knew. "Ye are from that wrecked *birlinn*, aye?"

He nodded.

Hope slowly unfurled in her chest. He was not a Ross! When she next opened her mouth to speak, he clapped a hand over it and grabbed her around the shoulders with the other.

"Dinna scream," he warned.

To Beverly Wymer, You're the best cheering section any author could hope for. I'm so glad you're mine!

CHAPTER 1

Scottish Highlands, 1410

Euan Brodie hauled on the sail and fought the wind as if his life depended on it. His did—his and his crew's.

They were nearing home. Though the Moray Firth was in a fine temper, he thought they could make port before nightfall. Then the wind shifted and began to howl, driving them northward, away from safe harbor. By staying out so late, they'd made a mistake—perhaps a fatal one. The fishing had been good, and they'd hoped to bring the joy of full bellies to their families. In this storm, they'd be the most fortunate of men to get home at all.

Wind whipped the sail, and rough rigging tore through his hands, stripping flesh he could not feel. Icy water sprayed over the *Tangie*'s bow as she fought her way into a swell toward the nearer shore.

"We're no' going to make it!" Eduard shouted, frustration pitching his voice high and ragged.

Euan grimaced as the others gaped, wide-eyed, at the normally steady first mate.

"Aye, we are," he insisted, commanding their attention and forcing confidence into his tone despite having to shout into a howling storm. They had to make it. *Had to.* "Haul that sheet tight and hang on. We'll soon reach the shore break. The tide will do the rest for us, and we'll take down the bloody sail."

Suddenly, lightning cracked, deafening Euan even over the tumult of the storm. He turned his head away as the freshening squall blew icy pellets into his face. *Almost there.* If they could hang on a few more minutes, they'd beach the *Tangie* and be safe until the storm blew itself out.

The wind shifted suddenly, from south to east. Too fast to save her, the *Tangie* heeled over, dipping the edge of the sail into the firth. It was more than she could take. For a moment, she lifted and hung, trying to roll herself upright, icy seawater dripping from the canvas. Euan shouted for the men to throw their weight to the high side, hoping to right her, but it was too little, too late. The wind gusted again, and the *Tangie* settled onto her low side, her pale sail a phantom carpet on the surface of the choppy sea.

Euan dangled for a moment from the rope in his hands, hearing the others cry out as the tide took the ship and pushed them shoreward. They should reach the shallows soon, he realized.

"Swim away!" he shouted and let go of the rope, sliding down the deck and into the icy water. He came up spluttering between the deck and the sail, the canvas now slowing sinking as rough seas sloshed over its surface. It would pull the *Tangie* down, and suck the men with it if they didna get clear. The others still hung from the upper side, frozen with indecision. "Dinna get caught under the sail!"

He swam for clear water. Once he was out of danger from his vessel, he searched the surface for his men. "Eduard! Dugal! Calum! Can ye hear me? James, where are ye, lad? Swim, ye fools!" A barrel floated nearby. He forced his numb fingers around the ends and hung on, the icy water making his body feel leaden. It seemed like hours while he searched the roiling surface and waited for an answering shout, but he knew it was only minutes. The crashing surf and cracks of splintering wood were all he heard as waves shoved the *Tangie* onto rocks. The men, and young James, barely twelve winters old, were gone.

With a heavy heart, he let go of the barrel and fought his way toward shore. He could let the waves push the barrel, and him with it, but if he lost consciousness from the cold, he'd sink below the surface and never be seen again. *Better to swim.* Though his mind was muzzy, he could recall an old sailor telling him the effort would warm him and might save his life. Waves crashed all around him, threatening to pull him under and keep him there. He gasped for air every time his head broke the surface, concentrated on moving arms and legs leaden with cold, and kept going. Eventually, something hard scraped his knees and he shook his head to clear his eyes of saltwater. The rocky beach beckoned, mere yards ahead. Somehow, he got his feet under him, but couldn't stay on them in the pounding waves, so he let the surf push him shoreward and fought against the undertow threatening to tug him away. In moments the waves propelled him onto a gritty beach. He dug in his elbows and crawled out of the water.

He lay there, panting, gripping pebbles and coarse sand in both hands, then gathered the last vestiges of strength in his frozen body and hauled himself to his feet. Shuddering, he swore through chattering teeth, too tense with cold to summon the howl of rage and despair he wanted to unleash. The *Tangie's* sailing days were done. She was gone, sunk below the angry sea—a loss Brodie could scarce afford. He'd wrecked the first ship he'd been allowed to captain, and likely killed the crew. One more thing gone wrong in his life, the latest —and worst—in a long list.

He should have gone down with them.

Rolling waves and sheets of wind-driven rain confounded him, but he refused to accept that his men and young James were gone as well. He called, again and again until his throat was raw. Nothing answered but the shrieking wind and the crash of waves. He was alone, half-drowned, in enemy territory.

MUIREALL MUNRO CAME AWAKE TO THE SOUND OF MEN shouting. She rubbed sleep from her eyes and rolled from her cot with a yawn. Disappointment nearly sent her back again. These were excited shouts, not battle cries, so this was not the rescue she prayed for.

She recognized the voices of some of the men from the Ross village. Donas, the chief, for one, and Teague, who had forced her fellow captive, Tira into marriage on the trip back to Ross from Munro.

Curious, Muireall threw her cloak around her shoulders and stepped outside the small cot she once shared with the other Munro captive, her friend Ella, but now had to herself. The pale pearl glow of early morning did not yet reveal the men, but she could hear them coming up the path from the cove.

Muireall joined the other women already gathered nearby as the chief's wife, Silas, spoke.

"I've nay idea," Silas was saying as her husband crested the hill with Teague, both soaked through. Between them, they carried hewn lumber.

"Shipwreck!" Donas announced, grinning. "We dragged as much as we could get to onshore. The incoming tide will carry more onto the beach during the day."

Thomas, who had recently taken Ella as his wife, arrived on their heels with others carrying loops of rope. "There's plenty more o' this, too heavy to carry. We'll leave it below to dry out for a day or two. Sailcloth, as well."

"And the sailors?" That from sweet Ella, answered quickly with hoots and laughter.

"Looking for a new man, are ye?" Silas asked with a grin. "Have ye worn out *puir* Thomas already?"

"Nay, but…" Ella blushed and dropped her gaze to her feet.

Muireall cringed, embarrassed for her friend by the coarse comments directed at her.

"Nay men," Thomas spat with a frown at his pretty new wife. "Must be dead."

Muireall hid a shudder. Had she been cursed with the kind of beauty Ella possessed, she might be the unlucky one under Thomas every night. As it was, no Ross had chosen her—yet. They awaited her next moonblood, to prove she carried no other man's babe before one of them got about putting theirs in her. If she'd counted correctly, she didn't have much longer to wait before she bled again. Then she'd be doomed.

"Bodies'll wash ashore in a day or two," Donas interjected, "and we'll see if they've got anything of value on them."

Muireall gave a grim nod to that pronouncement. Aye, they would. She'd heard these men boast around the evening fires about what they'd done when unpredictable winter storms pushed an unwary ship their way. There might be coin, or leather goods, even weapons worth the salvage, along with the ship itself, or what was left of it, not lying on the bottom of the sea.

"Come on, lasses, let's see what the lads missed," Silas ordered. Wed to their chief, her word was as much law as his. The women would look for food, crates of fish, metal implements—anything useful in the village, while the men focused on the ship, weapons, and dealing with survivors. Allies got escorted to the village. Enemies went back into the sea, throats cut for being foolish enough to live through a shipwreck onto Donas Ross's land.

Muireall's neck prickled at the thought of desperate strangers on the beach below, but Thomas had said there were none, so the women would be safe enough heading down to the cove.

Silas frowned at her and gestured, clearly giving her no time to dress. Obedient, she gathered her cloak about her and followed the other women down the cliff path. Now the roar of last night's storm was over, waves lapped at the shore. The men had not exaggerated. They'd reap a good, if grim, harvest from this wreck. From what she could see, there might be enough left of the *birlinn* to rebuild it without too much work. The men aboard her must have drowned, sucked below the waves in the darkness.

This morning, the sun pierced between remnants of leaden clouds. Shafts of brilliance danced on the crests of bigger waves out in the firth. The sea had yet to settle, so Donas could be right and more from this doomed ship might wash ashore over the next day or two.

Muireall headed downwind, in the direction the tide should have carried more of the wreck. Ella quickly joined her and the two walked the shoreline, happy to get away from the other women. They searched for small items in the cove and splashed along the water's edge, hoping to find something of value that would win Silas's and Donas's favor. Muireall expected the sea had carried the smaller, lighter things farther down the coast. The women she and Ella left behind might find little of use staying close to the wreck.

"They willna worry about us?" Ella fretted, looking back over her shoulder.

Muireall snorted. "Of course no'. There's nowhere to go from here." She pointed. Cliffs lining the next cove extended into deep water on the far side, blocking access to the northward coastline from the beach.

"I see Tira is sticking close to Silas."

Ella's frown was an expression Muireall had seen her wear all too often since they'd been taken, and more so since Thomas had claimed her.

"She's making the best of a bad situation, I suppose," Ella continued, charitably, which was more like the Ella Muireall knew.

"Teague aspires to Donas's inner circle," Muireall reminded her. "Tira must think gaining Silas's favor will help."

"It might, aye."

"And what about Thomas?"

"He seems more interested in enjoying his new bride than currying favor with Donas."

Ella's bleak tone made Muireall glance sharply her way. Her lips were pressed together and her fists clenched. Muireall took her friend's fist in her hand and tucked her fingers under Ella's. "I wish there was something we could do to get away from here."

"There is naught to do but learn to live the life we've been given," Ella replied. "At least for Tira and me. There's still hope for ye."

Muireall shook her head and kept walking, trying to put the Rosses out of her mind. She knew several of the men had their eye on her. She just didn't know which one Donas would award her to.

"Hope? The only hope I have is to die before one of them can claim me."

Ella stopped walking and tugged Muireall's hand. "*Ach*, Muireall, dinna say that. Dinna even think it. 'Tis no' so bad, truly. Thomas is kind enough…at least when he's no' around the other men. I just miss my family."

Muireall heard the lie in Ella's voice. She missed more than her family. She missed the life they'd had, and the prospect of marrying the man she loved, a future now lost to her. He'd think her dead, and if he ever found out what had happened to her, he'd wish it so.

"And ye ken I worry for Georgie," Muireall told her. "'Twas a selfish thing for me to say. I do so want to get back to him…" She let go of Ella's hand and turned away.

"Ye have tried. And suffered for it. Twice." Ella put a hand on her arm, stopping her. "Ye must give up trying to escape. Georgie is being cared for, I dinna doubt it."

Muireall thought of the nearly healed stripes on her back and stiffened her spine. "Nay, I'll never give up." The first time she'd snuck away, she'd been confined to the cot without food and little water for three days, a guard posted at the door. The second time, she'd run and been caught before she got out of sight of the Ross village. For that, Donas had given her three lashes, while stripped to her shift. It could have been worse—he'd threatened to strip her of the meager protection the shift provided, but Silas had intervened, so he'd told her the next time she would suffer more lashes. But she'd learned her lesson. The next time she ran, she'd be better prepared. Until then, she did everything she could to appear meek and cowed, unlikely to defy the Ross chief ever again.

She glanced back at the women blocking the climb to the village—and to the next cove behind them. That way lay home, just not today. "I canna escape from here this day, so let's make the best of our walk so we can get back to a warm fire."

Before long, she found a cook pot tumbling in the surf, and both she and Ella got soaked to the thighs retrieving it. They dragged it above the high tide line and set it in a depression in the sand to collect on the way back. If they were lucky, none of the others would have looked up from the beach at their feet to see them retrieve it. She hoped they would not notice it in the sand if they came this far, and claim the find for their own.

They moved back to the waterline. Then Ella went after something higher on the beach. Muireall, eager for solitude after their conversation, walked on, gaze darting from sand to surf and back again while memories of her life at Munro plagued her and filled her eyes with tears.

She was around the curve of the cove and well into the next beach before she realized how far she'd come. The cove was shallow, with a narrow strip of sand and rocks tumbled against the cliffs as if pushed there by the relentless tides. A glance behind her proved she was out of sight of the rest of the women. She kept going, enjoying the illusion of freedom the unexpected solitude gave her. When she saw a length of rope tossing in the surf, she waded out until the water was up to her hips, grabbed what she could reach and pulled it onto the sand. The men always wanted more rope.

By the time she noticed the tide encroaching on the footsteps she'd left in the scattered patches of sand, she'd collected an empty crate and a net bag. The canvas-wrapped package containing mushy, waterlogged bread she abandoned to the sea birds.

Suddenly, a memory of a tale told around the fire one evening chilled her. In the tale, this cove flooded to its walls. She looked back the way she'd come. The sliver of beach bordering the cliff dividing the coves was no wider than her foot, and shrinking fast. She was in danger of being cut off by the rising tide, and until the tide fell again, there was no exit from this cove save the one she'd just traversed.

She ran.

&

EUAN WATCHED THE LONE WOMAN WALK THE BEACH, searching, no doubt, for anything useful from the remains of the *Tangie*. Early on, when he'd heard the men approaching as the early morning gloaming lit the storm clouds, he'd retreated around a projecting bluff to the next cove. The cove where the *Tangie* foundered boasted sand, gravel and water-rounded pebbles all the way to the cliff face, with nowhere to hide. Tumbled rocks that gave him good cover lined this one. If he was not mistaken, its steep cliffs also boasted a sea cave or two he had yet to try to explore. *If* he could make the climb to them with his injured hands. One could serve as shelter for a few days, especially if it hid a spring or trapped rainwater. He'd be able to stay alive and undetected long enough to determine the fate of each of his men. Hope made him linger. He would delay as long as he could and risk capture rather than leave too soon and abandon them. Should any remain alive, once he found them, he'd steal a skiff or find another way for him and any survivors to make their way home. With luck on his side, they'd soon be back with families and friends.

The lass didn't look threatening, wrapped in a woolen cloak. Pretty enough, aye, but sad. Perhaps with her mind on the fate of the men on the wreck, having a heart good enough to mourn the loss of sailors she didn't even know. Or perhaps she was just wet and cold.

Don't be daft, he chided himself. This is Ross territory. Let the lass know a Brodie observed her and she'd start screaming out her lungs before he could reach her. Instead, he watched her slowly make her way across the cove, her attention on the waterline. Her cheeks were ruddy from the cold, her lips in contrast, pale. He could not see the color of her eyes, but they were framed by delicate brows that furrowed and slanted as she searched, signaling her excitement as she spotted something in the surf, then disappointment if she rejected it. The storm had tossed up plenty of sea grass and other odds and ends, little of use. Her cloak gaped as she squatted to go through a pile of detritus, and Euan realized she wore only her shift. The thin fabric, transparent from shapely thighs to hem from the wet, clung to her legs. Her feet bare, she'd been dragged from slumber to assist in the search, with no time to properly dress. What sort of laird led these Rosses?

Then she looked behind her, jumped to her feet, and started to run back the way she'd come. Her sopping garments tangled between her knees and slowed her down until she grasped handfuls of cloth and freed her legs.

The day revealed what the night had hidden from him. Waves crashed against rocks where she had crossed into the cove. The tide blocked her escape around the cliffs to the cove holding the *Tangie*'s remains. She was trapped.

And so was he.

Worried now, he searched for the high tide line and found it on the cliff wall, several feet above his head. Damn. And worse, the lass was attempting the surf, trying to make her way back to her kin. In the rushing seawater, her cloak and skirts tangled around her legs and brought her splashing down. She got to her knees, but not for long. A wave dragged her under the surface before she had a chance to scream for help.

With an oath, Euan broke cover and ran for the lass.

$\mathcal{M}$uireall awoke on her side, coughing and sputtering, gasping for air between blows to her back. All she could see was the surf a few yards in front of her. Dear God, she'd been dragged under. The last thing she remembered, besides the sting of seawater in her nose and throat, was the certainty she was going to drown and thinking it might be a better fate than the one that awaited her at the hands of the Rosses. But someone had pulled her out. She'd made it around the cliffs! She shuddered as she dragged in another ragged breath, not just from the cold and wet. She'd never before truly understood how good air felt in her lungs.

But she feared she would regret being saved.

A man knelt beside her, pounding on her back and muttering, "Spit it out, lass. Breathe. Ye are well." She thought she'd met all of her captors, but she didn't recognize his voice. She didn't want to owe any of the Ross men her life. That would seal her fate to his. Donas would give her to this man.

Grit clung to her face as she pushed up onto her hands and knees, still coughing up seawater. Her hair hung in damp tendrils to the sand, blocking her view of her savior, and his of her. At least he had ceased pounding on her when she'd moved. Her coughing eased.

Her wet cloak clung to her back and draped down her sides like a tent, but her shift, now soaked, was nearly transparent where it stuck to her skin. She sank onto her heels, gathered her sopping cloak around her for cover, if not for warmth, then scooped her hair out of her face and took her first clear breath.

The man sat back and regarded her with sea green eyes under russet brows. A stranger!

Muireall's gasp set her to coughing again, but she held up a hand to stop him when he reached for her back. "Nay!" she hissed, then got her breath back. "Give me a minute afore ye pound me back into the sand." She thought she'd seen every man in the Ross village. She hadn't seen this one. She would have noticed him. Even features, broad shoulders, and kindness in the glinting green depths of his eyes. He looked at her with care, not as if he wanted to rend her sopping garments and take her here on the beach.

A grin split his face, revealing even white teeth. "Arguing with yer leech so soon after he saves ye? Ye are well, then."

The man was possessed of a sense of humor, too.

She glanced around while she heaved another breath. *Ach, nay!* She was still trapped in the far cove with a rising tide. And a stranger. "Who are ye?"

The grin fled his face.

In that instant, she knew. "Ye are from that wrecked *birlinn*, aye?"

He nodded.

Hope slowly unfurled in her chest. He was not a Ross! When she next opened her mouth to speak, he clapped a hand over it and grabbed her around the shoulders with the other.

"Dinna scream," he warned. "I willna hurt ye. I just saved ye, for the love of God. We need to be finding a way above the high tide line or we'll both drown." He loosened the hand on her shoulder to gesture at the cliff face with one finger. "Will ye help?"

She gave a curt nod. One was all it took for him to let her go. As he moved his hand away from her mouth, she saw how raw and scraped it was, from wrist to fingertips. "That must hurt," she told him, softly.

He shrugged. "Least of my problems."

"Who are ye?"

"No one ye need fear, lass."

His eyes *were* kind, and he had just saved her from drowning. "Ye must have a name. I'm Muireall." She left it at that, certain he would refuse to reveal his clan.

"Euan, then." His grin flashed, then disappeared as fast as a lightning bolt from last night's storm as he glanced beyond her. "Are yer clan liable to put out to sea to search for ye? Surely they'll have missed ye by now."

"No' yet, I think. Given the chance, I'm apt to wander off on my own, so until the lasses gather what they've found to take back up the cliff path, they willna notice I'm gone." Or care. Unless they spotted the pot she and Ella left above the high tide line. Aye, the storm might have tossed it so far. Maybe. But Ella knew she'd gone in this direction and if she knew about this cove, she'd fear Muireall was trapped and might well beg for help. How soon would she raise the alarm? Would the Rosses bother to save a lass stolen from another clan nearly a month before?

The man gestured at the high tide line on the cliff face. "They ken this cove floods?"

"Aye."

"Then we'd best be about finding shelter. Ye may

wish to be found, but I dinna." He stood and offered one of his damaged hands.

Instead of clasping his palm, she grasped his forearm and let him haul her to her feet. His nod acknowledged her care. He tensed when she glanced toward the cove where her captors salvaged his ship, but she shook her head and stepped around him, toward the sea cliff behind them. Off to the side, she saw his shoulders drop. In relief? Perhaps. Or resignation. He thought she was one of theirs, and he was stuck with her until the tide went out—or until Ross warriors came searching for her and found him, too.

After that? Should she betray him to the clan in the hopes of gaining their favor, or let him go? Or *help* him go? She owed him the debt of her life, after all. Muireall shook her head and led the way into the rocks. She owed this man, this Euan, what help she could give him.

"Look, there," he said and pointed.

His voice so close behind her made her jump. She took a breath and looked along his index finger at a cleft in the rock nearly half a man's height above Euan's head.

"Is that a cave, do ye think?"

"I dinna ken. And how would we get up there to find out?"

"I could lift ye."

"Nay, ye couldna. Yer hands."

"'Tis the lowest of the two I've found that might shelter us. It is…barely…above last night's high tide. And if ye'll climb onto my shoulders, ye might be able to pull yerself inside."

"What about ye?"

"If ye say there's room, and if ye find a place to tie off that rope ye salvaged, I'll climb up. At worst, I'll wait for the tide to lift me."

"And if it doesna rise so high tonight? The storm drove it hard onshore last night, if ye recall."

His lips compressed into a thin line, making Muireall berate herself for a fool. Of course he recalled. His ship, and his men, had foundered in that storm. She'd hurt him with her thoughtless comment, and regretted it instantly. "I'm sorry…" she began.

"I'll manage, *dinna fash*." His response was curt, his jaw tight. He studied the rocks around them rather than meet her gaze. "Step up there, and there," he said, indicating the erstwhile rocky stair steps he'd chosen. "Then, ye can easily stand on my shoulders."

"And fall off just as easily."

"I'll hold yer legs. All I have to do is take a step or two toward the cliff and ye'll be able to see whether that cut in the rock leads anywhere."

Muireall pursed her lips, dubious his injured hands could hold her. But this man had survived the wreck of his ship and loss of his crew. He'd avoided the Ross men and wisely taken shelter away from the shipwreck cove. Somehow, she knew he'd do what he set his mind to, what he promised. Still, "Why not wait for the tide to lift us both?"

"Ye nearly drowned once today. Do ye wish to do it again? We need to ken, now, before 'tis too late, whether we can get in there. Whether there's room for both of us. Whether it leads anywhere. Once the water gets that high, if 'tis simply a crack in the wall, we willna have time to find another way to save ourselves."

"Verra well. But if ye drop me, I'll no' give ye another chance."

He flashed that grin and her heart tumbled over, shocking her. She was in no position to be taken in by an appealing grin. Saints forfend, she'd just hinted to Ella she'd rather die than let a man force her. Now she was trapped with one. One who'd saved her life, aye, but if he thought that gave him the right to more of her, she swore she'd run for the surf.

"I willna drop ye. Now, up ye go."

She gathered her composure and did as he bade, stepping from rock to rock and onto his shoulders, praying he didn't look up. Her cloak gaped and her shift clung to her legs, but she needed her hands for more than holding her cloak closed over it. Arms outstretched, she fought to keep her balance. He shifted his stance as she wobbled. But he held her fast and moved her closer to the cleft without complaint, despite how the salt-water soaked fabric under his hands must sting his wounds.

She was able to get a hand on the lip and steadied herself. "It looks deep," she reported. "Big enough for both of us. I canna see where it leads, but it might serve."

"Can ye pull yourself in?"

Careful of her balance, she reached, trying to hook an arm over the ledge. "Maybe."

"Get ready. I'll lift ye…"

"Are ye certain?" Muireall tensed. Could he stand grinding the sand on her feet into his wounds? She reached in again, searching for something to hold onto.

In answer, Euan wedged his hands under her feet and pushed her upward.

She squeaked, clamping down on the shriek she'd nearly released. It would have been sure to call attention to them. But with the lift, she got her torso into the narrow passage and wiggled her hips, clawing with her hands and elbows, until her legs were in, too. With a sigh of relief, she glanced around. Then she got to her feet, gathered her cloak, and leaned out. Euan's worried gaze met hers, his brows drawn down into a hopeful, wide-eyed frown. His hands, curled at his side, were dusted with sand and streaked with blood. Her gut clenched at how that lift must have pained him. "Aye, we'll fit. I'm going to see where it leads. There's a little light leaking in from somewhere above."

"Let's get the rope tied off first. Then wait for me to climb up."

EUAN STUDIED THE LASS, MUIREALL, AS SHE PEERED down at him from out of the cleft in the cliff, her face guileless and full of promise, her arms hugging herself and keeping the cloak closed over her wet shift. She needn't have bothered. When he'd pulled her from the waves, he saw all there was to see. And what he'd seen was nice. Very nice. He couldn't get the creamy pink tips of her pleasingly rounded breasts or the dark triangle at the apex of her thighs out of his mind. Fair of face, slender, and curved in all his favorite places. But her body was not where his mind should be right now.

Could he believe her? His life depended on her actions. If she found a way up through the caves and onto the clifftop, she could betray him to her clan. Or she might stumble into an unseen pit and lie there until help came…if it ever did. If the rising tide didn't lift him far enough to reach the cave, he'd drown, assuming he wasn't pounded to death against the cliff first. And no one would know where she was unless someone chanced to hear her scream. Everything he pictured was bad, worse and even worse. But really, what choice did he have? Either she was trustworthy and would aid him, or he'd die in the coming hours, one way or the other. Between drowning and torture by the Rosses, he'd prefer drowning, but he wouldn't give in just yet.

He uncoiled the rope, ignoring the sting from the salt and rough texture, thanking his lucky stars she'd found a manageable length washed up near the beach and had sense enough to pull it ashore. He tied a knot in one end to give it more stability for his throw. "Are ye ready?"

"Aye. Dinna look at me," she warned as she freed her arms.

Of course, the cloak would not remain closed, and she knew her wet garment would not shield her body from his view.

"I'll do my best," he told her and locked his gaze on the rock above her head. "Dinna try to catch the knot. Grab it anywhere ye can." The length he gathered felt like lead in his arms. Still wet, damn it. "'Twill be heavier than ye think, so dinna lean out too far. Ye'll fall."

She nodded. "I'll do my best."

He would have laughed at the spunk she showed, echoing his words, but nothing about this situation was amusing. He didn't like feeling his life lay in another's hands, especially the small, weak hands of a woman. A woman who would grab the rope but also wrestle with her cloak at the same time. He'd be lucky if she didn't fall at his feet.

But as he was all too aware, he had little choice in the matter. He gauged the distance, knowing he had to keep the rope as close to the cliff wall as he could without hitting it. If it were possible, he'd toss the bloody thing into the cave, but nay, Muireall must catch it and secure it...somewhere.

"Here it comes," he warned. With that, he tossed the knot, aiming for a point a few feet above her head. If she didn't catch it on the way up, she'd have a chance as it fell back to him.

But the lass was quick. She got it on the first try, pulling the rope to her chest with one hand and forearm, stifling a cry as she wrapped the other arm across it and backed up a few paces. Then she turned so the cloak on her back faced him.

"Good lass!" Euan kept his voice down, but put all the approval he could muster into his tone. "Do ye see somewhere to tie it off?"

She disappeared from view, dragging the rope with her. As it slithered up the cliff face, the opposite end trailed past his feet and started climbing the wall. It paused at his waist, then started up again. Euan watched grimly. Was there nothing for her to tie it to? Or was she playing an evil game, making him watch while she took away his best chance at life? It was nearly out of his reach, and still moving. He debated grabbing it, but he needed to trust her—didn't he? In moments, the end of the rope disappeared over the lip of the cave into its darkness.

Euan's knees gave way, and he sat down hard on one of the stepping stones Muireall had used to gain his shoulders. God damn it! He was a fool. The rope was gone, and so, probably, was she.

She lived here. Likely she knew these caves and had known all along she could escape through them, if only she had a way up into them. A way he had provided.

And then he'd handed her the only tool that might save his life, not that he'd yet figured out how to use it by himself. Still, she'd taken the rope. Even if he tried to ride the rising tide, he was in danger of being dashed against the rocks or sucked back out to sea by an undertow.

He dropped his wet head into his hands and growled at the sting. At least there, his spirit would join those of his men, with the tangies his ship had been named for, sea sprites or kelpies, depending on which old tales you believed.

Hearing a slithering sound, he looked up, then jumped to his feet. The rope hung down the wall, swinging slightly in smaller and smaller arcs. She hadn't abandoned him! In another moment, Muireall peered down at him, arms wrapped around her middle, her cloak securely shielding her body from his view.

"I couldna find anything to tie it to. I wedged the knot in a fissure between some rocks. I hope it will hold ye."

Euan huffed out a breath. "I thought ye'd made off with it."

"What? Nay!" Muireall fisted her cloak and frowned down at him. "I didna want the rope to fall out of the cave until I secured it, so I pulled it all in. I've tugged as hard as I can."

Euan nodded, grabbed the rope and gave it a few tugs, ignoring the sting in his hands. It held. If his grip would also hold, he might survive the next high tide.

He clenched his teeth and climbed.

In moments, he was over the lip of the cave. He lay there, breathing hard and forcing his tortured hands to unclench. He left bright red streaks on the rope's rough surface, and the stench of copper filled his nose for a moment, cutting through the smells of sea and dank rock. Muireall, one hand clutching her cloak and the other over her mouth, watched him from a few paces further into the narrow cave, concern written in her pretty frown. No time for that, dammit! He hooked the rope with his elbow, rolled to his feet and pulled the dangling end in after him. "No sense advertising our presence," he told her, ignoring the way her gaze tracked the crimson blood smeared onto the cave floor's dull stone. "We may need it to get down again when the tide goes out."

Muireall gathered her damp cloak more tightly around her. "The cave is narrow, but it leads upward toward the back. Daylight is getting in somewhere."

"Let's go see." Euan gestured for her to follow him. "Watch yer step."

The passage was indeed narrow, but trended upward. Euan took care placing his feet—worried as much about what a turned ankle would do to his chances for escape as he was about falling into an unseen pit. Soon enough, the cave widened out and a thin shaft of light pierced the gloom and reflected around the space.

"That may be our best chance," Euan said, pausing to study the cave's ceiling and walls. They still gleamed wetly from last night's storm, proof that water had created this space. "That crack is high on the wall rather than in the ceiling, which means there's a hillside that slopes in that direction." He gestured, sweeping one hand at an angle down the wall. "If I can reach that opening, I'll be able to see how much rock is between us and the outside."

"The rope…"

"Leave it. If this doesna work, we'll need to climb down at low tide."

Muireall moved past him, farther into the cave. "This is the end."

"Then let's see if 'tis also our way out." The rock face directly below the crack was too wet to provide reliable hand and footholds. He moved a few feet to the side and started up, grimacing as he left bloody fingerprints. When he reached the crack, he made a fist and forced his hand through. He could feel blades of grass outside. "The ground is thin here," he reported. "But without tools…"

"If ye tug on it, will it cave in or hold?"

Euan stretched on his toes and got his arm through to the elbow. Bending it, he used his weight and forearm to pull. He felt something give. "I think there's only a thin layer of scree held together by roots. It looks ready to crumble. Anyone walking above would likely fall into this cave." He braced himself on one foot, held on and kicked at the wall with the other. He heard stones and gravel roll downhill. "'Tis breaking loose."

"Be careful. What if someone sees?"

Shite. "Ye're right," Euan agreed and climbed down. "We'll wait for the gloaming. I need a little light to see handholds. When I try this, I want ye back in the lower passage. If the hillside collapses, you'll still be able to get down the rope at low tide."

"We will, ye mean to say."

"Aye, if I'm not up to my neck in rocks and mud."

"If ye are, I'll dig ye out."

"If I am, I'll dig myself out. Ye will go back around the cove to yer clan, where ye'll be safe."

He couldn't decipher the bleak expression that crossed Muireall's face at that moment, but it gave him a hollow sensation in his belly. "That is what ye want, is it no'?"

She turned and headed into the lower passage.

He followed. "Is it?" Her silence puzzled him. "What are ye no' telling me, lass?"

"Nought ye'll want to hear." She kept walking until she reached the cave's opening.

Over her shoulder, Euan could see sunlight dancing on the firth. Water sloshed against the cliff wall as the tide came up, with a low, rolling sound he could feel through the rock under his feet. The water had climbed another foot in the time they'd been at the upper end of the cave. "We've an hour until high tide," he ventured. "Six hours more cruntil the tide goes out far enough for ye to get around the headland. And nowhere to go until near dark. Ye could tell me what's on yer mind. To pass the time, if nought else."

"Should we no' find a way to collect some of the rain water in the upper cave?"

"We'll be away from here and ye'll be back to yer clan before thirst becomes that much an issue. What we need is to stay warm and let our clothes dry. We've nought to build a fire, and smoke would give us away if we did. We'll huddle somewhere out of the wind."

Muireall nodded, shoulders dropping on a sigh.

"Come, lass. Let's find a place to rest."

MUIREALL WRAPPED HER CLOAK TIGHTLY ABOUT HER. Euan's scrutiny made her uncomfortable. She wanted to tell him. She just wasn't sure she should. After all, what did she know about him? Even though he'd saved her life and said he wouldn't harm her, she couldn't trust a man she barely knew. If he found out she had been stolen, he might use and abandon her when he escaped. Nay, she dared not tell him—not yet. She might be cut off from the Ross clan, but she was no nearer home. Instead, somehow, if they managed to avoid drowning this day, she had to convince him to take her with him.

She was full of foolish dreams.

But if Euan agreed, she'd be leaving Ella and Tira to their fate with the Ross men. Shame made her chest hollow and her eyes sting with unshed tears. Though she and Euan were still in trouble, she had hope. Ella did not, though Tira seemed happy with the man who'd taken her. Ella seemed resigned, aye. Happy, nay.

Why had their own clan not found them yet? That question tortured her every day. Had the surviving Munro men lost their trail? They'd been gone nearly a month. On the trip, with every mile further from home, she and the others had prayed for rescue. But no one had come for them. On the journey to Ross, Tira's latest moon blood finished and she had been claimed by a man named Teague. A week after they arrived, El-las's latest moon blood did, too, and soon after, Thomas had taken her to his bed. Muireall knew her turn would come within days. Married, as the Ross clan counted it. She counted it taken against their wills. They'd all be ruined and lose all hope of rescue. Her father would be furious, if he still lived, to see his plans for her to make an alliance with clan Grant had been ruined by Ross raiders.

What would she do if Donas's boast was true and her village had been destroyed?

Could she leave her friends behind? Save herself and convince Euan to return her to Munro to find out their fate? If her clan lived, would she be able to con-vince anyone to return for the other lasses? Come to that, if the worst had happened, would Euan? If her people were gone, what possible reason would he and his men have to fight for her clanswomen? They would be risking a war with Ross over women who meant nothing to them and a clan that no longer mattered to anyone but her.

She didn't know anything about him. If she, Tira, and Ella were to have a chance of escape, she needed to find out which clan he belonged to, what he cared about, and what he might do. She resolved to use the time they spent waiting to good advantage and learn all she could.

Euan led her to a small inset in the rock she'd missed in the path to the upper cave. It was large enough for both of them yet small enough to hold some of their body heat.

"Get in," he ordered. "Ye'll be warmer on the inside."

She didn't like the thought of being trapped in the small space, his body between her and freedom. "I have my cloak. When it dries, I'll be warmer. Ye should go first."

"Nay, lass." He tilted his head. "Ye think I'd corner ye in there?" His shoulders lifted and lowered as he glanced aside and clenched his jaw. "I told ye I wouldna harm ye."

"I..."

"I willna." He waved a hand. "If I wanted to have my way with ye, I could do it right here. In the upper cave. Out by the rope. Hell, I couldha done it when I first pulled ye from the water, before ye woke up."

"Somehow all of that fails to reassure me," Muireall muttered. But he was right. He'd probably seen right through the front of her wet shift when he rescued her, and he'd made no advances. She huffed out a sigh. "Verra well." She ducked in and settled herself, finding it more difficult than she expected to lean her back against the hard, cold rock.

Euan waited until she stilled, then joined her. Within moments, she realized having his body close by had a delicious benefit. He warmed her, and she fought the urge to snuggle closer.

"Tell me about yerself," she said, keeping her tone neutral enough he'd hear it as a request, not a demand. "Where are ye from? Why were ye out in that storm?"

Euan eyed her, then shrugged. "The fishing was good. We overstayed the day and the storm came up—too fast." He gestured with an open palm. "We raced for home, but the wind shifted, driving us toward the far coast—here. The wind...well, before we could get the sail down, the wind heeled us over. The *Tangie* capsized and went under and onto the rocks."

"Yer men?"

"If none of my men have been seen, then...they went down with her." He leaned his head against the rock behind him and closed his eyes. Little enough light penetrated to their sanctuary, but it allowed Muireall to see a muscle jumping in Euan's jaw.

"Yer men. Ye were captain, then?"

"Aye." He paused and swallowed. "My men, my ship, my fault."

"Surely, ye dinna blame yerself for the storm?"

He lifted his head and looked at her. "Nay. But we shouldha run for home as soon as we spied dark clouds piling up on the horizon."

"How could ye ken which way the storm would go?" she asked, shivering at the thought of how his men must have died, knowing they'd made a fatal mistake. "What's done is done, and no' yer fault."

He didn't react.

She tried a different approach. "Perhaps yer men made it ashore. Ye just dinna ken it yet."

He nodded. "I pray for that, but dinna hold much hope. I barely made it myself. And one was just a lad." He sighed and turned his hand over, studying the scrapes marring it.

Muireall winced. He had to be hurting, yet he'd done so much with those hands to save them, as if their wounds didn't exist.

"What about ye, lass? What can ye tell me about yer clan?"

He wanted information about the Rosses, no doubt, not her own clan. Instead of answering, she countered, "Tell me about yers first."

He shrugged. "Our laird is new this past year. And newly married. His wife, Annie, well, ye'd have to meet her to understand. She's every inch the daughter of a laird—headstrong as all hell and into everyone's business. No' the sort of lass I'd ever want to wed."

Muireall frowned. "That's no' very kind. So ye think all laird's daughters are that way? And none could possibly suit ye?" His words cut her, though he had no idea.

"*Ach*, lass, but ye didna let me finish. On the other

hand, she's everyone's friend. Hell of a rider and archer, too."

"A lass can do that?"

"What? Aye. Useful skills, would ye no' say?"

She nodded. "For a man, aye."

He waved a hand. "Your turn. So yer lasses dinna ride or fight. Tell me more."

If she were truly a Ross, what would she tell him? "What do ye wish to ken?"

Euan didn't look at her. "Where does the clan keep its boats?"

That was easy to answer—he'd find them on his own quickly enough. "In the cove on the other side of where ye…where the *Tangie*…washed ashore."

His shoulders stiffened and the hand he'd waved curled into a fist.

Instantly, she knew what he must be thinking. If he'd gone that way instead of this, he could have taken a boat, and he'd already be at sea, searching for his men along the coastline or headed home, not stuck in a cold, damp cave with a lass…who was not who he thought she was.

Dear God, she could not deal with his reaction to finding out she'd been stolen and needed his help. Not yet. Not now. If she gave him time, he'd think of reasons not to take her with him, and she couldn't bear the thought of being left to the fate she dreaded at Ross.

"How many boats? What kind?"

His urgent question snapped her gaze to his. His green eyes had gone cold as winter sea spray. She quailed and lowered her lids, focusing on her hands instead of his. She had to look somewhere, anywhere, else. If she kept staring at him, at the evidence of efforts to save both of them, she'd blurt out the truth. "Five or six in all. I dinna ken what ye'd call all of them. One *birlinn*, the rest smaller."

"Do they keep a guard at the cove?"

"Aye—a man to raise the alarm." She thought about it for a moment and added, "They're salvaging what they can from your wreck, so there might be more men about than usual." Donas Ross had big plans, most of which meant raiding neighboring clans to steal their wealth and women. In many ways, he was a fool, but not in the strategy and tactics of war. He'd snuck onto Munro land and stolen three women without anyone being aware until it was too late—or ever. Since no one had come, Muireall suspected no one knew where to look once they realized the three lasses were missing. Muireall clutched her cloak more tightly about her and glanced aside at Euan. His frown told her he was considering his chances of escape and not liking them one bit.

And that was before she told him who she really was and begged him to take her with him. And the other women. Nay, he wouldn't like that at all. But he was the first chance of getting help she'd had since she'd been taken. She'd wait for a better time to tell him. She just didn't know when that time would be.

CHAPTER 3

*E*uan woke with a jerk. His head hit the cave wall behind him, just hard enough to make him realize he'd dozed off. His chin had dropped to his chest, then snapped back. He blinked a few times to clear the fog from his mind and realized Muireall, asleep, wrapped tightly in her cloak, leaned against him, her head on his shoulder. His sudden movement had not disturbed her. She must truly be exhausted.

He took a moment to enjoy the warmth of her body next to his. Her scent filled his nostrils, something soft and sweet under the briny ocean and dank cave smell that surrounded them. Her pale skin caught the wavering light reflecting along the cave walls. Dark circles smudged the skin under her eyes. Aye, she was exhausted. And probably hungry and thirsty. At least, she would be somewhat warmed by leaning into him.

The light told him the day was waning, but it was not yet dark enough to try to escape from the upper cave. He'd let the lass sleep a while longer. Now that he knew where the Ross boats were kept, escape along the clifftop didn't hold the appeal it once had. Having to avoid the Ross village would slow him. Making his way across the beach would be closer, and faster, than traversing the clifftop.

Low tide would happen soon, and with it, the narrow stretch of sand around the headland would be revealed. But in another two hours, it would be fully dark, and he might be able to make his way around the headland and across the next cove unseen if he hugged the cliff wall. He wanted one of those boats Muireall mentioned. Any that one man could drag into the water and sail on his own would do to get him home to Brodie. But first, he'd head down the coast. If a Ross boat followed, the men on it would not be able to guess his true destination. And it would give him a chance to see if any of his men had washed up on a beach nearby. Their families would want to know and give them a proper burial, if he could retrieve them.

He had to trust that Muireall would not send her clansmen after him, at least not right away. But once they got out, she'd have to explain where she'd been overnight and how she'd survived. Would a story that she'd made it into the cave on her own be believed? Or would he be better off to take her with him—willing or not—because no one would believe she'd survived alone?

Nay, he couldn't. She'd slow him down, and as long as he didn't need a hostage, he had no reason to take her from her people. Even if he did, he couldn't countenance putting her in danger by forcing her to make a risky escape with him. His only concern was to get her safely to the next cove where she could make her way up the cliff path to her village. After that, his priority was staying free, and finding out what had become of his men.

That decided, Euan resolved to enjoy the woman's soft warmth as long as she slept...or until it was time to go. Just then, Muireall's head moved so slightly he thought he'd imagined it. Until it happened again.

"Nay, nay! Nay…"

Euan frowned down at the head on his shoulder, clearly tossing now with every mumbled word. Was she dreaming? Talking in her sleep?

"Muireall." He shrugged his shoulder, hoping to wake her from her dream with a gentle movement.

"Nay, ye canna…leave us be…"

What? "Muireall, wake up. Ye're dreaming. Ye are safe with me."

"Nay…dinna take us…"

That came out as a wail, so Euan jostled her again and was reaching for her hand when she suddenly roused and sat up, then rubbed her face with both hands.

"I'm sorry. I didna mean to use ye as a pillow."

"*Wheest*, lass, all is well. Ye were dreaming and talking in yer sleep. Ye seemed upset, so I thought it best to wake ye."

"Talking…" Her expression went from muzzy to worried in the space of that one word, eyes widened under drawn-down brows. "What did I say?"

Her cheeks pinked as he watched. "Ye kept repeating "nay." Then ye said "leave us be" and "ye canna take us." I thought ye'd rest better away from such a dream."

She nodded, refusing to meet his gaze.

That convinced him. "Or was it a memory? Is there something ye havena told me?"

Muireall heaved a heavy sigh and rubbed her face again, then fisted her hands over her cloak. "Aye."

"Then perhaps this is a good time for confession."

Just then, Euan heard a man's scream. Though agonized, the voice sounded familiar. He rolled out of their inset, stood and ran to the seaside entrance.

There, he leaned out and listened. The wind was blowing their way. The next sound was another man's shout, a demand if he judged the timbre correctly. Then a hoarse cry broke the stillness. It couldn't be! This time, he recognized Calum's voice, his cousin's agonized tone.

As he grabbed for the rope he'd left coiled on the floor of the cave, Muireall came up behind him and placed a hand on his shoulder. He shook her off. Waves still broke against the headland between this cove and the next. Calum needed his help, and he couldn't get to him without risking drowning as Muireall had. He'd never get there fast enough. Yet even if he could, without weapons, what could he do? Perhaps something the lass had collected before the tide came in would make do—and would still be on the sliver of beach starting to show below them.

Another hoarse cry cut off abruptly.

He froze.

The silence that followed lasted long enough for Muireall to seize his fist and softly cry out at what she saw. "Ye've made it bleed again, ye daft man."

"I need to get around that headland. One of my men survived. They're torturing my cousin."

Rough laughter blew in on the wind and Muireall's shoulders dropped. "I ken that laugh. 'Tis Donas." She clutched at her throat with one hand. "I'm so sorry. I fear yer cousin doesna need yer help any longer. They've killed him."

"Nay!" Euan covered his mouth with his arm to muffle the sound and heard the cry as if it came from another. The wrenching pain in his chest confirmed it was his.

"Likely he was half drowned and couldna tell them what they wanted to know," Muireall told him softly, then bit her lip and turned her gaze to the water and continued, "so they killed him and tossed him back into the firth."

Furious heat rose from Euan's chest to his face. His breath whistled through his nose as he grabbed Muireall's shoulders and glared at her through a red haze, heedless of the pain in his hands. "Your people just killed my cousin." He shook her, then let her go, leaving bloody prints behind on her cloak.

"Nay, no' my peo...." Her voice broke on a sob.

She denied what they'd both just heard? What she'd just described?

"Nay? No' yer...what? Yer people?"

She shook her head, misery in her gaze.

How convenient. "Did ye make me think ye talked in yer sleep in case something like this happened?"

With a growl, he left her there and charged into the upper cave, grabbed the first hand-sized rock he found and climbed, then began chipping away the limestone imprisoning them, swearing with each blow against the pain in his hands and his heart.

Muireall was only moments behind him. "Stop!" she cried. "If there's a patrol on the clifftop, they'll hear you. Someone will see what ye are doing." She tugged on his boot, unsettling him and making him lose his precarious hold on the wall.

He fell, knocking her down, and landing beside her on his knees and palms. He was too angry to feel the damage, though he could see blood dripping from his fingers as he straightened up. "See what ye have done!" He glared at her and stood.

She scooted away and got to her feet, clutching her damned cloak around her and wincing.

"I ken ye are angry, but ye must hear me. They are no' my people. No' my clan. I was stolen, nearly a month ago."

"Ye lie. Ye'll say anything to save yerself." But the red

haze dissipated a little. Was that why she'd been sent to scour the shoreline in her shift? And seemed less than eager to return to what he thought was her clan?

"Ye must believe me." She grabbed his arm.

He twisted out of her grip and demanded, "Who's Donas?" as she stumbled aside.

Whatever else she meant to say was lost to her cry as she fell. Then her head smacked against the cave wall and her eyes rolled back.

She went limp before he could catch her with his injured hands.

Horror filled him. What had he done? He'd only meant to break her grip on his arm, not to shove her into the rocky wall. He fell to his knees and gathered her up. "Muireall, nay. I'm sorry! I didna mean to harm ye." Frantic now with regret and fear for her, he ran his bloody fingers through her hair and found the lump behind one temple. Then he bent and kissed her forehead. "Muireall, lass, wake up. I will no' harm ye. I swear it." For good measure, he kissed the lump on her head, too, then pulled her cloak together to cover her. Her shift was drying but still damp enough to reveal what lay beneath. She'd be angry about the lump on her head. Angrier still if she thought he took advantage of her and looked.

She stirred and muttered, "No' your fault...ye didna mean to..."

"Ah, ye're still with me." He rocked her in his arms, then kissed her face as he would to comfort a child. "*I'm so sorry*," he crooned, smoothing back her hair. "I didna mean to hurt ye."

She yelped as his fingers again found the knot. Though her eyes remained closed, she lifted her hand to her head, frowned and tucked her face against his neck.

"I saved ye from the firth," he murmured into her

hair, thinking of how he'd pulled her to safety and wishing he could have done the same for his men. "I canna have killed ye, now." Her breath warmed his throat and gave him a small measure of comfort as he stroked her head.

She gave a soft moan at the last, then pushed up until he helped her to sitting, then met his gaze. "Now will ye listen to reason? Ye canna fight the whole clan alone. We must escape." She stopped talking to take a breath and blinked, then added, "I've tried twice and failed."

He could scarce deny the resolute tone ringing in his ears. She'd meant what she said earlier. She was no Ross.

Her lips thinned. He attributed her pained expression to the lump on her head.

"I…we…need yer help. Then ye can return to take yer vengeance."

"We?"

"Aye." She glanced down, then continued. "Let me tend yer hands. I'll tell ye the tale while I do."

MUIREALL TOLD HIM ALL OF IT WHILE SHE CLEANED HIS wounds with rainwater from a shallow depression in the floor of the cave, dabbing at them with a wet strip torn from the hem of her shift. Then she wrapped his hands, covering the wounds and hoping to protect them long enough for him to return home to his own healer's care. It hurt to relate how the raiders had come while she and the other two, Ella and Tira, were washing clothes at the burn, taking all three lasses away with them. Their captors left behind a village of ghosts, they were told, killing all they didn't steal. Before she was done, tears streamed down her face, and she spoke around sobs that threatened to choke her. "Perhaps a few survived who were out hunting, or children playing in the woods away from the village. I canna ken."

"Perhaps all survived. Have ye thought yer captors might have told ye such a tale to keep ye hopeless of rescue. Ye say ye've been here nearly a month. I'd say their tale did its job."

She wanted to believe him. More than anything. For Georgie's sake. "God, how I hope ye are right. But we've had nay chance to escape, though I tried…twice. And if our men live, why have they no' come for us?" Because she and the others had been abandoned.

"Perhaps they looked, but lost the trail. Or never had it."

"Or perhaps they are all dead."

He traced her cheek with his fingertips, the only part of his hands not covered by strips of her shift.

Despite his injuries, his hands were strong. He'd abused them over and over in his determination to save them both. Euan's looks pleased her, and she couldn't deny his bravery. Nor could she help how she was growing to feel about him, though she knew she was beyond foolish even to imagine he could ever feel anything for her. She was a burden to him, nothing more.

"Once I discover the fate of my men, and return home with the news, I'll take ye home."

She thought about the way he'd wakened her with his frantic kisses. He cared for her at least a little. He felt responsible for her. Surely, she could convince him to do as she asked. "Where is home for ye?"

"Across the firth—clan Brodie."

Hope made her bold. "Munro is closer. We should go there first. Our healer could tend to ye."

"Nay."

Her face fell and her shoulders slumped.

"Ye ken why I canna," he said as he took in her reaction to his refusal. "I must return to carry the news. My men had fathers and mothers, two had wives and children. They need to ken what happened to their men."

"Just as I need to ken what happened to mine. And if they still live, to tell them what happened to us." She dropped her head into her hands. "I've hoped and despaired for so long. Yer people have only had a day to wonder..."

Euan rocked back on his heels, and Muireall feared she'd pushed too hard. It was within his power to leave her here, after all.

He pressed his hands together and winced as if he'd forgotten his wounds. Then he said the thing she most feared. "I should leave ye here with the Rosses, where at least ye'd be safe. I could return for ye in a few days. Ye could meet me..."

"What makes ye think I'd be safe here? In a few days, Donas Ross could give me to one of his men. I'd be ruined and never be able to leave. Or ye could decide once ye are gone that I'm no' worth the trouble to retrieve." She shook her head. "I canna risk that. Ye must see why."

"Aye, I suppose I do. What about yer friends?"

"They are both married now. Tira seems happy. I'm no' certain about Ella. If I could, I'd ask her if she would like to come with us."

"That ye canna do—ye risk her telling her husband. It will be dangerous and hard enough for two of us, much less with a third who is no' certain she wants to leave."

"That's just it. I think she would, if she could. If we could find a way..."

"Forget it, lass. I'm sorry."

She studied the floor, lips pressed together to hold back the pleas he would only ignore. "I'm sorry, too."

AT LOW TIDE, EUAN STOOD AT THE CAVE'S MOUTH AND watched Muireall dunk herself in the surf and go around the headland alone. They'd argued while the surf retreated, until a thin strip of sand appeared there and began to widen. She feared her captors would be on the other side, waiting for the chance to discover if she yet lived, or to retrieve her body, had it not been swept out to sea.

"If ye go with me, ye would be captured and all hope would be lost," she'd told him. "I've thought about what ye said. 'Tis better I go alone. If no one waits, I can come back to tell ye."

He fought the idea, preferring both of them to wait a while in the cave and see if anyone came looking for her, but the more he thought about it, the more he saw what she said made sense. Time was not on their side. Not if any more of his men were alive to save. They had to get out before the next high tide or be trapped again, without food or water, for long hours more.

"They willna have any reason to search this cove if I return," she'd argued. "Ye'll have a chance to steal a boat and get away. I could still go to the beach in a day or two."

"I couldna leave without seeing ye were safe, lass." He'd known it was foolish even to say, but he'd come to care for her.

"Nay, that's too dangerous. We have agreed ye must go if ye are to search for yer men."

"Once I see ye are safe, I'll go. But I'll keep sailing back until ye appear on the beach, alone, or with yer friend Ella," he swore, meaning every foolish word. He didn't want to be saddled with a lass—his duty to Brodie drove him to find out what happened to his men. But he owed her. She'd helped save both of them from the incoming tide. "No matter what happens to ye, I willna abandon ye." He didn't want her to take the risk, but he couldn't see another option that might save them both—and any of his men he chanced to find.

Somewhere in the midst of their argument, she'd also made him swear that if another week went by and she didn't appear on the beach, he'd cease risking himself and forget about her. She was sure by then Donas would have given her to one of his men and her fate would be sealed. He swore to himself he'd free her before that happened.

Just before dark, when she ran out of sight around the widening strip of sand, Euan prayed as he never had before. She had to appear eager to reach safety with the clan, if indeed they waited on the other side. He stood in the cave mouth, rope pulled up out of sight, watching and ready to duck back in case she returned with an escort demanding to know how she'd survived. She planned to make use of climbing the rocky steps to stand on his shoulders and say she'd managed to pull herself up onto a rock, and each time the tide rose, she swam to a higher one. The only thing she couldn't explain is why no one had heard her scream for help.

Returning alone to her captors was perhaps the bravest thing he'd ever seen anyone do. She couldn't be certain he'd return for her, despite what he'd promised.

Seconds dragged into long, breathless minutes, then even more, yet still she did not return. He forced himself to practice patience he did not feel, and fought the growing urge to climb down and go after her. That would be foolhardy in the extreme—and a waste of her sacrifice. Where was she? Why had she not returned for him? He couldn't believe they'd harm her. They'd stolen her for a reason—for a life that would be much the same with the Rosses as any lasses' would be with any clan, married and raising a family. Aye, if he had any sense, he'd leave her to make her future here.

But he knew he would not abandon her. A sweet face and pleasing form could catch his eye, and she had that. But rarely would a lass hold his interest for more than that moment of appreciation. Muireall, though, had begun to fill his thoughts. He'd never met a more valiant lass—or one more desperate, he supposed. But desperation did nothing to negate the spirit she showed him with every word she spoke and everything she'd done to help them both survive since he'd pulled her from the surf. A strange sensation—respect for a lass he barely knew—filled him at the thought.

The sea was clear of boats for as far as he could see. No one waited offshore, looking for movement in the nearby coves, ready to signal to warriors where to pick up survivors of the wreck. That was what he would have done, but perhaps the Rosses figured it was too late for anyone lost at sea the night before.

If he waited until the tide started coming back in, he'd be trapped for another twelve hours. After a night and a day with no water and no food, another night would leave him too weak to save himself, much less Muireall or any of his men who might remain alive and free. It was time to take action. Yet, the fact Muireall seemed to have disappeared without a sound troubled him. He should have heard voices, glad cries or an argument...something to let him know she'd been met and would be taken back to the Ross village.

"I may be the biggest fool yet born," Euan muttered as he kicked the rope over the side. He kept an eye on the headland, knowing with his luck, now the rope was down, a group of her captors would cross the narrow strip of beach and spot him. "But the devil hasna taken me, yet." He sat at the cave opening, grabbed the rope in sore, stiff hands, levered himself over the side, and clung to it as he dropped down. For a moment, he debated whether he should toss the rope into the cave, but feared he'd need it again, so he'd have to accept the possibility of it being discovered hanging down the cliff face.

To his relief and worry, he was still alone on the beach. Showing himself had not signaled a horde of Rosses to come pelting down on him. So where was Muireall?

Despite the sense of inevitable doom that hung over him, he made his way quietly to the thin strand of beach that marked the way to safety—or death. Nearby clifftops were empty.

Had Muireall gone back to the village and left him to make his way home? Nay, she wanted to escape as much as he. If she'd found the shipwreck cove empty, she would not have chosen to climb to the village. She would have come back for him. Which meant she'd been taken, without a chance to make a sound to warn him.

They had her. Now, he had to get her back.

*D*onas's broad hand had clapped over Muireall's mouth and nose as soon as she came around the headland. She struggled in his grasp, but he prevented her from making more than a squeak and nearly prevented her from breathing at all. Then they waited, eerily silent for so many men, for long minutes, as if Donas expected someone else to round the headland behind her.

Finally, when no one came, he canted his head. One man ventured the way she'd come, soon returned, and shrugged. The saints be praised, he hadn't seen any sign of Euan.

They moved, three men before her, Donas, hand still clapped over her mouth with his other gripping her arm tightly enough to bruise, and two more behind. She stumbled as they started up the cliff path. Donas's rough treatment weakened her knees and made stars dance in front of her eyes, much as they had when she hit her head on the cave wall. She could not see where she placed her feet.

With an oath, Donas hauled her onto his shoulder, bruising her ribs and forcing the breath she'd gasped out of her lungs. He kept climbing as though she weighed nothing while she fought for breath.

What would Euan do? Would he have time for it to get dark enough to sneak away before Donas and his men went looking for him? She had to buy him as much time as she could. No matter what Donas did to her, she would not tell him about Euan.

At the top of the cliff, Donas dumped her off his shoulder. She landed in a heap, adding a bruised backside to her list of complaints.

"Did ye swim all day?" he demanded, grinning at her gaping cloak.

"Ye ken I couldna do that," she answered, shoving her wet hair over her shoulder and pulling her cloak tightly together in front of her. The wind whipped damp strands of hair back across her face.

"Then why are ye still alive? We know that cove floods. Did ye have help?"

"Nay. I climbed on a rock until the sea rose, then a higher one. Each time the sea lifted me I swam to a higher rock. I hit my head once," she added, lifting her hair to show the lump. "'Twas a long, terrifying day."

"And how is it no one heard ye cry for help?"

"I did cry out once," she lied, "but I dared no' do it twice. The rocks were so slippery, even a deep breath made me fear to fall. I didna ken how many times I would have the strength to climb out of the water if I fell." At Donas's skeptical expression, she knew she must dare more and turn his questions back on him. "I prayed someone would come for me in a boat. Why did ye no'?"

Donas snorted, sending fresh chills down Muireall's spine. "Risk a boat on those rocks, or against that cliff, for such as ye? Ye are daft. I'd sooner toss ye off this cliff and be done with ye."

Muireall gasped. Blood drained from her head,

leaving her pale and shaky. She tried to scoot away from Donas, and away from the cliff's edge, but her wet garments only tangled around her, holding her in place and throwing Donas and his men into fits of laughter.

"What do ye think, Erik?" Donas asked when he got his breath back. "Do ye think ye want this half-drowned lassie to wife, or should I kick her over the edge?"

Muireall didn't know what to react to first: Donas's threat to kill her, or the revelation that he planned to give her to Erik, his second-in-command. She didn't dare look at the man in question. Of the Ross men, Erik was one of the most pleasing to look at, large and well-muscled, with dark hair and dark eyes, but he had a dark and silent disposition, and she'd been told, a fearsome temper to go with them.

So, provoke Donas into killing her now, or let Erik do it later? She had little hope for anything better. She was trapped between the cliff and the village. Between Donas and his men. Euan could not possibly free her from this village. One man against all of these? Nay, better he steal a boat and sail for home, and never think of her again. Muireall dropped her head into her hands. Perhaps, if she was fast enough, she could throw herself over the cliff and settle the matter, once and for all.

Then someone grabbed her elbow and hauled her to her feet. Blinking she looked up, and up again, into Erik's grim countenance.

"She'll come with me," he said and led her away, their progress followed by the guffaws and jeers of the other men.

Ach, nay. He couldn't mean to do what she feared. Her next moon blood had not come yet. The men all waited for that to prove a lass was not heavy with another man's child. Muireall's mind whirled furiously as

Erik dragged her along, trying to think of an argument that would prevent what she saw coming.

To her shock, when they reached the center of the village, he handed her off to Silas. "Clean her up and get her warm. Donas says she's to be mine in a few days."

His gaze raked her and made her feel naked as well as chilled.

"She's no good to anyone in this condition. Worse if she sickens from spending the day wet and cold."

At his surprising kindness, Muireall's knees folded, and she dropped to the ground. Erik cast one disgusted look in her direction, then turned back to Silas. "Do it now."

Muireall didn't see Silas nod, but in moments, the woman was calling for the clan's one wooden tub and clean water to be heated in the large pot someone had found on the beach. Hers, she supposed...or Euan's. Either way, it seemed fitting that its first use would be for her.

Silas walked toward the cliff, leaving Muireall in her cold, sodden heap. She wrapped her arms around bent knees, her thoughts on Euan and his whereabouts. Long minutes passed while she recalled all the ways he'd ignored his own pain to save her. She prayed he would be safe and away from danger, if not by now, then very soon. She barely noticed when a lad ran up to Silas and urgently but quietly spoke to her, gesturing down toward the men and the beach.

Silas turned and gave her a long look.

Muireall frowned, waiting to hear the worst; that Euan had been found and killed.

Silas just shook her head and sent the lad away.

Helpless to do anything else, Muireall rested her head on her knees. Despite her discomfort, fatigue made her doze until Silas pulled on her arms.

"Get up." Her tone brooked no argument. Preparations must be complete. Then she knelt and unclasped the cloak from Muireall's shoulders. "Up, lass," she commanded and rose, taking Muireall's arm, pulling her to her feet. The tub sat, steaming, a few feet away, not in her cot, as she'd expected, but in full view of the entire village. The men—arms crossed and grinning—had arrayed themselves around it—and her. Several women stood behind them, peeking between broad shoulders and jabbing each other in the sides with their elbows. Muireall quailed, but couldn't prevent Silas from plucking at the torn hem of her thin shift, and stripping the useless garment over her head. Naked and covered in chill bumps, Muireall wrapped her arms around herself and fought the urge to cry.

"Why..."

Donas gestured and Silas handed him Muireall's shift. He examined it, then tossed it aside. "Ye sat on a rock all day...by yerself?" He looked her up and down, and angry glint in his eye, but a smirk on his lips. "Yet the sun failed to color yer face. Did the rock tear yer shift?"

She froze, hope and fear filling her at the same time. She knew why she'd been stripped bare in front of the entire clan. Euan had left the cave.

"So," Donas continued, "where did that rope come from that we found hanging from a cave, and how did it get there, I wonder?"

Muireall looked around for an ally, but all she found were angry faces, or hungry looks that scared her more than the angry ones admiring Donas's handiwork.

Silas took her arm and led her to the tub. "In," she commanded.

Muireall set one foot in the water and yelped.

"Yer betrothed wanted ye warmed up. That'll do it,"

Silas said, with no trace of pity or remorse. "Now get in or I'll let him throw ye in."

Betrothed. Muireall gulped. She got her other foot in the hot water and dropped to her knees, fighting not to cry out at the painful heat. Her skin reddened alarmingly. She feared she'd have blisters, but in a few moments, her body adjusted to the temperature, and it became if not comfortable, at least soothingly warm.

"Dunk yer head."

That was Erik. So he wasn't missing the chance to inspect his prospective bride, and to see to it that she met with his approval. She wanted to glare at him, but knew she'd regret it, if not today, then later. She kept her head down and curled onto her side into the tub, hissing as the hot water hit her back and breasts. Then she held her breath and dropped her head into the water, rinsing the salt out of her hair, all the while wondering if Donas would decide to hold her down and drown her. That would be ironic, after Euan fought so hard to save her.

As she came up for air, someone grabbed her hair. She fought, clawing at large hands. But rather than forcing her face back underwater, they yanked her head back.

"Who helped ye?"

It was Donas, of course. Was he going to shove her head underwater again and again until she gave him the answer he wanted? Erik stood nearby, but made no move to help her...or Donas.

"I dinna ken..."

"We checked the cave. Nay sign of anyone being there for long. So it was someone from that wreck, aye? Ye tore strips from yer shift. He's injured. Or did he rip that before he got between yer thighs?"

Muireall let her silent disdain answer for her.

With an oath, Donas released her hair and turned to

the other man. "She's yer problem, now, Erik." Then he waved an arm in a broad sweep. "The rest of ye, back to work. There's a man somewhere nearby. Find him. And ye," he pointed to one man who'd stood at the back of the crowd, "I told ye to stay with the boats. Get back down there before one goes missing." Without another word, he stomped away.

Muireall glanced at her intended. A small crease between his eyebrows gave her the only hint of what he was thinking. But he wasn't frowning at her. He was watching Donas. That interested her. Was she the source of tension between the chief and Erik?

Silas handed her a palmful of soap as the men filed away, several giving her assessing looks as they went.

"Who knows," Silas taunted. "Perhaps ye'll be wed at Candlemas. I hear that's lucky."

Muireall ignored her and washed her hair, doing the best she could to keep the rest of her body below the surface of the water, more or less out of sight. Not that Erik—and most of the rest of the clan—hadn't already seen all there was to see. She needn't have bothered. Silas ordered her to stand, then at her direction, two other lasses poured clear, cold water over her head and body. The shock of it made Muireall gasp.

One of the lasses was Ella, tears in her eyes. She had witnessed Muireall's humiliation, and worse, been forced to be part of it. Muireall caught her gaze and shook her head, slightly, trying to tell her not to cry. Ella had already been through much worse in Thomas's bed.

But worse waited for Muireall, a few days hence, once Erik got his hands on her. If what she'd heard about his dark side was true, and if she was lucky, he'd kill her quickly. Not that her luck had been very good over the last month. Maybe that changed when the *Tangie* broke up in the firth and Euan washed ashore.

If only she knew what had happened to him. Had he gotten away?

❧

CALUM'S BODY WAS NOWHERE TO BE FOUND. AS EUAN made his way to the cove where the Rosses beached their boats, he searched as quickly as he could, all the while watching for a Ross patrol or even a lone guard. The tide must have pulled Calum out into the firth. Surely the Rosses hadn't carried his body up to the cliff for burial when the sea was so much closer at hand. So much simpler.

As Muireall had described, there was one large *birlinn*. Several smaller craft were pulled above the high tide line. But unlike what Muireall had led him to expect, no one watched over this cove. Where were the Ross guards? Based on what she'd said, he expected more, not fewer...or none. Because of Calum, they had proof someone had survived the shipwreck. Why would they fail to post a guard over their boats, especially as night fell? The lack made him even more uneasy than prowling around Ross coves already had. Did they know he was here? He blended into the deeper darkness near the cliff and stood as still as he was able. Where could they lay in wait for him? The boats were as empty as the pebbled ground around them. There were no other hiding places.

Nothing moved but the eternal rush and slide of the waves against the shore.

He was sorely tempted to take one of the medium-sized sailboats and head out. His first loyalty had to be to his men. If any had survived and, unlike Calum, avoided the Rosses, they would have made their way down the coast, intent on getting around the firth and back to Brodie. He might find them, or he might find their bodies washed up on shore.

Muireall's silent disappearance still worried him.

His gut twisted with indecision. Take a boat and go now? Or delay and risk capture?

Staying won. He had to know if she was dead or alive. He couldn't just abandon her to the men who'd snatched her from her home and family, and who planned to force her to wed one of them. He'd take his chances on stealing one of these boats when the time came to leave.

Euan continued down the beach. As he went, the clifftop rose even higher than at the Ross coves. He doubted any of his men could have climbed here. They would have continued down the beach if they were able. Then, in a little over a mile, a slope trailed gently down to the water, forming a hillside covered with dry grasses, winter-brown shrubs and starting about halfway up, small leafless trees. This looked promising. Avoiding sandy areas in favor of gravel and water-rounded stones that would hide his tracks, he ascended the slope.

He wanted to approach the Ross village from the landward side. They would not expect shipwreck survivors to go inland, but to stay near the coast to search for fellow sailors, and to hope for rescue by a friendly boat. The chance to come at the village from higher ground was an opportunity he hadn't foreseen. With good cover, he might be able to overlook the village and actually find out what had happened to Muireall from a distance. From there he could double back using any cover the land offered to avoid Ross patrols and look for his men. Only then would he steal a boat and leave. It was a good plan, but he'd fought enough battles to know how seldom any plan survived being put into action.

Even in the early darkness the view of the coastline from the clifftop was spectacular, if unrewarding. The sea sparkled whenever moonlight broke through the clouds scattered across the sky. The beach gleamed, a pale ribbon between the restless sea and the dark cliffs. He saw no sign of wreckage or bodies from the *Tangie* past the coves he'd already searched. Nor could he see the Ross village on the clifftop below him for intervening hillocks and trees, but the wind had shifted and carried the scent of smoke. Cooking fires, most likely.

He turned away from the sea, carefully crossed a meadow filled with chest-high grasses, and entered a sparse grove of evergreen trees. Trees meant water. He needed only to find a downhill slope where trees grew taller and thicker to find a burn. Or take his chances and head directly toward the Ross village. There had to be a burn or small loch near it where he could slake the thirst that was becoming a fine torture, more painful even than the hollow pinching of his empty belly. He knew he'd regain some strength if he could find fresh water, but he'd rather not have to do it on an enemy's doorstep.

A rustle in the undergrowth alerted him and he crouched next to a tree trunk, barely daring to breathe. Was it an animal? Or a Ross sentry? All too quickly, he could become the hunted rather than the hunter. Other than his damaged hands, he had no weapon. He'd left the rope hanging from the sea cave nearly two miles down the coast. He'd lost his dirk in the firth, along with his ship and his men...most of them. Not Calum. Pain filled his chest at the thought of what had happened to him, making him wince.

The rustle sounded again. Euan held his breath and watched. He couldn't let himself be distracted, not with his survival at stake—and more. Muireall counted on him to rescue her, and he had to get home to tell his clan what became of his crew.

A shiver of movement in the undergrowth gave away the position of whatever made the noise. A Ross patrol would have no reason to hide in the under-growth so close to their village. They'd search openly and walk confidently in an area they likely knew very well.

Hope flared in his chest and he nearly stood, so strong was his need to see another of his men. Calum was dead at the hands of a Ross. If they'd made it to shore, the others might be alive—and one of them might be just a few feet away.

Whoever it was made a soft choking sound, then moaned. At that, Euan got slowly to his feet, careful to keep the tree trunk between him and the person in the brush. They sounded troubled—injured or ill, he couldn't tell. He peered around the trunk, but could not see enough to recognize one of his men. He was going to have to take the chance and get closer.

MUIREALL WAS GRATEFUL WHEN ELLA STAYED BEHIND her from the tub to her cot, shielding Muireall as much as possible from the men's view with her full skirts. Laughter followed them until they got inside and Ella firmly shut the door.

"*Ach*, Muireall...yer back..."

Muireall held up a hand. "Dinna start, please. If ye think to number all the insults against me up to this day, ye'll have me weeping, too." She went to the small chest in the room and pulled out a kirtle and under-shift. "I'm going to clothe myself and act as though none of that ever happened. I must be strong."

"No matter how strong ye be, Erik will be stronger."

"Aye, and there's nothing I can do about that. But I can, I hope, gain some small measure of respect by not cowering in front of the clan. He's a prideful man. Perhaps he'll treat me better for it." She pulled the shift over her head and continued through the cloth as the kirtle followed it, billowing over her head and down her body, "'Tis no' as if I have anything else left to me."

Ella's uncharacteristic silence made Muireall turn to her as soon as the dress was on her shoulders and she could see.

Ella stood off to one side. The cottage's door was open, filled with Erik's large body.

He glanced at Ella as he stepped inside. "Out."

She nodded and moved carefully around him, then ran out the door.

Erik's lips quirked in what Muireall suspected could have become a grin, if he'd let it. Instead, he closed the door and faced her, expression solemn as a priest.

"I heard what ye said. About gaining the clan's respect."

Muireall clasped her hands in front of her. Would he taunt her, or worse, punish her, for her pride?

He leaned against the door and crossed his arms. "Ye would make me a fine wife. Ye have spirit. And ye are comely enough to please any man."

Muireall barely heard anything he said past the word *would*. She frowned up at him, leaning, confident and completely at ease, on her door. "Would?"

"Aye. There is another I intend to wed."

"No' a Ross, then?" Or Donas and Silas would know about his plan.

"Nay. No' a Ross. A Rose lass I met in Inverness before ye...arrived. Fiona."

Muireall crossed her arms, knowing that made her look defensive, but needing the comfort. His choice of words rankled. *Arrived*, had she? "Where does that leave me?" If he met Fiona Rose before Muireall was taken—nearly a month ago—what had he been doing since then? Why hadn't he asked Donas to offer for this Fiona? Maybe he had, and Donas had put him off, saying he'd have to marry her instead. Maybe all this time, Erik had been trying to find a way out of doing as his chief bid him do.

Erik studied her so intently, Muireall nearly took a step back. Instead she tightened her belly and stood her ground. When her chin lifted, Erik chuckled.

"I dinna ken. But I think ye'll do fine, no matter who ye wed." He paused, then stood away from the door, a thoughtful look on his face. "Only, dinna anger Silas. She never lets a slight go unanswered."

"Thank ye for the warning. But what do ye think Donas will do when he finds out ye seek to defy him?"

Erik's expression turned fierce and something dangerous flashed in his eyes. "Ye'll no' say a word to Donas unless ye want trouble from me."

Muireall planted her fists on her hips. "I dinna want trouble from ye or any other Ross. I'll no' tell yer secret. All I want is to go home, and take Ella and Tira with me."

"They canna leave. They're married. They're Rosses now."

"And I can?" She snorted. "So will ye take me home in return for my silence?"

"Yer silence is more easily bought than that, lass."

His big hands clenched into fists and ice suddenly slid down Muireall's spine. "Ye wouldna." This time, her nerve failed her and she backed up a step. "Is that why ye came here? To get rid of me, so Donas willna object if ye marry another?"

"Nay, but 'tis no' such a bad idea," he growled.

"'Tis a very bad idea," Muireall assured him as she eased away. She couldn't help herself. She knew there was nowhere to run, no way to escape Erik if he truly intended to choke the life out of her, but she backed up another step, anyway.

Suddenly, Erik's fists relaxed and he laughed.

Muireall frowned up at him, speechless.

"Heed me, lass," he told her and slipped out the door.

Muireall's knees went weak. She collapsed in a heap on the earthen floor, shaking, her hands over her mouth and her pounding heart. What had just happened?

And why?

CHAPTER 5

*A*nother groan from the form in the grass pulled Euan from behind the tree. Not yet willing to throw caution completely aside, he approached carefully, moving as quietly as he was able until the darker shape of a man lying on the ground came into view.

"Calum!" Euan knelt beside his cousin, who at first glance looked bad, at second glance...terrible. "I thought ye were dead."

"Water..."

"Aye, but we'll have to go a bit farther to find it."

"Bloody hell..."

Euan helped Calum sit up, wincing at his yelp of pain. Calum cradled his left arm—broken no doubt.

"Just my luck," Calum added, "I've gone about as far as I can go."

"Did a Ross do that to ye?" Had the blood on his hands not dried into stiff scabs that would hurt like hell to crack and tear, Euan would have clenched his fists.

Calum must have heard the fury in his voice, for he was quick to answer and his reply held some of his well-loved humor. "No' unless the rocks in the cove are named Ross." He shook his head. "As the *Tangie* went down, I heard ye yell to get away from the ship." He stopped for a moment as though trying to swallow, then continued. "So being the excellent follower of orders that I am, I swam clear." He waved his good arm. "I found a piece of the wreckage afloat and hung on." He tried again swallow but only managed a weak cough. "With the tide coming in, I thought I would float to shore." He paused and took a few breaths, shaking his head. "I expect the others did the same. Have ye seen them?"

Euan shook his head, sadness a heavy weight on his heart, and worry another on his head.

Calum cradled his arm and continued. "Well, ah, the waves pushed me into some rocks. My bit of salvage became my enemy, slamming my arm against a rock. That might have been when it broke. I couldna get clear right away. The waves kept pounding..." He pursed his lips, then continued, "I had to protect my head." He shrugged one shoulder—not the one attached to his broken arm. "A small price to pay to keep breathing, I suppose."

"I thought I heard ye this morning..."

"Aye, well, as to that," Calum said and huffed out a breath. "The Rosses found me on their beach. When I couldna tell them where the rest of the crew had gone, they knocked me out and tossed me back in the firth." He nodded at his arm. "Thinking, I'm sure, with this broken, I'd flounder and drown." He paused to breathe again.

"Good thing they didna cut yer throat."

"I'm no' so easy to kill, praise all the saints and sinners. I woke up spluttering. Water up my nose, aye? Damn thing still burns."

"Ye are fortunate the Rosses didna stick around."

"Aye, or they woulda finished the job instead of counting on the firth to rid them of my handsome corpse. I made it back to shore a cove or two down. I lay there like a beached kelpie for what seemed like hours."

"Then ye climbed up here, looking for fresh water."

"And if I wasna dry before I told ye my tale, I certainly am after the telling. Since I have nay choice, shall we go?"

"Aye." As Euan helped Calum stand, he told him, "When I heard ye scream, and then the sound o' yer voice cut off, we...I...thought they'd killed ye. I'm glad to see ye, cousin."

"We? I though ye said ye'd seen nay more of our men."

"'Tis a long tale. Let's walk and I'll tell ye."

Euan kept up a low-voiced rendition of his adventures since the shipwreck and, without going into her history, Muireall's assumption that the Rosses had killed their captive. He also kept a careful watch, knowing Calum would not be much help defending them if they ran into a Ross patrol.

Calum punctuated his tale with grunts of pain as they began to descend the uneven ground of the far side of the hill. "I wish we'd bound this bloody arm before we started this trek," he complained.

Euan sympathized, but knew that could wait. Calum's arm was not bloodied, so the broken bone had not pierced the skin. Once they had drunk their fill of water and perhaps found something to eat, he would do what he could for his cousin.

"That lass I told ye about, Muireall..."

"Aye?" Calum stumbled and Euan held him up by his good arm, earning him a grateful glance and a nod.

"I have to find her and get her away. The Rosses stole her and two others from Munro nearly a month ago. The other two have been claimed. She fears she will be, very soon, and wants to escape."

"Claimed?"

"Aye, wedded and bedded against their will."

"Something no Brodie would ever do."

They'd been following a thickening stand of trees down the hill. Now Euan heard what he'd been listening for—the sound of rushing water. "We're nearly there. I hear a burn."

"Good. That is good."

Calum sounded exhausted, and looked it, too. He'd spent more time in the water than Euan. Chilled and in pain, he'd suffered even more mistreatment and exposure at the hands of the Ross men. "I'll get ye there," Euan promised, and breathed a sigh of relief when they reached the rushing burn.

Both men dropped to their knees. Euan began scooping water up to his mouth, frantic to ease the thirst he'd ignored for so many hours.

Calum tried it one-handed, gave up and stretched out on his good side, then rolled to his belly, yelped and rolled back. "Damn," he muttered, digging into his shirt and down his side with his good hand. He pulled out a slingshot. "I forgot the damn thing was there. I couldna think of another way to keep it with me once I kenned we were going in the water." He turned it front to back, frowning as he studied it. "I dinna expect it'll be much use, me with this arm. Shouldha kept my dirk, but I would been pulling it out of my gut by now. Or worse," he added with a grin and a glance at his crotch.

"Ye would ha stabbed yerself in the leg, no doubt. There's little else in the way." Euan's droll tone expressed his doubts as he reached out a hand. "Here. Let me have that. I can try it," he offered. He'd seen Calum use it often enough, mostly to frighten persistent seabirds away from their catch on other fishing trips. His aim was deadly, but he preferred clipping their tail feathers with a small pebble, a supply of which he usually kept in a pouch at his waist, to shoo them away.

Calum tucked it into his belt on the outside of his shirt this time. "Nay, ye canna. Ye've never been any good with it. Like as no', ye'd hit me rather than what ye're aiming for."

"I'm no' that bad."

"Aye, ye are." With that, he plunged his face into the cold, clear water. When he came up for air, he pushed his hair out of his eyes and dunked his entire head. "Try it," he said when he came up again. "It feels good to get rid of the salt."

"That may be so, but dinna think to bathe in it. Yer clothes are dry now. Ye'll be better served to remain that way."

Calum rolled onto his back, cradling his broken arm on his chest.

"Ye could put that arm in the cold water. It might numb the pain for ye, and make it easier for me to set."

"Worth a try…" Calum agreed and rolled back to his stomach. He supported the break with his good hand and extended his arms into the chill water, resting his head on his shoulder. After several minutes, the pinching around his eyes eased.

Seeing that, Euan left to find some stout straight sticks. When he returned, he tore strips from the hems of their shirts, much as Muireall had done for him from the hem of her shift. Thinking of her made him anxious and eager to be on the move.

By then, Calum reported the arm was numb. Euan gave him one stick to bite down on, set the arm, and then bound it tightly, using the other sticks to keep it straight. By the time he finished, Calum was pale and sweating, but the job was done. "That should do until we get home and Mhairi can take a look at ye. Put it back in the stream and let it get numb again. The wet binding will hold the cold a bit longer, too." Euan tied two wider strips together and fashioned a sling to support the arm once Calum felt able to travel.

Without comment, Calum did as Euan suggested.

Euan let him rest. "This burn flows down toward the Ross village," he mused after a while. "I can follow it and bring Muireall back here. 'Twould be best if ye stayed."

"And if they capture ye, how am I to sail for home with this arm? Nay, I'll go with ye, to keep ye out of trouble."

Euan eyed him. "I dinna plan on getting into any trouble."

Calum snorted. "Ye never do. Yet how do ye think we wound up here?"

THE NEXT DAY, EVERYWHERE SHE WENT, MUIREALL KNEW someone watched her. Sadly, the eyes on her were not Euan's. Always a Ross. Donas's announcement that she was Erik's to claim had put a stop to the speculative looks from the rest of the men, but those had been replaced by suspicion and mistrust after her return from the sea cave. She didn't welcome the attention, not when she hoped to escape.

Oddly, only Erik seemed not to care how she'd spent that day in the cove. His mind was probably on the lass he did want to marry. He seemed determined to avoid being seen with Muireall, though he'd passed through the village between patrols.

The Rosses still hunted for the shipwreck survivors.

Muireall hoped Euan was long gone, but since no one had reported a boat missing from the Ross cove, he must still be in the area. Worse, she feared he would make his way nearby, looking for her. She stayed outside as much as possible, trying to be visible in case

Euan hid in the woods surrounding the village on three sides. She hoped once he saw she was unharmed, he would sail for home. If he stayed close, he would be captured, and she could not bear to see him tortured—or killed.

She settled in a sunny spot behind her cot, where the light fell on the needlework in her lap and tried to look busy. In truth, her gaze kept returning to the edge of the woods, searching for any movement that might betray Euan's presence. Ella soon joined her, and even Tira settled on her other side.

"Ye ken they're all talking about ye," Ella told her, low-voiced.

"Donas is waiting for Erik to claim ye and punish ye as ye deserve," Tira added.

Muireall's mouth fell open. What a thing for Tira to say. Did she mean it or was she simply repeating what she'd heard?

At that moment, Erik moved across the village center, and Tira sighed. "Ye might be the luckiest of the three of us," she said, her gaze following him. "I wouldna mind being punished by that one."

"Tira!" Ella gasped. "How can ye say such a horrible thing? Ye ken what Donas did to Muireall. Besides, I thought ye were happy with Teague."

"Aye, happy enough, I suppose, but I'd rather have had time to choose a man, if that had been possible, rather than be taken by the first man wanting a woman on the way here. Just look at Erik. Ye're getting the handsomest man in the village, Muireall. And the one most likely to follow Donas as chief."

"Perhaps," Muireall responded, knowing Tira would misinterpret her comment. She wasn't thinking about his looks. If he had his way, he would marry another, not her. She let a little of how that pleased her show on her face, knowing Tira would misinterpret her expression, too. And as for the rest of the Ross men...Muireall fought to still the instinctive urge to shake her head, denying those possibilities. Of the lot, Erik was by far the best choice. For a fleeting moment, she thought it a shame he wanted someone else. Then sanity returned. Being forced to marry him—or any other Ross—made her stomach turn. She hoped, with Euan's help, to escape that fate, and soon.

It was a shame, too, that Erik was not already chief of this clan. She suspected things would be very different with him in charge. Silas had lied about him. She shouldn't be surprised - Silas and Donas lied about many things. Making her terrified of the man Donas threatened to give her to must have been a game to them. One she'd fallen for. And lost sleep over, until Erik had proven them wrong. Despite his rumored temper, Erik had shown her respect and been honest about his intentions. That encounter should have made him more attractive to her, but it did not, not in that way. It did make her willing to trust him, at least a little, and to believe that all of the Ross villagers would be better off under his leadership than under leaders like Donas and Silas.

Suddenly, Muireall wished Euan was close by, ready to steal her away from here.

She picked up her stitching and bent to work. Out of the corner of her eye, she saw Ella frown at Tira, still watching Erik. He'd paused to speak to another of the men. Then Ella glanced her way and shrugged, as if she'd accepted there was no point in discussing anything about their new lives with Tira. Likely anything they said would be reported back to Silas at Tira's first opportunity.

While Muireall didn't like being spied upon, she couldn't blame Tira for wanting to make the best of her new situation. Teague had led the raid on their village and claimed her on the way back to Ross territory, before Donas could give her to anyone else. He wasn't the biggest or the best-looking warrior among the Ross men, but he was smart and quick, and he did seem to dote on his stolen bride. If Tira took advantage of his infatuation to claim certain freedoms—and to cozy up to Silas—that was her concern, not Muireall's. She and Ella would have to remember that Tira might have come from their village, but she was all Ross now.

They worked silently long enough for Tira to complain she had other tasks demanding her attention today. Muireall suspected she was bored.

Tira left. Ella stood and stretched then sat back down. "Thank goodness she's gone. Honestly, I used to like her, but now I dare no' say anything around her unless 'tis something I want Silas to ken."

Muireall saw an opportunity to sound out Ella. "Keep yer own counsel, then, or talk to me—quietly. There are more ears than Tira's in this village." She glanced around. They were as alone as they'd ever be, Tira having given up her duty to keep an eye on them. "Have ye thought about leaving, if the opportunity were ever to arise?"

"I'm married now. I canna leave."

"Ye were married against yer will."

"Do ye think that makes a difference?

"Do ye think it does no'?"

Ella sighed and dropped her mending in her lap. "I dinna ken. I didna chose Thomas, but he does take care of me. And who else would have me, after this?"

"Is he kind? Affectionate? Does he love ye? Do ye love him?"

Ella laughed softly. "Kind? Aye, even affectionate at times, I dinna ken if he loves me, and nay, I dinna love him, though I may grow to...someday. I dinna have much choice in the matter, do I?"

"What if ye did? What if we could leave? Would ye go?"

Ella frowned at her. "Does this have something to do with yesterday? The shipwreck survivor you tried to deny exists?" Her hand flew to her throat. "Is he coming for ye?"

Muireall shook her head, anxiety a spike in her belly. "I dinna ken. But if he does, I would go. You could, too."

Ella's head fell against the wall at her back. "Nay, Muireall, dinna make me wish for something that will never be." Then she lifted it and looked directly at her friend. "Besides, ye ken less about that man than ye do about these Rosses. Tira's right about one thing—ye could do much worse for a husband than Erik."

Muireall wondered if she dared tell Ella what Erik had said. Nay, she'd promised to keep his secret, and she would, at least while she remained here. "No' if I have to live under the rule of the likes of Donas and Silas," she finally answered.

Ella pursed her lips. "I see what ye mean. But men die in battle all the time. Donas loves to fight. And ye could help Erik take over the clan."

"If it ever comes to that, I think Erik will be quite capable of doing that without me."

"Aye, ye are right, of course." Ella picked up her stitching. "May that day come soon. Then ye'd be wife of the chief."

Muireall shook her head, though she knew her friend would not see the gesture. Her gaze was on the needlework in her hand. "Ella, forget it. It will never happen."

"So ye have made up yer mind to go." Her tone was sad, resigned.

Muireall knew she was imagining being left behind to face the life they now found themselves in. She laid a hand over Ella's. "Aye. And to take ye, as well, if ye wish it."

"I'll think on it, but I'm not sure running away will improve anything." Her hands tightened into fists. "I'd rather stay with Thomas than take a risk that may get us both whipped, or killed." '

"Dinna take too long," Muireall cautioned. "But if ye decide to stay, then change yer mind, find a reason to spend time on a beach in one of the coves."

"Why?"

"Just trust me. And dinna say anything to anyone about this. Lives depend on silence—yours and mine included."

❧

EUAN AND CALUM HAD TRADED OFF SENTRY DUTY through the night, though Euan slept with one eye open. Calum's injury might keep him awake and restless, but exhaustion might cause him to nod off. Fortunately, the night had passed uneventfully. After several hours sleep each, Calum wanted to hunt.

"I think I can manage this well enough to take down a bird for our breakfast," he boasted, pulling the slingshot from his belt along his side.

"And clean the bird and cook it? Or do ye fancy eating it raw? Smoke from a cook-fire will give us away."

Calum frowned and looked away. "Raw it is, then."

"We'll wait," Euan told him, wondering if Calum was becoming feverish. "Ye willna starve in a day's time."

"'Tis already been more than a day..."

"Dinna remind me."

They crept closer to the village and found a good

vantage point in one of many clusters of low-growing evergreens along its north side.

Once the sun came up, though Euan stayed especially alert for Ross patrols, his real quarry was Muireall.

By late morning, she appeared. Euan spotted her immediately as she left one of the small thatched dwellings that made up the village. She took a seat on the ground in a patch of sunlight and rested her back against the building, facing out toward the trees. A lass soon joined her—one pretty enough to be her friend Ella. They were soon joined by another lass Euan supposed might be the third Munro, now Ross. They worked on some mending as they talked, too far away for him to make out what they said, then they fell silent for a long time. When the third lass left, Muireall and her friend resumed a conversation. They looked so serious, Euan became convinced this was Ella, and that Muireall was trying to find out if she wanted to leave the Ross village, too, despite her forced marriage.

Muireall's gaze kept lifting to the woods.

He doubted she could see him, but he could change that in an instant, simply by standing. Should he?

He glanced around at Calum, who knelt at his back, attention on the woods around them. Though still exhausted, and not yet capable of running for his life, should that be required, Calum had the sharpest ears in the clan. So far, so good. Calum had not given the alarm, so no one approached, despite how close they were to the village.

Muireall appeared to be fine. As much as Euan wanted to get her away from her captors, and take her in his arms, this was not the time.

"Which one is Muireall?"

Calum's low voice at his back startled Euan into a

frown. "The one with auburn hair. The other, I think, is her friend, Ella."

Calum huffed out a breath. "My God, she's gorgeous."

"Muireall? Aye."

"Um, aye, she's pretty enough. But Ella…"

Euan slanted him a frown. "She is married to one of the men here."

"Against her will, ye said."

"True. But Muireall's no' certain she'll want to leave."

"I wouldna mind a chance to help her make up her mind." Calum straightened, still on his knees, then put a foot forward and started to rise.

Euan grabbed his good arm and hauled him back down. "No' now. Until ye are stronger, 'tis too dangerous. I've seen that Muireall is safe and unguarded, if no' unwatched. We need food and more water before we can fight off anyone who might try to stop us."

"And swords. Even a dirk would improve our odds. But mine's on the bottom of the firth."

"Mine, too. We'll figure something out. Look, they're leaving." The sun had moved far enough their spot was becoming shaded by the building behind it.

Euan watched the lasses gather up their mending, stand and move away. But wait, hidden beneath Muireall's skirts until she stood was a bundle. She left it behind. It looked like a sack of more mending, but what if…"

"That's got to be for ye," Calum whispered. "Food. Maybe even a dirk."

"It doesna matter. I've seen what I needed to see. We should leave."

"'Tis no' safe to move during the day. And if she's as braw a lass as ye think, she's canny enough to have left ye what ye need. Food, at least. Maybe a weapon, too."

Euan nodded. Calum was right about one thing. They'd be too easy to spot in daylight. And they didn't know the land as well as the Ross warriors, who might have vantage points he hadn't yet recognized. He thought back to how he'd found Calum. The slightest movement, the slightest sound, would betray them. And if they were unlucky enough to be seen by a Ross patrol, they'd be easy prey. "It will have to stay there until dark, or until something draws the clan to the other side of the village. Then I'll retrieve it. Get comfortable. We're going to be here a while."

CHAPTER 6

The bundle was still in place after the sun set. No one from the village had wandered behind this cot since Muireall and her friend left. Eventually, Euan judged it dark enough, and late enough—and he was well past hungry enough—to risk retrieving it. Calum had dozed off hours ago. Euan let him sleep and kept watch, praying no one discovered them, since they had no weapons. In a fight, Calum's broken arm would only make a bad situation worse.

Euan put a hand over Calum's mouth and shook him gently. "'Tis time," he whispered. Calum opened his eyes and nodded his understanding. Though the bundle was only a little more than a dozen yards from their lair, most of those yards were open ground, where any movement would be instantly visible if someone chanced to look that way.

He had to risk it. They'd been days without food. Yet they still had to make the trek back down the beach, overpower a guard, and steal a boat. After that, they would have to row until it was safe to raise a sail, then stay alert for pursuers for hours more until they reached Brodie. Going after the bundle Muireall left behind was safer than hunting game anywhere near the

Ross village. The hunter could quickly become the hunted. And even if they were not discovered, they would not dare risk a fire to cook anything they managed to kill. Though his belly was empty enough to pinch, the thought of raw meat made it turn. First, he'd see what Muireall left him.

Calum sat up, then took up position to keep watch. Euan crawled out of their lair and stood, slowly and silently, dreading the alarm that would announce their presence to the clan. When no call broke the stillness, he crept away from their cover toward the edge of the trees, then paused. The usual night noises continued, reassuring him. Heartened, he crouched and covered the distance to the back wall of the cot in fleet seconds, picked up the bundle, and returned to the tree line.

Nothing disturbed the stillness of the night but the sound of his heart hammering hard enough to beat its way from his chest. He'd gladly take on an enemy face-to-face, suitably armed, of course, than repeat that stealthy run.

He moved deeper into the woods and joined Calum in their lair.

"Let's see what Muireall left us," Calum greeted him.

"After we move away from here, aye?"

They headed back to the burn and settled in a clump of bushes. Euan unwrapped Muireall's bundle and revealed what he'd hoped for: a round loaf of oat bread, a fist-sized hunk of hard cheese and several apples. Even better, stuck in one of the apples, a small eating knife! A feast for two starving men—and a weapon. Small, awkward for throwing but useful for close quarters fighting, it wouldn't be much help against a claymore or even a dirk, but it was better than nothing.

Given the amount of food she'd provided, he wondered if she hoped he'd come across more of his men or just thought he'd be that hungry. Either way, he was grateful. If only she could have left him a bigger blade. But even a dirk would have caused her problems if the bundle had been discovered in her possession. An eating knife made sense and was safer for her to include.

"Take it slowly," he advised, as he broke the bread in two and handed half to Calum. He used the knife to divide the cheese. "This may have to get us through tomorrow, unless ye fancy eating raw whatever we can catch."

Calum nodded and took a bite out of his share of the cheese. His eyes rolled back in his head as he chewed, then swallowed. "Bloody good."

Euan ate slowly, and left more than half his portion for later. Calum did the same, though Euan could see he wanted to finish off everything Muireall had left. Euan handed him an apple. "Drink some from the burn, then rest a wee. In a few hours, we'll make our way to the Ross's boats and steal away before the dawn."

"Ye're going to leave those lasses…"

"Only for two days. They're safe for now. The rest of our men may no' be. We will sail straight out into the firth, then come back along the coast with sunup to see if we can spot any of our men north of Ross. If we dinna see anyone, I'll get ye home with the news, then return. If I'm right, somewhere on one of those beaches, one or both of those lasses will be waiting for me."

"No' by yerself…"

"Nay. In another boat and with a small crew. No sense sailing a Ross skiff right back into their clutches."

Calum considered it. "Aye, that's a good plan. If they see a boat they recognize as theirs, they'll follow it along the coast and ye'll no' be able to retrieve the lasses. A strange fishing boat will get less notice. Give me a few hours with the healer and I'll come back with ye."

"Ye are in no condition to handle a sheet, much less a sword."

To Euan's great relief, Calum nodded and moved to the burn. When he came back, he said, "I slept earlier, so I'll keep watch for the next while. Get some rest."

Euan saw the sense in that and agreed without commenting. Instead, he stretched out on the ground, knowing Calum would wake him all too soon. But sleep wouldn't come. Memories filled his mind of the *Tangie* going down, of Eduard, Dugal, and James's faces as they gripped the lines, peering down at the frothing firth and their sail sinking below the waves. He hoped they'd made it, but couldn't shake the certainty they'd gone down with the ship. His only consolation was the knowledge that he'd thought the same of Calum.

&

MUIREALL GOT UP DURING THE NIGHT AND QUIETLY stepped out of her cot, hoping the darkness would shield her movements as she made her way around it.

The bundle of food she'd left was missing. She smiled in satisfaction.

Despite the fact that she'd told Euan not to come near the village looking for her, she'd known he'd do exactly that. She hoped he had the bundle. If he did, he was safe, and fed, and free—so far. She felt certain no animal had dragged it off. There was enough starlight for her to see if bits of the contents had been scattered over the ground. They weren't, nor did she see the shawl she'd used. No animal would have dragged it far once it got to the food in it.

Was Euan still nearby? Watching and waiting for

her? Nay, he had better sense than to remain so close to the village. Checking on her was one thing. Staying nearby long enough to be discovered by Donas's men was quite another. Besides, they'd agreed she would find a way to be down on a beach in a few days, and knowing he'd kept watch over her made her confident he really would sail back to retrieve her. And Ella, too, if Muireall could convince her to leave Thomas.

"What are ye doing back here?"

Muireall choked back a gasp as Donas's demand sounded behind her. She hadn't heard him approach. She turned to face him, casting about for some explanation that would satisfy him. On the way to relieve herself? Nay, all the cots had chamber pots. "I just needed some air. The sky is so clear, I thought to enjoy the stars for a few minutes. Is there a problem?"

Donas stared her down, but she kept her head up and her gaze on the ground at her feet. She couldn't bear to look at him, and didn't dare. He wouldn't take kindly to any lass staring directly back at him. Even less if she was the one daft enough to issue that kind of challenge.

"Three lashes were no' enough for ye? I told ye there'd be more the next time ye tried to run again."

Muireall shook her head. "I wasna..."

"Nay? So ye're waiting for the man from the wreck. Was I right? Did he have ye while ye waited for the tide to turn?"

Muireall shook her head again and backed away. Donas was playing with her, and she didn't know the rules of the game, only that he always won.

"Ye should be in yer bed."

His tone had turned beguiling with this comment about Euan taking her. Muireall shuddered at what must be running through Donas's mind. She had to get away. "Aye, well, I'll go there now," she replied and made to go around him.

He grabbed her arm. "No' so fast, lassie. I've been wanting a taste of ye. Now's as good a time as any, seein' as how we're all alone back here."

Muireall tried to pull her arm out of his grasp, but he was too strong and she only succeeded in making him pull her closer.

"If ye want to live, no' a sound out of ye, do ye hear me?" he growled, giving her a little shake as he bent closer. "I'd like nothing better than to hand Erik my soiled goods. He's gettin' above himself lately. Thinking that he's ready to replace me as chief. That willna happen any time soon." He chuckled and bent toward her. His mouth landed on her ear as she turned her face aside. "Dinna be coy, lass. I'll have that taste, and a whole lot more, I'm thinkin'. Instead of giving him my clan, I'll get to watch him raising my bastard. How about that?" Donas chuckled again, put a hand on her arse and pulled her against him. "Ye shouldha stayed tucked in nice and safe and warm in yer cot."

"Release me!" Muireall put as much force into her demand as she could, hoping to distract him, while still keeping her voice down. If she screamed, he'd snap her neck like a twig. "Silas willna appreciate what ye have in mind."

"Silas will never ken. If ye think to speak a word of this, ye'll regret it."

Muireall shook her head. "Then let me go, and we'll both forget this happened."

"Ye're a cheeky lass. But I've seen ye without a stitch on, and I'm thinking I'll have some o' that, right now." The hand on her arse delved between her legs. His other hand left her arm and traced her throat down to her breast, then squeezed.

Muireall reacted out of instinct. No rational

thought would have led her to such a foolish action. She drew back a foot and kicked him as hard as she could.

With a laugh, he let her go.

She knew she'd only surprised him. She couldn't possibly have hurt him. Nonetheless, the opportunity was too good to waste. She ran.

Even this late in the year, the woods were thick with undergrowth and low branches. She heard Donas's heavy tread coming after her, then heard him swear, and swear again. Finally he must've stopped because the next thing she heard was laughter. She paused to catch her breath and listen, surprised he'd given up so easily.

"Go on wi' ye," he taunted. "Ye'll have to come back, and when ye do, ye'll be mine. If no' tonight, then another time, but I'll have that taste and more."

Muireall collapsed against a tree and wrapped her arms around her middle. That tore it. She could not go back. Not ever. Bad enough to be wedded to Erik, but to submit to Donas pawing at her and worse? Nay. And if she told Erik and he failed to kill Donas, Donas would take his revenge, then kill her…eventually. There were too many places Donas could take her to have his fun, then finish her off. She was certain Silas would have no say in the matter.

Nay, the only thing she could do now was to make her way to the boats and hope Euan had not left yet. She could go with him. She'd have to leave Ella behind, but if Euan meant what he said, and she believed he did, they could come back for her later.

Mind made up, she stood and began walking, moving slowly and carefully through the woods. The last thing she needed was to attract the attention of another predator. Some of them walked on four legs.

CALUM JOSTLED EUAN'S SHOULDER, SURPRISING HIM OUT of slumber—he hadn't thought he'd sleep—but then Calum's low-voiced warning froze Euan in place.

"Someone is near."

Euan nodded slightly. Message received. Except for the far-off hoot of an owl and the ever-present gurgle of the rushing burn, the night was silent. He'd chosen this spot not only for the water, but because the sound of it would capture the attention of anyone approaching, so he and Calum might stand a chance to hear a patrol before it got close enough to discover them. "What did ye hear?" he whispered close to Calum's ear.

Calum shrugged.

He wasn't certain what he'd heard. Euan got that. It was actually good news. Man was not the only animal that hunted at night. Some predators preferred the dark. Without weapons, other than the wee eating knife, he'd still prefer a badger or a wolf over a Ross right now. It was late for a deer to be about, but not impossible, especially if one sensed their presence as it searched for safe haven. All in all, he'd rather a deer wander near them.

But Calum had said "someone" not "something." And his instincts were very, very good.

Euan waited, alert to any movement, any sound, that might penetrate the blackness around them. Finally it came, a slight shuffling noise and hiss of indrawn breath, as though someone's foot slipped on leaves. The slope leading down to the burn was uneven. Scattered tree roots and rocks made the descent treacherous unless you could see where to put your feet. Whoever was out there could not.

Someone was sneaking up on them. They were about to be ambushed. How the hell had they been found this deep in the dark woods? He cast about for a weapon—a stout stick, a rock, anything. Nothing but pebbles came to hand.

Just then, the person stumbled and let out a soft cry. A woman's cry.

Muireall? Euan had to have imagined that. His longing for the lass was making him hear her voice at the oddest, most stressful times.

"Damn thorns!"

The voice was closer and held a note of pain. This time, he could not mistake it. Muireall. Here. Was she searching for him? Alone, or did someone —the Ross chief, perhaps—have a dirk to her throat?

"Who...?" Calum asked, softly, but too loudly to suit Euan's level of anxiety.

"*Wheesht,*" he breathed and waved Calum to silence. "Stay still. 'Tis Muireall, but I canna say if 'tis her alone." The eating knife was where he'd left it. He palmed it and moved carefully away from his cousin. He paused by a broad tree trunk, then made his way toward the lass, hoping to spot any danger before it could find him—and Calum. Damn his lack of a decent blade. Any longer blade would do. The one he had in hand was little more useful than a wee *sghian dubh*. It gave him more of an advantage than mere surprise, but only barely. That and stealth were all he had now to protect them.

Then he saw her, standing in a patch of starlight, one hand on the slim trunk of a young pine, one foot feeling for the ground before her. She appeared to be alone. He moved closer. "Muireall..." He called her name softly, in case a horde of Ross warriors waited just out of sight.

Her head lifted and she turned toward the sound of his voice. "Euan? Thank God."

He stood and started toward her. "Aye, I'm here. What are ye doing in the woods in the dark of night?"

Muireall met him halfway. "I'm so glad I found ye."

He folded her in his arms, relief flooding him to have her near. "I'm glad as well. Now ye have come, we can make our way to the boats and be gone from here. But what about yer friend?"

Muireall looked up at him and shook her head. "She hasna decided yet."

His heart sank, hearing the regret in her voice. "Ye ken we canna wait."

"I do. I told her what to do if she ever wants to go. I hate to leave her behind, but I ken we must—for now."

"Aye. The longer we delay, the more likely we'll be discovered."

"Ye have already waited too long." A man's voice echoed among the trees, seeming to come from everywhere at once.

"Donas!" Muireall hissed.

Euan instinctively shifted Muireall behind him as he struggled to pierce the darkness. Where was the Ross laird? And how many men did he have with him?

Donas stepped out of the deeper darkness between several trees. Three other men stepped out a moment later, one to Euan's right, one to the left, and one betrayed himself by the snap of a twig somewhere behind Euan. Donas nodded and crossed his arms. "Ye led us right to him, lass," he gloated.

Euan mentally kicked himself for focusing on Muireall. He'd failed to keep his guard up. As soon as he'd heard her voice, he'd been aware of nothing else. He knew better, damn it.

Muireall whimpered, "Nay! Euan, ye must believe me, I didna ken…"

Euan tugged her to his side and kept an arm around her. "'Tis no' yer fault, lass."

"Yer attack was but a ruse," she spat and glared at the other man.

"Aye. I expected ye would lead us to the man with ye in the sea cave."

Muireall sagged against Euan. "If only I hadna stumbled upon ye. I could just as easily have led them away from ye."

He tightened his hold on her.

Donas gestured. Two of his men stepped forward. One set the point of his sword against Euan's chest. The other yanked Muireall out of Euan's arms.

She shrieked.

Euan grabbed for her and felt the sword point bite through his shirt into his skin. He twisted away from it, still reaching for Muireall. "Let her go!" he demanded, following the line of the sword to the man who held it, looking for any advantage, any way to get it away from the Ross and into his hands. The man eyed him and shifted his stance. There was none. "She's done naught to ye," he said, turning away from his captor and glaring at the Ross chief.

Donas lifted his chin, his gaze sliding past Euan.

His attention was so tightly focused on the threat in front of him, he almost missed hearing the third man come up behind him. He'd barely turned to defend himself when the man knocked him to the ground, then drew his dirk and laid it across Euan's throat. The man with the sword stepped back, his weapon held at the ready.

"Ye are in no position to make demands," Donas growled. "Now, who are ye and why should I no' let Garrick there slit yer throat?"

Euan didn't take his gaze from the chief, but he could hear Muireall struggling against her captor and demanding to be released. Good lass. He hoped she got free and ran for the woods. Calum might be able to find her and take her home. He didn't want her to see him killed. "My name is Euan," he answered as the edge of the dirk bit lightly into his skin. He hissed against the sting. "From the shipwreck ye found."

"So ye willna tell me yer clan?"

"Only a fool would put his kin at risk for no reason."

The man snorted and crossed his arms over his chest. "Yer presence here is reason enough."

"I'm no' here to do harm to yer clan. I'm trying to get home."

"With one of my lasses."

"No' yers!" Muireall shouted.

Donas turned toward her. "I can do whatever I wish with ye, lass, so for now, I suggest ye *haud yer wheesht*, or I'll let Robbie there have at ye." He jerked his head at the man who'd held Euan at sword point. That man joined Robbie to subdue Muireall.

Euan's heart sank. She had even less chance of escape now, held between the two men. He shifted, casting about for a way to save them both, but only succeeded in making the man behind him hold the dirk more tightly to his neck.

"Ye were bluffing before. Ye are now. Ye wouldna give me to another man," she argued, continuing to struggle. She got one arm free and nearly doubled over one of her captors with an elbow to his side. "Ye've already promised me to Erik," she taunted as the man grabbed her arm and got her under control.

"But ye dinna belong to him yet." Donas glared at the man she'd momentarily bested, then laughed. He moved to stand in front of her and grabbed her chin. "I've been known to change my mind. Dinna tempt me."

Muireall gasped and stilled.

Euan tried to catch her gaze, to make her understand she would only make things worse by baiting the man. But she refused to look his way.

To get Donas's attention off of Muireall, he had no choice but to draw it back to himself, and damn the consequences. "If ye kill me, eventually ye'll have to answer to yer chief. The Earl of Ross will not like ye starting a war with another clan."

Donas released Muireall and stepped toward Euan. "The Earl will never ken. And yer clan will assume—correctly—that ye and yer men were lost at sea. If ye want to live, ye'll tell me where the rest of the crew is, and what were ye carrying, besides fish, aboard the sunken ship?"

Euan knew better than to trust that Donas would allow him to live, no matter what tale Euan told him. He debated fabricating a story about the *Tangie's* cargo, but couldn't see what good it would do. The man was smarter than he'd given him credit for. Euan prayed Calum would stay silent so he could get away when the Rosses finished doing whatever they planned. Unarmed and with a dirk to his throat, Euan didn't expect to survive the encounter, despite Donas's offer. But Calum could, and he could get the truth back to Brodie. "Fish," he replied. "A lot of fish."

Suddenly, Euan heard a whoosh and a thunk. With a groan, one of the guards holding Muireall dropped to the ground. Before anyone could react, another thunk broke the night's stillness and the other man fell, too. Calum! Thank God for his skill, though how he managed it with a broken arm, Euan didn't take the time to fathom.

He used the distraction to roll clear of the dirk at his throat. Still moving, he kicked the man's knee and heard the crack of breaking bone. The man screamed and went down. Rising, Euan grabbed the sword out of the sheath strapped to the man's back. He had only a second before Donas charged, his blade swinging right for Euan's heart. Euan sidestepped and parried, knocking the blade aside.

"Clever," Donas congratulated him. "Ye had another man under cover all this time. But 'twill make nay difference in the end."

After what Muireall had told him about the Ross chief, and after Calum's tale of being tossed back into the unforgiving firth, Euan knew he was in a fight for his life.

"Yer men are alive," he insisted as he swung around, hoping it was true. "We can leave with no lasting harm to anyone. Ye'd best let us go while they—and ye—still live."

Donas answered with his blade, his swing aimed to remove Euan's head from his shoulders. Euan ducked, then fell back. If he appeared weaker than he truly was, he might gain some advantage.

Muireall, he noted out of the corner of his eye as his opponent found his footing, had taken cover behind the trunk of a stout tree. Good lass. Calum was still out of sight.

Euan had to stop Donas, or they'd never get away. Yet he knew he could not let this battle go on for long. His hands were bleeding again, making his grip slippery. His strength was not fully restored on one meal and some water. And he doubted his opponent would make the mistake of letting him get close enough to knock him out, not without the risk of being gutted himself. Why hadn't Calum used his slingshot to take Donas down?

Then Euan realized Donas was working his way toward Muireall.

Her gaze darted around, watchful, yet she was clearly unaware of her danger.

The big chief could kill her easily, but first he'd use

her to bring Euan to heel and force Calum out of hiding. Then he would kill them. Euan couldn't let that happen.

He charged, swinging the borrowed sword with everything in him, surprising Donas and catching his blade on his own. Heedless of the danger to himself, he forced his blade up his opponent's steel until the hilts clanged together.

Donas growled and fought to free his blade.

Euan kneed him, jerked his blade free and kneed him again. Doubling over, he still managed a wild thrust, which Euan easily avoided. Counting on Donas's agony to hinder his ability to fight, he took the risk and moved in, knocked aside another thrust and impaled the Ross chief.

The disbelief in Donas's eyes slowly faded away on a rattled gasp. He dropped his sword and fell to his knees, silent, gaze fixed far away. In a moment, he was dead.

Euan pulled his blade free and allowed the body to fall to its side. He took a deep breath as Muireall came out from behind the tree and slowly approached.

"Is he truly gone?"

"Aye. We'd best take advantage of the hours of darkness we have left and go." Euan glanced at the men, still laid out on the forest floor like so many dropped shirts. The man whose leg he'd broken was unconscious, as were the two Calum had knocked out. He picked up Donas's sword and called softly, "Calum, where are ye?"

"Here." Calum stepped out from behind a tree, tucking his slingshot inside his shirt with his good hand. "'Tis good ye didna need my help. He wouldna stay still. I couldna throw at him without the chance of hitting ye or the lass."

Euan clapped him on his good shoulder. "Glad I am ye devised a way to use that. I thought for a moment ye would have to find yer way home without me." He glanced around. Off to one side, Muireall shivered, arms hugging herself and gaze bouncing from him to Donas's body and back to him. She'd been so brave. He had to help her.

"Calum, this is Muireall." He handed the sword to Calum, then put his arms around her. "She's a braw lass." He kissed her temple, pleased to feel her shivering subside. "Ye are safe now," he murmured. "We all are." Calum stepped forward but Euan spoke before Calum had a chance to greet her. "Lass, ye and I will take their blades," he said, gesturing at Donas's men. She nodded but didn't move out of the circle of his other arm. He decided to give her another minute and signaled to Calum to retrieve the dirks while Muireall stood, still unmoving.

After a moment, she heaved a breath, nodded and gave him a hint of a smile, then stepped out of his arms and bent to retrieve the nearest man's dirk.

Euan kept a claymore and tossed the remaining swords into the darkness.

"What about them?" Muireall asked.

"When they wake up, if they decide to give chase, they willna be armed," he replied.

"Perhaps they'll take the man with the broken leg back to their village, instead," she said.

Euan nodded. "Let's hope so. For his sake and ours."

Then he spared Donas one last look, regretting the necessity of killing the Ross chief. He didn't know what trouble would follow, but had no doubt Donas Ross's death would bring more.

Calum followed his glance and shrugged as if to say he didn't know, either.

Euan took Muireall's hand and gently tugged. "Let's get moving."

 *M*uireall tugged her hand too easily from Euan's. When she did, dampness slid across her palm. She dug in her heels and turned his hand over. The bindings she'd made from the hem of her sleep shift were still in place, but smeared with blood. "Is that Donas's, or are ye bleeding again?"

"*Dinna fash.* Ye can tend me later." He pulled his hand free.

"Wait." She added a frown warning him not to move, then bent and sliced up the length of the sleeves of Donas's shirt, tugging the fabric out from under his arms to cut it free. She tried to ignore how she jostled the dead limbs, focusing instead on the practical matter of Euan's need for bindings. Donas had fallen with his arms outstretched, so the sleeves were less bloody than the rest of his clothes. "This should do," she muttered. She split one sleeve in two, quickly and efficiently, and wrapped each over the strips of her shift already covering Euan's hands. When she was done, he nodded.

"Ye are full of surprises, lass."

She grimaced and tucked the other sleeve in her bodice, loath to have Donas's smell anywhere near her, but she could wash that away in the sea. Given what she'd seen of Euan, she expected to need more bandages before long.

"I'd do the same to them, but they might wake up. Let's go before they do."

Euan gave her a nod and took her arm.

As they headed out into the darkness, she didn't know whether to try to forget the image of Donas falling under Euan's blade, or revel in it. The Ross chief was dead. That could only be good for the clan and for her. And for the Brodies who flanked her and led her through the dark night toward the cove where the Ross clan kept their boats. Now that the two men were armed, and despite Calum's injury, they made a large and fearsome escort. With them, and with a dirk in her hand, she felt safe for the first time since she'd been stolen from her home.

They were going to make it.

Once they made their way down a hill to the beach, Euan called a halt. "From here on, no' a word, no' a sound. If we're discovered, we have no cover and nowhere to run. And if there's a guard at the boats, surprise is our best advantage."

Muireall nodded her response.

Calum gestured her forward with his good arm.

Euan took up position to her right, the better to swing his borrowed sword, she knew, should the need arise.

Calum followed.

She supposed he'd keep an eye out behind them and warn if anyone appeared on the slope they'd just come down.

After ten minutes of silent pacing, Euan dropped back to have a whispered consultation with Calum. She heard the word *Brodie*, but that was all. It miffed Muireall that she couldn't make out what they were saying, but she knew if she stopped to let them catch up, they'd cease speaking, and she still wouldn't know what they discussed. Grateful for her rescue, she nonetheless felt a burn of anger building in her chest. She needed to find out whether any in her village survived. Once away and on the firth, she'd appeal again to be taken to Munro, though she knew she'd be wasting her breath. She couldn't blame Euan for being determined to find his survivors, if any remained. Or for wanting to take Calum back across the firth to be cared for by the Brodie healer, but that way lay even farther from her home. They'd had this discussion in the cave, before he'd known whether any of his clansmen lived. Now that he knew one had survived, he'd be even more determined. Others might still be alive, as well.

She pressed her lips together and kept on, gaze skimming the clifftop above them, alert for watchers.

Before she realized what happened, she found herself sprawled on the sand. She'd tripped! She struggled to her hands and knees, wondering why the men had not rushed to help her up. She glanced around and met Euan's and Calum's grim expressions. Then she realized the impediment underneath her was not driftwood, but a body, still damp and cold from the sea. She scrambled up and sank back on her heels, clearing the body before her. "One of yers," she murmured, knowing there could be no doubt of that. "Oh, God, 'tis only a lad!"

Euan knelt by her, wide-eyed, and with gentle fingertips closed the eyes that no longer saw the stars above them. Muireall knew his heart was breaking. She jammed a fist against her mouth to stop her cry of sympathy, tears pricking her eyes.

"James," Calum muttered an explanation. "I saw Eduard and Dugal with him on the ropes as the *Tangie* went down."

Euan nodded, pain tightening all his features into an

immovable mask in the starlight. "Likely the undertow pulled them out into the firth, or they'd be here, too." He reached out a hand to Muireall and helped her to her feet, then kept his arm around her. "I'm sorry ye found him in this way, lass. Ye wouldha liked the lad."

"What will ye do?" She was certain they could not leave him lying on the beach. Nor did they have time or tools to bury him.

A muscle jumped in Euan's jaw. "Keep on as we are, and once we have a boat, come back for him." He squatted by the body for a moment, then stood and glanced around, as if he was fixing landmarks in memory. "His family will want to bury him properly."

"Even if we're seen taking a boat?"

"'Twill be a risk we'll have to take. The lad must go home to his family."

Behind Euan's back, Calum, his gaze on the clifftop, shook his head, whether in disagreement, or in dismay over the fate of their young friend, she couldn't know. His lips were pressed into a thin line, mirroring Euan's grim expression.

"Let's go," Euan ordered. "Morning will come all too soon." Without a backward glance, Euan continued down the beach.

Calum gestured her forward.

She followed Euan the rest of the way to the cove where the Rosses kept their boats. At the entrance, both men knelt behind rocks. On the far side, the tide drowned the narrow strip of beach leading to the cove where she and Euan had been trapped. She was glad. A band of Ross warriors could not be lurking there, waiting for anyone who dared steal from them.

"That one," Calum whispered, pointing to a skiff sitting just out of the encroaching tide. Euan nodded his agreement, then pointed out the guard, sitting in the sand, back propped against the cliff wall behind him.

He appeared to Muireall to be sound asleep. Positioned behind the two Brodies, she had to strain to see what the men indicated in the cove, so after spotting the guard, she kept an eye on the clifftop above them. Nothing moved. The stillness there should also make her happy, but somehow, it only increased her anxiety. Surely by now Donas's companions had woken up, discovered his body and reported back to Erik with their injured clansman. And surely Erik would guess where the castaways would go next.

Euan signaled for her to stay put, then he and Calum made their way into the cove. Using the boats for cover, they moved carefully, the soft sand mixed with pebbles muffling the sound of their footfalls. In moments, they flanked the sleeping guard. Euan cracked him over the head with the hilt of his dirk, sending him into a deeper sleep.

That thunk sounded like the fall of a blacksmith's hammer on a wooden stump, startling Muireall and making her even more vigilant about movement on the clifftop. But the night remained still and quiet, save for the gently lulling surf. Donas's guards must still be unconscious, or slowed by their injured man.

They put the swords in the craft they'd chosen. With Calum's one-handed help and Muireall pushing, Euan dragged the skiff into the water and beckoned for her to get in. He lifted her into the bobbing boat, then helped Calum before pulling himself over the side and grabbing the oars. "I dinna want to raise the sail yet. It will be too visible from the clifftop."

"I can row," Muireall told him. "With Calum to help," she added, with a glance at Euan's companion. After his nod, she added, "We can take one side and ye the other. It might spare yer hands."

"Aye, we can," Calum seconded and took a seat beside her on the bench. Euan relinquished one oar without comment.

Before long, her arms shaking and hands stinging, Muireall knew blisters must be forming on her palms, but she gritted her teeth and gamely kept time with Calum. The pain in her hands kept her mind from the twinges in her back as each pull on the oar pulled her newly formed scars. Euan seemed to be allowing them to set the pace, mindful of Calum's injury and her lack of strength—or because gripping the oar with his injured hands was too painful. Despite their grim errand, she was glad to let the tide push them onto the beach to retrieve James's body. Euan allowed her and Calum to rest while he did what had to be done.

All too soon, they were back on the water, this time fighting the tide as they rowed for distance from shore. But before long Euan raised the sail, letting them ship the oars. As soon as she caught her breath, Muireall pulled Donas's sleeve from her bodice and dunked it over the side. The salt water stung her palm and fingers fiercely, making her realize how brave Euan had been. Her few blisters hurt, but his hands were scraped and torn and bleeding, and had been for days. She shuddered, imagining how badly his must hurt. His need to find the rest of his men and return home drove him to ignore his injuries, but he couldn't do that much longer.

Still, she had to ask. "I ken ye feel honor-bound to return home as quickly as ye are able," Muireall ventured while she washed Donas's remaining sleeve, "but I feel the same and Munro begins only a few miles down the coast. Ye could get help with yer search…if anyone is left alive there."

"Your Munro village is several miles into the Cromarty firth and inland, aye? I hear ye, lass, I do," Euan told her. "But ye ken what my answer is, and why. I'll no' take another chance with Calum. Or James. Or ye gettin' trapped on this side of the firth and back in to Ross hands. We go to Brodie."

"It makes nay sense to sail across the firth…" she told him, wringing out the cloth and wincing. She reached for Euan's hands to check whether the bindings still protected them, but he drew back.

"To ye, perhaps, but I am the master of this vessel. She goes where I decide."

Muireall glanced at Calum's profile. She'd find no help there. He had to be in pain, and eager for this misadventure to be over. But by sea, her home was so close! She opened her mouth to argue, but after another glance at the lad's body laid out in the prow, she wisely clamped her mouth shut.

Irritated, she'd been tempted to point out how well Euan had done as master of his last vessel. That really wasn't fair, not after the storm they'd ridden out. They'd almost made it to shore, likely mostly due to his skill. Perhaps a bad decision had kept them on the water too long, but bad luck had killed his crew, and Euan had no escape from the reality of their deaths, not while James's body sailed with them.

EUAN KNEW THEY WEREN'T THE ONLY BOATS ON THE firth this night, and the Rosses weren't the only ones who could be unfriendly, so they kept a close watch during the dark hours of the crossing to Findhorn Bay. The sun was rising in their faces by the time they beached their borrowed skiff and made their way, Euan carrying James's body over his shoulder, to the Brodie village and keep.

Shocked stares and silence greeted them as they passed through the thatch-roofed cots on their way to the chief. With a murmured word as they passed her, Calum added the healer to their party. He had to be using the last dregs of his strength, and his arm needed tending yesterday.

Muireall appeared as dazed and exhausted as Calum. Despite the grievous burden Euan carried, she stayed close by his side as they made their way through the villagers. Euan decided it would be best to leave her with the healer. She could keep Calum company and get some rest away from the curious eyes of the clan.

By their presence, it was clear that the others were not coming home. Euan could not meet the resigned gazes of the families of the men he'd lost. When they reached James's family's home, the lad's parents and younger brothers quickly took charge of his body, relieving Euan of the physical burden. But the emotional burden would not be lifted so easily. Euan made his apologies to the tearful family, Muireall and Calum by his side. Calum looked pinched and white around the mouth, so they went next to the healer's cot, where he ordered both Calum and Muireall to remain.

He would face the laird alone, as was his right and his responsibility.

Now lacking an escort, he trudged up the last slope into the keep and found Iain in his solar, standing by the open window overlooking the path he'd just trod.

"I saw ye coming up from the beach," Iain said by way of greeting. "I'm glad to see at least two of ye made it back."

Euan expected sorrow and anger, so the ambiguity of Iain's greeting surprised but did not sway him from his purpose. "'Tis my fault we lost James. Eduard and Dugal, too, as far as I ken. We stayed overlong and the storm four nights ago caught us..."

"That storm came up so swiftly, I misdoubt yer boat was the only casualty that night." He indicated they take seats. Once they'd settled, he said, "Tell me what happened."

Euan crossed his arms, reluctant to relive that night, yet fully aware he owed his chief an explanation.

"The fishing was good. We had nearly a full load and wanted to bring home as much as we could carry." In truth, even though they'd noticed black clouds piling up on the horizon at sunset, Eduard had argued they had hours yet before a storm would reach them, and Euan had let himself be persuaded, seduced by the idea of bringing in such bounty. "The storm rolled in so fast, we had only an hour from the time it appeared before it blew us out across the firth. When the wind shifted, we fought the sail and tried to take it down, but the *Tangie* heeled over and sank off the Ross coves."

Iain shifted in his seat. "Were ye caught? Is that how Calum was injured?"

"Nay. Calum said waves tossed him against rocks and snapped his arm. I found him the next day after... well, 'tis a long story that involves the lass ye saw with us."

"Before ye get to that, what happened to the others?"

"We...I...dinna ken. I saw them last clinging to the ropes as the *Tangie* went over. Once we found James, we became convinced the others drowned and are lost in the firth. We searched along the shoreline for as long as we dared and saw no sign of them."

Iain sighed. "Good men, and a good lad. Years of sailing experience lost in Eduard alone."

Euan nodded. Of all of them, Eduard should have been savvy enough to survive, yet he was among the missing.

"And the lass?"

"Stolen by Ross with two others from Munro. Only she remained unclaimed—unwed—and determined to escape. She aided us, but Donas Ross and some of his men followed her and found us hiding. They dinna ken who we were, only that we were shipwreck survivors on their land. I never named my clan." Euan tensed, expecting his next words would break through Iain's calm demeanor. "We fought. I killed him."

Iain reared back. "The Ross chief?"

"Aye."

"God. Ye canna help yerself, can ye? Trouble follows ye like…" he paused and grimaced. "I was going to say a dark cloud, but…" He shook his head. "If the tales I've heard are true, ye did his folk a favor."

Euan accepted the censure. "If the tales ye have heard are anything like Muireall's, I did, though I dinna ken whether they'll see it that way. Especially his widow, Silas."

Iain stood and paced to the window looking out over the firth. "Damn it. We dinna need a war with Ross."

Euan cringed, glad Iain had his back to him and could not see how those words stung. *There* was the reaction he'd expected. Not only had the men on the *Tangie* died, his actions put even more Brodies at risk if Ross found out who had killed their chief. He'd brought another disaster home.

"What of the men who you said came with him?"

"Calum and his slingshot…even with a broken arm he was able to knock out the two holding Muireall. He distracted the one with the knife to my throat, and I broke that man's leg getting free. He passed out. But Donas was determined to kill me. I had nay choice but to grab a blade and fight."

Iain nodded. "I'll send Kenneth and some men to sail the Ross coastline and see if they can spot any sign of our two lost men."

"I should go."

"Ye should rest and eat and take care of the lass ye brought to us."

"About Muireall. She wants to go home to Munro. Donas Ross told her they killed her people."

"Until we ken what the Rosses are likely to do, I'll no' send more Brodies ashore on that side of the firth save to rescue one of ours. Nor will I have ye seen by a Ross and known as a Brodie. No' yet. But I will speak to her...nay, no' now," he added as Euan stood, intending to fetch her. Iain waved toward the door. "Get ye to the healer and see to Calum and the lass, then get some rest."

Euan frowned. "I'd rather ye give me leave to go with Kenneth. And to find out about Munro."

"I will no'. He'll do better without ye. And Munro will have to wait while we search for our own men. Now get ye to the healer."

Euan stood and left the room, seething. If anyone should continue the search for the missing men, it was him, but Iain was right. He was trouble.

MUIREALL SPENT THE DAY UNDER THE HEALER'S watchful eye. She'd ordered her to rest and eat and help her keep Calum on the same regimen. Calum complained at regular intervals that he didn't need their coddling. He needed to help find their missing men. When word came down that the chief had sent others to do that job and that Euan had been ordered to the healer's cot, Calum had gone silent, his complaints overruled by the chief's action.

Only then did he stretch out on a pallet and turn his face to the wall.

She knew he had to be hurting, and not just his arm. Left behind, and too injured and worn out to attempt to change the laird's mind, he could only do as ordered —eat, rest and heal. She wanted to comfort him, but had no idea what would ease his pain. And with the healer's watchful eye on her, she dared not approach him.

She was a stranger. And while the healer gave her the same gentle care she gave Calum, there was still that hint of distrust, of distance, in her demeanor that kept Muireall from feeling truly comfortable in her new circumstances.

Voices from outside the cottage carried wails of grief, and Euan's name, spoken angrily.

"Where is that laddie?" the healer muttered.

Muireall supposed she was asking the air, since neither of her charges were privy to that information. Where was Euan, indeed? Avoiding her? Or had he stowed away on a Brodie *birlinn* in hopes of being there when their men were found. Or their bodies recovered. If so, she wished him well. His laird would likely have his head when he found out, but in the meantime, Euan would be doing what he thought was right. And if she knew one thing about Euan Brodie, besides how he made her breath catch and her heart beat faster, it was that he had a strong sense of honor, of right and wrong. He felt responsible for the loss of his men and his ship. He wouldn't take kindly to waiting like a bairn for news of their fate.

Once Calum started snoring, letting them know he was asleep, the healer bade Muireall to wash. Someone had brought in the tub earlier and set it by the fire, so the water was still warm. With a glance at the sleeping Calum, Muireall stripped and laid her gown over her cot. Despite her having tripped over James's body, some sand and salt spray from sailing across the firth were all that marred the cloth. Then she noticed a few spots of blood on the back of the skirt and paled.

Discovering her monthly bleeding had come was disconcerting. A few days from now, as soon as her courses finished, if Donas Ross had been alive to have his way and she was still his prisoner, she would have become Erik Ross's unwilling bride. And he her un-willing husband.

She told herself her narrow escape didn't matter. She was safe now. But the shock of it made safety feel tenuous and unreal.

The healer saw the blood and gave her a sympa-thetic nod. She fetched what Muireall needed from a chest, then moved behind her to the tub to rinse the blood from her skirt.

Muireall knew the second the healer got a look at her back. How could she have been so careless?

The woman kept her voice low, but her shock and anger were evident in every hissed syllable. "My God, lass, who…"

Muireall shook her head, dismayed, embarrassed and praying Calum would not pick now to wake up. "Dinna tell anyone," she pleaded in a whisper, forcing herself to make eye contact. "What's done is done, and it doesna matter anymore. The stripes are nearly healed."

The healer gave her a long look, frowned, and nod-ded. "I'll keep yer secret, but whoever did this to ye should answer for it."

"He already did." Those three words felt final, as though they should have allowed her to put Donas and all he had done utterly and forever behind her. But with her eyes closed against the healer's watchful gaze, she could still see her hands cutting away the sleeves from his dead arms as if watching someone else do the deed. If that image stayed with her, how much worse a vision did Euan see when he closed his eyes?

Keeping her gaze on the glowing coals in the hearth,

she got in the tub. Her skin prickled and she forced herself away from thoughts of her last bath, under the angry and lustful stares of her captors. This time, no one watched, and it felt good to rinse the salt from her skin, even if she had to put on the same dress she'd worn for the last day.

Nonetheless, she bathed quickly, dried off and made use of what Mhairi had given her for her bleeding. Then she pulled on her shift and slipped the damp dress over her head. Shivering from reaction, Muireall sank onto the stool by the fire to let her clothes dry. She hated that a stranger now knew she bore permanent scars from what had happened to her.

The healer surprised her by picking up a comb and running it through her hair. The scratch of the teeth along her scalp felt wonderful. And Mhairi's gentle ministration lulled her. Eventually, she succumbed, moved back to her cot and slept. She roused some time later to the low rumble of Euan's voice and the higher pitch of a woman's. A pretty blonde lass held Euan's arm. Muireall's sinking heart stirred her enough to note the bandages on his hands were new and clean. The healer must have found him, after all. But who was the lass? And who was she to Euan?

Both he and the lass left Mhairi's cot before Muireall could sit up and ask. The healer bustled in.

"Ah, ye are awake. Good."

While Muireall sat and scrubbed her face with her hands, Mhairi woke Calum. A glance at the window told Muireall it was past midday.

"'Twill be time for a meal soon," she heard the healer cajole Calum. "I ken ye are hungry."

A meal meant meeting more of the clan. And seeing Euan with that lass? Was she important to him? Or worse, his wife? She thought back over the way Euan had treated her. In the light of her new circumstances, she realized he'd been caring, concerned, but never forward, even when she'd fallen against the cave wall and woken up to his kisses on her face. He'd promised he'd never hurt her, and he hadn't, not deliberately. He'd never said he had a lass at home, but she'd never asked. She'd been falling for him and simply assumed.

But her father had other plans for her future.

If her father still lived, she would never be Euan's. She suddenly needed to get outside in fresh air. With a nod to Mhairi, Muireall stood and stepped out of the cot into the afternoon sunshine. But from the healer's doorway, she had no idea where to go or what to do.

CHAPTER 8

*E*uan paused while Annie started up the hill to the keep. He wasn't ready to go that way yet. A glance in the other direction gave him the firth in all its deep blue beauty, sunshine gleaming on the surface. Without thinking, he turned and started down the path toward it. Dolphins leapt in graceful arcs as he neared the beach, but he barely noticed them. His hands hurt and his mood was better suited to storm clouds and rough seas. He could understand where Iain was coming from, *he could*, though he didn't like his chief denying him what he most wanted to do. Annie had done her best while she and the healer tended his hands to smooth his ruffled feathers, but damn it, the missing men were his responsibility. Yet here he stood, staring across the wide blue water, unable to do a bloody thing to help them. To find them. Or to bury them, if that would be required. He clenched his fists and groaned as the bandaging pulled at his abraded skin. Then he set off, pacing down the beach, balancing on the uneven footing of sand and pebbles. Brodie boats lined the shore, pulled above the high tide line. Just below that watermark, the skiff he'd stolen from Ross waited for someone to sail it away and hide it. Or sink it. What if he took it?

He slowed as he reached it and paced around it. Could he pull it into the water without help? More important, could he sail it by himself? He glanced up at the sky. Clear and blue. As lovely a day as could be found on the shores of the Moray firth. And about as far from the weather that had sunk the *Tangie* as weather could be. The surface of the firth was calm, even flat, looking more like a lake than a broad body of water open to the northern sea.

He could do this. If he could get her in the water, that is.

He reached for the stern.

"Ho, Euan!"

Euan lowered his hands and turned to face the man who'd called out to him. Kenneth, damn it. Iain's right hand. Annie must have sent him, or Iain had. "Kenneth." Euan contented himself with the man's name, nothing more. If Kenneth had any idea what he'd been about to do, Euan would not admit it. And if he didn't, Euan would not enlighten him.

"Iain told me to hide the Ross skiff," Kenneth announced with a grin. "She's been sitting here too long already."

So he did know.

"I could use some help."

Euan held up his bandaged hands.

"Ye sailed her here, did ye no'? I think ye can crew with me well enough."

Euan narrowed his eyes. "And ye are certain there's no one else to do that for ye?"

"No' at the moment. And since ye are here..." Kenneth answered with a shrug and pushed the skiff toward the water. "We need to get this beast out of sight."

Euan lent his shoulder and between them, she was quickly afloat. "Where to?" he asked.

"Ye ken the caves I have in mind. North…"

"Toward Inverness, aye. And how do ye plan to get back?"

"We'll no' swim all the way, if that's what concerns ye. Angus is bringing horses to meet us. We'll be back before the evening meal."

The afternoon was as perfect for a sail as Euan had imagined. When he left Mhairi's care with Annie, Muireall was sleeping and didn't need him. As pinched as she'd looked, he expected she'd sleep for hours yet. He nodded.

They made good time, and saw no other boats they recognized as belonging to Ross. None approached them and by the time they took down the sail and rowed for shore and the cave Kenneth chose, there were no other boats near enough to see them.

They rowed into a cave they knew well. The back took a sharp turn, which meant they could tie off the skiff where it could not be seen from the outside. That done, they dropped over the side into the water.

At first, Euan's hands stung, but the cold water soon numbed them. Or perhaps given how often he'd gotten sand and salt in his wounds he was getting used to the sensation. Either way, his hands were the least of his troubles. As he swam toward the cave's entrance, he became aware the water in the cave was not still. It ebbed and flowed, tugging at him and reminding him of the surf the night of the *Tangie*'s shipwreck. All too quickly, he lost himself in the memory of the salt water in his nose and mouth. Before he could stop himself, he started thrashing, fighting a surf that didn't exist.

Finally, he managed to break the spell and resume swimming smoothly without Kenneth, who was well ahead of him, becoming aware he'd been in trouble for a moment.

They swam out along the cliffside without incident to the rough trail leading from the waterline to the top. Euan pulled himself up onto a rocky shelf and sat, fighting to control his galloping heartbeat. The sound of gentle swells slapping against the cliff face brought back the storm and how the water had sloshed over the *Tangie*'s side as he shouted for his men to let go of the ropes and get away from her. Euan pushed his hair out of his face and took a deep breath, glad to be out of the water and back on solid rock.

Kenneth stood and offered a hand.

Euan reached up, grateful Kenneth grabbed his forearm instead of his bandaged hand, to pull him to his feet.

They climbed.

Atop the cliff, the view stretched nearly to Inverness in one direction and to Brodie in the other. They started walking back, the wind making quick work of drying their clothes, but not before chilling them even more than the water had.

Kenneth shuddered. "Where the hell is Angus with those horses? I'll be glad to get home and finish drying out before a fire."

Euan nodded and managed to answer, "Aye, before a fire would be brilliant," without letting Kenneth hear his teeth chatter.

Before much longer, they heard horses approaching. Angus appeared over the next rise, leading two mounts by their reins.

"So whose idea was this?" Euan accused.

"Annie's. When she saw the way ye headed, she wondered if ye would willingly swim again. That lass is wiser than her years."

Euan grunted agreement. "She decided I needed to get back in the water?"

"Or ye might never wish to, aye. I told ye, the lass is…"

"Wiser than her years," Euan chorused. *Shite*. If he'd really panicked during the trip, would Kenneth have thought to let him off where they climbed the cliff before rowing inside the cave?

"Are ye lads dry yet?" Angus greeted them.

"Aye, and ready to stop walking, thank ye," Kenneth answered.

Euan swung wearily onto the back of his mount, turned it homeward, and let it have its head. Suddenly, exhaustion took him, every reserve of energy he'd ever possessed expended. He wasn't used to being the beneficiary of such care and concern from Kenneth and even from Annie. He didn't deserve it. Nor did he know what to do about it, so he pushed his feelings aside and just rode.

The horses kept pace with each other and made good time. Much to Euan's relief, as Kenneth had promised, they were back before the evening meal.

When they reached the stable, Euan dismounted and gave his horse to a lad to care for it. Kenneth dismounted and touched Euan's shoulder. "Annie may have sent me after ye, but I am grateful for yer help and yer company, nonetheless."

"Thank ye," Euan replied. "I'm for a fire and a wee dram. Will ye come?"

"That's the best idea I've yet heard today. Angus! Are ye with us?"

"Nay, damn it. I've got to see these lads take proper care of the horses."

Kenneth shook his head and gestured for Euan to precede him.

By the time Muireall left Mhairi to deal with Calum, Euan had disappeared. Muireall couldn't help wondering where he was. She was tempted to walk up to the keep in hopes of finding him, but Muireall didn't want to see him if he still accompanied the blonde lass. If she was something special to him, Muireall would not be able to bear it. She was too shaken by what she'd already been through to find out Euan had a mistress or a betrothed or a wife. Not yet.

Instead, she turned downhill, through the village. She'd had no real destination in mind. Just a hunger for fresh air and sunshine. And to give Calum some privacy.

Childish shouts and laughter drew her on. Children chased each other down the path toward the beach. Some—lads and lasses—wielded wooden swords, or child-sized bows, blunted arrows clutched in the opposite fist. She couldn't imagine such taking place at Munro. Lads were taught to fight and to use weapons, not lasses. Would the lasses eventually be called upon to help defend the keep here, firing arrows down on a siege force, or invaders?

How would she feel about doing that, had she been trained in archery?

She'd seen battles, and the aftermath of battles. She'd tended wounded warriors and helped prepare the dead for burial. But she'd never thought to be part of the fighting force herself. The idea frightened her, yet at the same time, excited her. To be able to hunt for food, and to defend herself, her clan and her keep—how powerful would she feel? Would she have been able to prevent the Ross men from stealing her, Ella and Tira from Munro land? She shook her head. Fruitless speculation. She could do none of those things, and likely never would. And a bow and arrow would not have stopped the Rosses. But, oh, if she could have!

She watched for a few more minutes, then something else caught her attention.

Cats. Several of them. Sleeping in the sun, wandering from one cottage to another, trotting after the children toward the beach. No mouse would dare approach this village. She nearly laughed out loud at the thought, when she felt a tug on her skirt.

A young lass stood there, holding a kitten. "Could ye help me?" the lass asked, holding up the kitten. "I've lost her sister. She looks just the same. And she's too young to be out in the cold once the sun goes down."

Muireall smiled and stroked the kitten's head. "She's a beauty. Another just like her, ye say?" She looked around and spotted another kitten sleeping in a sunny spot on top of some rocks marking the boundary of a fallow garden.

"Is that her?" She pointed, but when the lass nodded and took a step in that direction, Muireall stopped her. "I'll fetch her. She's too far into the rocks for ye to venture near."

In a moment, she returned with the kitten, now awake and complaining about having her nap disturbed.

"Thank ye, Lady," the little lass told her. "Would ye like to see the rest of them? They're in the byre."

"I would."

The lass led her to a small byre next to a cottage, where the mother cat lounged and three other kittens nursed. Muireall set her kitten down and it immediately found a spot and joined its siblings at their meal. The little lass did the same with hers, then stood back with a satisfied smile.

"What's yer name?" Muireall asked.

"I'm Janie, and those are mine."

"All of them?"

"Aye. I take care of them. Except that one," she said and pointed to the one Muireall had retrieved, "keeps sneaking away."

"She likes the sunshine, I suppose."

"I dinna want one of the hounds to eat her." Her lower lip puckered at the thought.

"I dinna think they will, but ye had best keep her with the others, just the same."

"Janie, is that ye?" A lad's voice from outside interrupted them.

"Aye," Janie answered. She frowned and her shoulders slumped.

Muireall could guess what the lad was going to say before he said it.

"Yer ma is looking for ye. 'Tis nearly time for supper."

Janie looked up at Muireall. "I have to go."

"I do, too. Thank ye for showing me your kittens."

"Ye can visit them whenever ye like. And if ye see that one outside," she continued, pointing at the escape artist, "please bring her back."

"I'll do that. Now, go on. Ye'd best find yer mother."

Janie nodded and ran off.

Muireall smiled at the mother cat and her hungry kittens, then stepped outside. The view out over the firth was stunning and drew her gaze. A boat bobbed just offshore, two men raising the sail. Euan! She started running, calling his name. Why was he sailing away? If he could sail, he could take her home, couldn't he? Before she'd gone very far, she realized running after him was foolish. The boat was too far away. He'd never hear her. She slowed, angry that while playing with kittens, she might have missed a chance to go home.

She continued down the path to the beach and settled on the sand with her back against a rock to watch the sun set. The rock was warm, the breeze cool, and before long, Muireall found herself nodding. Visions of playful kittens and snuggling kittens filled her mind. She roused after the sun dipped behind the hills on the firth's opposite shore. The rock was still warm at her back, but her front was chilled. She pulled her woolen shawl tighter around her and stood. She should return to the keep and find out about supper.

"Muireall! There ye are!" Euan ran to her. "Everyone is searching for you! The healer said ye left her care hours ago and no one has seen ye since."

"I...I'm sorry. I dozed off. Where did ye go? I saw ye sailing away."

"Hiding the Ross's skiff." He took her hand. "Let's get ye back. Were ye here the whole time?"

"Nay," she answered as they started back up the hill. "I wandered about the village. Oh, and visited a cat and her kittens with a lass named Janie."

Euan nodded. "I ken the lass. One of the cats had an early litter."

"She was quite serious about their care."

"More than I have been about yers." He stopped them outside the healer's cottage. "I am sorry about leaving ye alone this afternoon, but Kenneth needed my help. And I'm sorry, too, that I must leave ye with the healer while I tell the others ye are found. I'll see ye soon at supper."

He left her before Muireall could frame an answer. She leaned back against the healer's door and watched him hurry up the path to the keep, thinking about his last statement. He thought himself in charge of her care. Was that all? She had begun to hope for more, but then she recalled the blonde lass who'd been clutching his arm. Perhaps it was already too late.

CHAPTER 9

It was time to meet the rest of the clan.

When Muireall and Calum entered the keep's hall for the evening meal, her heart leapt into her throat. Euan! He stood, talking to some other men, and frowning. In the short time since he'd left her, he'd cleaned up and no longer looked as rough as when he'd found her on the beach. Granted, over the last few days, he'd been shipwrecked, starved, and attacked. Now, somehow, his face had lost the drawn look of exhaustion from the exposure he'd suffered.

He glanced up and saw her. His frown smoothed away and transformed into a welcoming smile. But he held up a newly bandaged hand to stave her off and went back to the discussion he was having.

She wondered what was so important. Were the searchers back? Was there news?

And where was the lass she'd seen with him earlier?

Calum had noted the unspoken exchange and said, "I see he's busy. Let's find a seat and he can join us when he's free, aye? From the look of that group, he could be there for a while, and I'd rather spend that time sitting than standing. Would ye, as well?"

"I would." Muireall followed Calum to an empty

bench. In moments someone brought trenchers of food and ale. Calum wasted no time digging in, but Muireall kept an eye on Euan and contented herself by sipping her ale. She'd wait for him. Surely he wouldn't be as long as Calum feared.

Someone refilled her cup by the time Euan joined them. He sat opposite her and looked her over as food was placed before him. "Ye look rested," he told her.

She smiled. Euan had a lovely soft halo around him. She felt Calum at her side shift to study her.

"She hasna eaten yet. Waiting for ye," he told Euan.

"Ye daft lass." Euan chuckled and pushed his trencher across to her. "Eat, or ye'll hate yerself in the morning."

She picked up a bit of fish. It went down, but she wasn't certain it would stay there. "I think I already do."

"Try the bread. It'll soak up some of that ale."

She nodded and wished she hadn't. Suddenly she was back on the skiff, only in rougher waters than they'd crossed last night.

Euan reached across the table, broke off a piece of bread and handed it to her. "Why did ye no' eat?"

She took his offering and got it down. It seemed more content to stay put than the fish had. "To wait for ye. 'Tis no' polite to begin before my host."

"Calum clearly had nay such compunction."

"He is yer clansman. Ye are no' his host."

"*Wheesht*, lass," Calum broke in. "'Had I paid attention to more than my empty belly, I wouldha talked ye out of that fool notion."

Muireall stiffened. "I am no' a fool."

"Nay, ye are no'," Euan told her with a narrowed glance at Calum. "No' as long as ye finish that bread. Then we'll see how ye fare."

"Where were ye all day?" Calum asked as Muireall

picked up another hunk of bread and took a bite. "We heard Iain had sent ye to join us in Mhairi's care."

"I had other things to do."

"I see they didna involve stowing away with the searchers." Muireall realized that voice was hers and clamped a hand over her mouth.

Calum reared back, then leaned away. "Ye're no about to spew, are ye?"

Muireall shook her head and winced as the room moved a bit side to side after she stopped. She hadn't drunk that much ale. She must be hungrier than she thought.

Euan sighed. "Nay, they didna, though I would have preferred to join them. But Iain would have banished me had I defied him."

"Ye are wise, as well as honorable." Muireall cringed. She'd done it again. Every thought she had about Euan Brodie flew from her lips. Clearly she had no business drinking Brodie ale. It made her mouth run ahead of her mind.

"And ye have had too much to drink for having nought to eat. Try some more bread, lass."

Euan's tone contained no censure, only concern for her well-being. Just as it had from the moment he'd pulled her from the surf. He'd been taking care of her for only a few days, but it felt like he'd looked after her for years. He'd saved her life, after all. She felt closer to him than to any other man, save her father and brothers. Poor Georgie. If they were still alive. That thought brought tears to her eyes. *Oh no*, she could not cry, not here in the middle of the Brodie clan, with all eyes on her, the strange lass Euan had rescued. She took a deep breath and got her roiling emotions under control by forcing down the last of the bread Euan had broken for her.

"Are ye ready for more?"

She risked a glance at him. The room seemed steadier and he seemed a bit more in focus than he had only minutes ago. "Aye, I think so."

"Then try a bit of cheese." Euan signaled for a serving girl and asked for some soup and a pitcher of clean water for Muireall to drink.

His kindness set her thoughts to racing again. She knew him well enough to believe his concern was genuine. But was it only out of polite regard for a guest rather than attraction to her? In Muireall's eyes, he was warm and caring and perhaps the most handsome man who'd ever paid attention to her. Did she feel that way because he'd saved her life, and rescued her from the Rosses? Or was there something true and perhaps lasting in her feelings?

Who was the lass who'd been holding his arm?

It didn't matter. She couldn't expect Euan to want to get involved with her. She needed to return to Munro.

Once she had more food in her belly, she felt much better. Looking around the room and at the people in it no longer made them wobble. The high table stood empty. Either the chief was away or he'd chosen to sit elsewhere. The rest of the Brodies sat as she did at long tables. Many benches stood empty.

"Where is everyone?" she asked.

Euan answered. "James's family and the families of the men still missing are keeping private. Iain, our chief, sent a dozen men across the firth to search the northern coast for them. And Iain prefers not to use the high table save for formal occasions. He's over there."

Euan nodded toward a tall man whose dark hair glinted with coppery highlights standing a few tables away, deep in conversation with a man and a woman whose backs were to Muireall.

"He'll make his way here before long."

Muireall was afraid of that. She wasn't sure she was up to convincing the Brodie chief to send her home. Euan had said he understood why she wanted to go, though he'd refused to take her. Here, he had to follow his chief's orders. But with Euan near her, his green gaze locked with hers, leaving seemed less urgent somehow.

&

As much as Euan wanted this day to be over, he wanted to remain in the hall even more. He had two reasons—to await news from the men Iain had sent across to the Ross coast and to shield Muireall from Iain's interrogation. Iain had said he would talk to the lass, and Euan knew what that could mean.

Guilt still wracked him over the loss of his men. If Iain's crew returned with even one of them alive, a heavy weight would lift from his shoulders. But the longer it took to find them, or their bodies, the worse he felt.

Muireall was barely recovered from their escape. While she'd been braver than any lass he'd ever known, he knew Iain too well. If Iain thought she knew more than she divulged, he could be intimidating. Euan had seen grown men quail under Iain's scrutiny. It was one thing to face his chief's interrogation himself, another to stand by and see Iain question the lass, especially on her first day here.

Euan hoped they'd gotten enough food into her to counteract some of the effects of the strong Brodie ale. She might not have known better, but Calum did and should have stopped her, or made her eat. Another failure on Euan's part—he was her host and he'd let her down again.

Under the circumstances, his interest in Muireall

seemed wholly inappropriate. He'd succeeded in avoiding her all day, yet now that she sat next to him, all he wished to do was see her face, touch her hand, and inhale the fresh scent of her skin.

Yet he was about to be denied those small pleasures. Iain and Annie were headed toward their table. Calum, on Euan's other side, leaned closer and whispered, "The fun is about to start. Is she up to it?"

Euan gave him the frown he deserved.

Iain and Annie reached their table and sat across from them while Euan made the introductions. "Welcome to Brodie," Iain told Muireall, a friendly smile on his face. Either Iain was in a good mood, or Annie had warned him to charm the new lass.

Euan held his breath and looked from Iain to Muireall. She had stiffened as Iain and Annie approached. Well, meeting the clan's laird and his wife for the first time would do that, he supposed. But she relaxed under Annie's friendly gaze.

"Thank ye," she said and returned Annie's smile. "I saw ye with Euan in the healer's cottage as I woke up earlier. I'm grateful for yer hospitality, and for everything Euan and Calum did to help me escape the Rosses."

"Aye, well..." Iain began, then paused on a sharp glance from Annie.

Iain gave Euan a look that let him know Iain was thinking about Donas Ross and the trouble that might bring to Brodie. Euan pressed his lips into a thin line and didn't comment.

Calum, at his side, shifted but also remained silent.

"And," Muireall continued before anyone had a chance to speak, "I will be grateful for your assistance in returning me to my home."

Euan bit back an oath but Iain only canted his head,

which Muireall must have taken for encouragement, because she kept talking.

"Donas Ross told me most of my people were killed in the raid when Tira, Ella, and I were taken, but Euan thinks that may not be true. I need to know..."

"And ye shall," Iain interrupted, "but no' before 'tis safe, both for ye and for Brodie, to return ye to that side of the firth, even to Munro land."

Euan tensed, not liking that Iain had interrupted Muireall. If that was a sign of how this interview would go, he'd better find a way to put a stop to it.

"No harm will come to me..." Muireall countered firmly, straightening up in her seat.

Annie spoke up then. "I was told ye were stolen from yer village. Is that correct?"

Usually Annie's intervention would serve to lessen the tension in a discussion—especially Iain's. But her question merely restated what her husband had implied—that Muireall had no guarantee of safety, even at home.

Muireall's shoulders dropped. "Aye, Lady."

"Then perhaps ye must admit caution is warranted," Iain said. He glanced aside at his wife, then back at Muireall. "Ye will remain here for now."

Iain's mild tone surprised Euan. Usually the chief did not exercise such restraint. Then he noticed Annie squeeze Iain's hand. Ah, Annie at work again. Well, they'd made their point and done so without rancor. Though Euan hated to see Iain force Muireall to accept the truth of her situation, someone had to. She hadn't wanted to listen to him or Calum refuse to take her home. When he wanted to be charming, Iain had a persuasive way about him—and support from his wife. When that failed, he had the power of his position to enforce his will. As long as Iain said she would remain at Brodie, she would do just that.

Iain's gaze shifted to Euan, and he held himself still in anticipation.

"I dinna need to remind ye that as yer guest, the lass is yer responsibility and ye will see to her comfort and safety."

Euan could read the intent behind Iain's words. There were to be no unauthorized trips across the firth to deliver Muireall to Munro, no matter how the lass pled her case or what inducements or enticements she offered to convince Euan to take her home. Euan met Iain's gaze fully and nodded. He'd gotten the message.

"Verra well, then. I'll leave ye to see to it." He stood, but Annie stayed put.

"A chamber has been prepared for yer use while ye remain with us," Annie told Muireall with a sympathetic smile. "If there's aught ye need, ye have only to ask."

"Other than an escort home, ye mean."

She said it so quietly, Euan at first thought he'd imagined it. Surely she hadn't mean to speak such thoughts aloud to the Brodie chief.

Iain's eyebrows lifted, then lowered into a frown that he turned on Euan.

Euan tensed, ready to defend the lass. He glanced aside at her as Muireall's hand rose to cover her mouth, her gaze lifting to Iain as she realized what she'd done.

Euan held up a hand to forestall the angry reaction he expected, intending to remind Iain the lass was still exhausted and not thinking straight. He thought it wise to leave out the part about the ale she'd consumed without eating.

But Iain only chuckled. "Other than that, aye," he said, cocking an eyebrow at the lass. "For now." He gave Euan another stern glance before taking his wife's hand and leading her away from them.

CHAPTER 10

*E*arly the next morning, the rumble of voices awakened Euan. In moments, he heard someone shout, "They're back!" Those words could mean only one thing. The searchers Iain sent across the firth had returned.

He pulled on boots and wrapped an extra plaid around his shoulders before making his way out of the keep to join the throng headed for the beach.

The *birlinn* had already been pulled halfway over the high tide line, and the men walking away from her showed no sign of excitement. Nor could Euan see either of his missing men. Gasps and moans greeted the returning sailors. As they reached the crowd come to meet them, they shook their heads. "No sign of them," Kenneth announced and hung his head, then looked up again. "We fished all along the coast, as long as we had light. No sign of our men, and no sign of a struggle to show they might have been captured. Nothing. They're gone."

Iain arrived in time to hear the last few sentences. "Could ye see any of the Ross village?"

"Nothing that looked out of the ordinary," Kenneth answered.

A sob followed that pronouncement.

"But 'tis too far back from the bluff for anyone out on the water to be able to see much more than chimney smoke," Kenneth continued as more cries of grief sounded around them.

"If Ross had them, there'd be something to let us know," one of the men muttered angrily. "They'd taunt us with something that could be seen from offshore."

"So they're really dead, then." That from a woman Euan couldn't see in the crowd.

Iain held up both hands for silence. "We have to accept that they are gone. That does not mean that we will not be fishing on that side of the firth over the next few days. We will. But after so much time, no one can expect they still live. I'm sorry."

Euan balled his hands into painful fists. He should be the one apologizing to the clan. To those men's families. But his throat closed up so tightly he could barely breathe. Iain met his gaze and nodded. No doubt Euan's rigid posture told Iain what was going through his mind.

Iain spoke more softly than before, "We've much to do to grieve their loss, but also to do as they would wish and live our lives. To start with, on that boat, there's a catch to unload. Let's get to it."

Someone clapped Euan on the shoulder and urged him toward the *birlinn* along with everyone else. Calum. What did his friend expect to be able to do one-handed? Mhairi had warned him she would inflict a slow death if he removed the sling she fashioned to replace the one Euan made.

"No one blames ye," Calum told him quietly as they walked.

"I do." Euan stood in line and watched baskets full of fish being lowered to waiting hands.

"Ye shouldna. I was there. I ken what happened,

first-hand, and I dinna blame ye. Ye mustna take on yerself what the storm wrought."

"So you think my guilt stems from pride?"

"I think 'tis yer way of grieving. Ye feel responsible for the sun rising every morning. Ye must learn there are things ye canna control or ye may never be able to sail again."

Euan pondered Calum's words as they moved toward the *birlinn*. Was he right? If so, Euan's only course would be to speak to Father Innis and join the clergy as quickly as he could. Maybe then he'd be able to leave everything in the Lord's hands.

The more he thought about it, the more he knew Calum was wrong about him. No man went to sea without confidence that he could control his vessel, that he and his crew were experienced in the ways of the tides and the wind. But, he'd been overconfident, and he'd assented to Eduard's urgings to stay and fill their hull to the brim. Even though Eduard was a more experienced sailor, Euan was responsible.

When it was his turn, he took a basket loaded with fish, wincing at the pressure on his wounds. This should have been how his fishing trip ended, with a bounty of food for the entire clan, not a loss to grieve them all.

Calum stayed by him as he turned to take his burdens—real and internal—back up to the keep. He opened his mouth to argue the point some more when Calum's eyes widened. Then he saw the reason.

Muireall? She approached with several other lasses, waiting their turn to help carry what they could. Euan headed her way.

"Steady," Calum warned him. "I see yer jaw jumping. She only wants to help."

"She shouldna be here. She's a guest."

"She's also had a rough few weeks. Maybe she needs to feel useful, too."

Euan put his basket down at her feet, effectively blocking her way. "Ye dinna need to do this, lass."

"I ken that, but I want to. This is one way I can contribute."

"Ye dinna need to contribute. Ye are my guest."

She glanced at the lasses beside her and waved them on, then looked from Euan to Calum and back again. "What is it with the two of ye? Do ye never go anywhere one without the other?" Her lips quirked just for a moment, then she sighed. "To tell the truth, I'm bored. I'm not used to having nothing to do. Even in the Ross village, I had to work, and I had a friend I could rely upon." She shrugged. "Those two lasses invited me to come along, and so I did."

Euan nodded.

"I gather the news was no' good?" Muireall looked from him to Calum, who suddenly studied his own boots, then back to Euan.

"Nay, there's no news. My men are presumed lost." Euan's belly tightened at having to say the words.

"I'm so sorry." She put a hand on his arm.

A prickle of heat ran into his chest from where she touched him. "Ye had nothing to do with it."

She lifted her hand and drew back, clearly disconcerted by his gruff tone.

"What he means to say," Calum broke in, "is to thank ye for yer kind concern and bid ye go on with the lasses." He gave Euan a look that could not be mistaken. *Stop being such an ass.*

Euan crossed his arms and nodded. "Aye. I'm sorry, too."

Muireall nodded and then froze, her gaze fixed on something behind him.

Euan glanced behind him, then turned in surprise. Kenneth approached with Muireall's friend, Ella. When Ella spotted Muireall, she broke into a run to her friend.

"When...?" Muireall choked out while hugging Ella tightly.

"Yesterday," Ella said, releasing her. Then she glanced aside. "Ye must be Euan. Some of your men found me on the beach, waiting as Muireall told me to do. They said they'd been told to look for a lass waiting there and bring her back with them."

Euan traded a glance with Calum. He'd gotten the word to Kenneth after his interview with Iain. If he couldn't make the trip, he could at least honor Muireall's promise to her friend.

"I didna think ye had made a decision to go," Muireall said.

"I hadna," Ella replied, turning back to her. "Until I realized ye were gone. Suddenly I felt so alone...I couldna trust Tira. And Thomas...well, I couldna bear the thought of staying. So I went to the beach."

"Excuse me," Kenneth told them, without taking his gaze from Ella. "Now ye are with yer friend..."

Ella whirled to him and offered her hand. "Aye. Thank ye for taking care of me."

Kenneth kept her hand for a beat longer than Euan thought necessary, then nodded and moved away.

A frown creased Calum's face, making Euan smile.

"Ella, this is Calum," Euan told her, giving Calum the introduction he so clearly craved.

"I'm honored to meet ye..." Calum trailed off as Ella turned her smile to him.

"Thank ye," she replied as Calum colored. "I'm pleased to meet ye, as well."

"Let me escort ye to the keep," Calum offered and lifted his injured arm in its sling. "I'm of no use unloading the boat."

"Oh, I'm so sorry ye are hurt," Ella told him, placing a hand over the sling.

Euan fought not to laugh as Calum steered her away.

"He's still smitten by her beauty," Euan informed Muireall.

Calum moved with Ella as if in a trance.

"We saw her with ye, sitting behind a cottage the day ye left food for me." Euan turned his head to follow Calum's progress and make sure he didn't walk into anyone. "Her and another lass."

"Tira." Muireall pursed her lips. "I'm sorry for him, then. As far as I ken, Ella is still married to Thomas."

"But she left him," Euan objected.

"Aye, but she hasna said whether they pronounced their divorce before she did." Muireall shrugged. "I'll find out more later. But before I climb back up to the keep, I'm going to get a basket of fish. I may as well make the trip worthwhile."

Euan nodded and turned from following Calum's departure to watch her walk away. He could wait for her, but why? Her friend was here now, and before long, Iain would agree to send them home, so Euan saw no sense in continuing to hunger for Muireall. She would never be his.

He picked up his basket and continued toward the keep, his melancholy returning. He had spent long days and nights holding out hope for his men. There was nothing he could do for them. His only obligation now was to return Muireall to Munro—Ella, too, if she wished to go. If he could convince Iain to let him take them.

&

Once Muireall delivered her basket to the kitchen, she went in search of Ella. Calum hadn't taken her friend very far. She found them in the Great Hall, talking and laughing over bread, cheese and ale. She joined them and grasped Ella's hand. "I canna believe ye are here!" Muireall exclaimed, earning a hint of a frown from Calum. "I'm so happy to see you."

"I'm relieved to see ye, too," Ella told her. "When I got on that boat, I wasna certain it would take me to ye, though they said they'd been told to pick up any lass—or two—waiting on the beach. The captain, Kenneth, seemed trustworthy. And he said all the right things, except for telling me his clan. Where exactly are we?"

"Clan Brodie," Calum spoke up. "Across the firth from Ross…and Munro."

Ella clasped her hands together. "Ye will take us home, aye?"

Muireall wanted to cheer as Calum nodded. Though his expression was grim, that nod lifted Muireall's heart. Euan had promised her, and now Calum had promised Ella. No one had ever denied Ella anything, so it would happen. She just couldn't say when.

"Come on," Muireall said, tugging again on Ella's hand. "Let's get ye settled and then we can talk. I want to hear about what's happened at Ross since I left."

"As do I, and so will Euan," Calum broke in. "Perhaps we could meet back here in an hour? I'll find Euan." Calum did them one more service and waved down the steward, who led Ella to a chamber across the hall from Muireall's.

"I hope ye'll be comfortable here while ye bide with us," the man told Ella, smiling all the while.

Once he'd gone, Muireall snorted. Ella's beauty hadn't lost its ability to charm every man in sight. Muireall might as well have been invisible. She wasn't surprised.

Ella sat on the bed and looked around the chamber.

It was just like Muireall's—simply furnished with the bed, a chair placed by the small hearth, a chest, and a side table. Muireall walked to the small window. It looked out on the bailey over the walled garden. A pleasant view, if somewhat limited. A chill breeze blew in, but with the shutter closed, the chamber would be comfortable and warm. She closed it and turned to face her friend.

"Why did ye leave Thomas?" Muireall asked after deciding she might as well get right to the point.

Ella pursed her lips and shrugged. "Before ye left, after what ye'd said about going with your shipwreck survivor, I was torn. The idea of leaving, despite the way we'd been taken, frightened me. I couldna imagine what would happen to us. Whether we'd be better off, or worse. If we'd even survive. And God help us if Donas Ross recaptured us. What he did to ye after yer second attempt to escape and after yer night in the cove would be nothing in comparison."

Muireall crossed her arms. "I was worried, too, but I couldna bear to stay when Euan offered a way out."

Ella nodded. "But then ye disappeared. And word came Donas had been killed. I feared if ye had something to do with it, the clan would take their anger out on Tira and me."

"Nay!" Remorse filled Muireall and she couldn't think. In her desperation to leave, had she considered that?

"Even if ye didna, they might think so. Silas was inconsolable. Mad with her grief. And ye were gone." Ella looked away. "I felt more alone than ever I have in my life."

Muireall moved to the bed and sat beside her, then took one of her hands. "I'm so sorry."

"Ye have nay reason to be sorry. Ye offered. I wasna

ready. After I realized leaving would not be so bad, especially if it brought me to ye...and eventually home, I took advantage of the chaos in the village. Silas had taken to ranting and screaming out Donas's name, setting everyone on edge."

"How awful."

"The men could leave at will—hunting, or hunting for shipwreck survivors. The women would do anything to get out of the village—searching the cove for more from the shipwreck or even going into the woods to look for herbs everyone knew were out of season." She gave a mirthless laugh. "I went along with them to the cove, then just wandered away and kept going. I hid in some rocks down the beach until they left. When I saw a boat approaching near the shore, I walked to the water and waved. It was that simple."

"My God, Ella, they could have been anyone..."

"Before they got close enough to beach the boat, they asked if I was yer friend." She shrugged and patted Muireall's hand, then pulled hers free and wrapped her arms around her middle. "So, I went with them. Now, I wish to go home. If we have a home any longer."

Muireall nodded. "I worry about that, as well. Euan thinks Donas lied to us, to keep us from trying to escape. We were taken so quietly, he said the Rosses likely never came near our village or our keep. We never heard any fighting. He thinks our people live, and probably searched for us, but had no idea what happened to us, or where we might be."

"Which would explain why no one came for us. Aye, I like that explanation better than Donas's."

"I, too."

"Well," Ella said, rising, "I have no belongings to unpack. I suppose we might as well meet Euan and Calum, as Calum requested."

"Before we go downstairs, let's go to my chamber.

Annie, the laird's wife, found some dresses for me," Muireall told her. "One or two might fit ye. If not, others will be found, I'm sure." She led Ella across the hall into her room. As she pulled the clothes she'd been given out of her small chest, she explained. "The Brodies have been kind to me. The laird is Iain, and his wife Annie is from clan Rose. Euan said she's...unusual, though she seemed kind to me. I think ye will like her."

Ella reached for a blue dress and held it up in front of her. "What do ye think?"

"That's one I had in mind. 'Tis too large on top for me, so it might work well for ye. And it appears to be long enough. Do ye want to change? *Ach*, I didna think to ask if ye'd like a bath first, after yer voyage."

"Nay, I'm fine as I am. I'll save this dress for later."

"This one, too, I think," Muireall said, holding up a yellow satin gown trimmed with deep blue embroidery. "The skirt is also too long for me, and the color will suit ye." As if Ella needed any more help capturing the attention of every man in a room.

"Thank ye," Ella told her, fingering the frock "I've never had a dress so fine."

"Nor I, but it doesna fit me very well." Muireall sighed, envying Ella's taller and curvier shape. "Let's put these in yer chamber and go to the hall."

A few minutes later, they met Euan and Calum near the hearth at a table set with sliced venison, cheese, bread, and cups of ale.

"I thought lady Ella might be hungry after her journey," Calum said.

Muireall smirked. She hadn't missed Euan's elbow in Calum's ribs. Suddenly, he needed encouragement to speak to Ella? He was even more smitten than she first thought.

"Thank ye, I am," Ella told him and favored him with a smile.

Calum colored, then Ella did, too.

Muireall traded a raised-eyebrow glance with Euan, then turned to Ella. "While we eat, tell them what ye told me has happened at Ross since I left."

"The clan has been much like an anthill stirred with a stick," Ella began as she placed food on her trencher. "Silas is furious and bent on revenge. But there are cooler heads among the warriors."

"Cooler heads?" Euan asked, giving her time to take a bite and chew.

Ella swallowed and nodded. "Some were becoming vocal about being glad Donas no longer controls the clan. But Silas and her followers have taken control, at least until someone calls the council together, or defies her and calls for a vote. So far, no one has."

"No' even Erik?" Muireall was certain he would have no trouble gaining the position. So why wait?

Ella shook her head while she nibbled on some cheese. "She's kept him out on patrol, looking for..." her gaze shifted to Euan and back to Muireall... "ye two, I suppose. Erik must be furious to lose his intended bride."

Muireall bit her lip. She'd told no one what Erik had said to her that day he'd ordered Ella out of her cottage. She kept her promises. Even to Erik.

When Muireall failed to respond, Ella continued. "Thomas...well, he favors Erik, but has held his tongue. Waiting, I think, for Erik's return."

"Sensible," Euan said.

"Aye. 'Tis one of the things I came to like about Thomas. He has a good head on his shoulders."

Calum's mouth opened, then closed, but no sound came out.

Muireall bit back a laugh at his reaction to Ella's praise of the man Muireall suspected Calum would rather Ella forget. Then she asked the question she suspected Calum had sense enough not to ask. "Then why did ye leave him?"

"Why?" Ella's eyebrows arched in surprise. "Ye must ken. He helped steal us. He…married…me against my will."

"But ye just said…" Muireall goaded, earning a frown from Euan. She nodded. She'd behave.

"Nay, he's no' all bad," Ella was saying. "He could be kind. I've told ye that before. But I canna forgive the things he did. Once ye were gone, I realized what my future would be…with him and with Tira doing her best to curry favor with Silas. Even once I heard Donas was dead and gone, and there was hope for real change at Ross, I realized I couldna stay. I didna wish to stay."

Muireall nodded in sympathy.

"Do ye think we have a home to return to?" Ella directed that question to Euan.

"I do. And we'll take ye…both…home as soon as 'tis safe."

Ella grasped Muireall's hand. "But will they take me…us…back?"

"I dinna ken," Muireall told her. "But I hope so. They canna hold what happened against us."

"Aye, they can. Dermott will want nothing to do with me. I'm ruined."

Muireall winced, anticipating Calum's reaction to hearing of another man with a claim on Ella. "If he loved ye before, he'll love ye still."

Ella shook her head. "I dinna believe he will."

Muireall snuck a look at Calum. His stricken expression made her wish Ella's betrothed had never been mentioned. Calum clearly didn't hold what happened to Ella against her. Dermott, knowing him, probably would. Ella was right. She might face a cold reception at Munro.

Muireall pursed her lips. So might she. She had not

been taken, but only her virgin's blood would prove that, and who at Munro would take the chance and marry her to find out?

She glanced at Euan. His gaze was fixed on her. He nodded and gave her a smile. If he hadn't promised to do as she asked and return her to Munro, she might believe he wanted her for himself. But he had promised. And he would take her home. She had no future with him.

❧

ONCE THEY FINISHED EATING AND TALKING, ELLA WENT to her chamber to rest. Euan and Calum disappeared outside. Muireall returned to her chamber to fetch a shawl, thinking a walk outside would be pleasant, when she heard Euan's voice rising from the bailey. She went to her window and looked out.

Euan stood below her, watching a group of lads practicing combat with wooden swords. After a moment, he moved to one of the pairs and spoke to them, then took one lad's arm and moved it slowly through a sequence, then again. After a few words, he had the lad demonstrate it, then again, faster. With a nod, Euan stepped back and gestured for the lad to continue practicing with the other lad.

Muireall bit her lower lip. The smaller of the two lads reminded her of Georgie. She wondered how he was faring without her. Did he miss her? He must. Tears threatened at the back of her eyes. He needed her, and she'd been gone more than a month.

She shuddered and wrapped the shawl around her shoulders. She'd been that close to being wed to Erik. Her unwilling groom. She wondered if he had ceased searching for her by now. Had he sent an offer of marriage to the Rose for the lass he wanted, Fiona, or been too busy getting the clan under his control? She wished him well. Truly, she did.

He'd intimidated her, but he'd also shown her the respect of his honesty. That was a kindness she hadn't expected, and she shivered, recalling how he had shocked her. Now, days later and at a safe distance, she could see the most threatening of his comments as gruff teasing. He hadn't touched her, hadn't even moved closer to her. Merely told her, mildly, that he could silence her if he wished. She had no doubt he was able. But he hadn't been willing, and for that she was thankful.

She wrapped the shawl tighter around her shoulders and went down to Euan and the lads.

He smiled when he noticed her approaching.

"They're doing well," she said, glancing over the mock combat. "Did ye train them?"

"Nay, Iain's master at arms does that. But he's away from the keep today, so I stepped in to help. The more they practice, the stronger they'll be."

"I see."

"And this probably willna surprise ye: I'm a better fighter than I am a sailor." His brow creased, but he kept his gaze on his charges.

Muireall clamped a hand on his arm. "How many times must I tell ye no' to blame yerself?"

"Aye, well, many more, I suppose." He turned his head to look at her. For long seconds, he didn't speak, just stood there, his gaze moving slowly over her face.

She waited, wishing his fingers were caressing her face, not just his gaze.

His muscles shifted under her hand.

She didn't release his arm, but met his gaze with every bit of courage—and longing—she had in her. "Euan..."

"Muireall..."

They spoke at the same time. Unfortunately, the sound of their voices got lost under the anguished cry of one of the lads. The wee one Euan had helped while she watched from her window now held his wrist, his wooden sword on the ground at his feet. His sparring partner stood by, looking frightened, his elbows clamped to his sides and his posture stiff, as she and Euan approached. The other lads paused their practice to watch.

"I dinna mean to," the bigger lad protested as Euan knelt by the smaller one. "He…"

"I dinna care what he did, or ye, right now," Euan said, cutting the lad off as he ran careful fingers along the smaller lad's wrist. "I dinna think ye broke it, Angus, but 'twould be best to let the healer have a look, aye? Ye can practice some more tomorrow if she says ye may."

Muireall's heart broke to see how determined wee Angus was not to cry. She squeezed his shoulder and smiled, offering what comfort she could. She didn't want to embarrass him in front of the other lads.

He gave Euan a brave nod and her a sideways glance before he took himself off to the healer's cottage. Muireall wanted to go with him, but Euan saw her take a step to follow and shook his head. Muireall sighed. Part of toughening the wee lad was getting him accustomed to dealing with his hurts. She knew that, but she didn't like to see it.

Euan stood and watched him go out the keep's gate, then turned to the other lad. "Now tell me what happened."

"I dinna ken. We were practicing, then all of a sudden he yelped."

"'Twas yer responsibility to help Angus learn. Ye ken ye must be careful of a smaller lad, aye?"

"I do. I will."

Muireall nodded, glad the lad showed enough maturity not to argue with Euan and try to defend himself.

"Very well. Pair off with young Gowan over there. He's more yer size, and I see Cook has come to fetch his partner."

"I should leave ye to watch over these lads," Muireall said, but Euan took her arm.

"Nay, stay with me."

She fell in beside him as he walked back to the edge of the practice area.

"Ye must have younger brothers," Euan said. "Ye were very good with Angus. Ye lent him comfort yet didna mother him too much in front of the other lads."

"Wee Angus reminds me of a lad at home, Georgie."

"Georgie?"

She kept her gaze on the lads while she talked. "He's one of the reasons I must go home. Georgie's an orphan," she lied. She couldn't tell Euan the truth without revealing more about herself. Things she knew he wouldn't accept, after some of his comments in the cave. "He's a wee lad, small for his age. The other lads... well, they can be very unkind. He has no one to defend him, to help him. I need to ken someone has taken care of him since I...disappeared."

"What do ye mean, the other lads can be unkind?'

Euan's abrupt tone startled her, and she shifted her stance to face him. "They chase him and beat him. Worse, they laugh when he tries to join in the training. He's too small to defend himself, and the arms master thinks he's too young to start training. He willna accept that Georgie is as old as some of his lads, just smaller and weaker."

Euan's expression surprised her. Distant, as if he focused on an old pain, yet fierce, brow drawn down and jaw tense.

"Euan?"

He shook his head. "I'm sorry. 'Tis a familiar story."

A heavy sense of dismay started to fill in from the edges of her belly. "Is it?"

He glanced at her, then went back to watching the lads. "Aye. But ye needna fash. By the time ye get back, ye may find wee Georgie has learned to take care of himself…one way or another."

"What do ye mean?" She didn't like the sound of that. "One way or the other?"

"If the other lads havena beaten him to a pulp, he will either have learned how to fight using his small size and quickness, or…"

"Or what?"

"Or he'll be gone. Run away. Unless someone else has taken over protecting him."

"Oh God." Muireall closed her eyes. If Georgie believed she'd abandoned him, he might well have run away. How could he survive on his own? The thought made her belly cramp.

"*Ach*, lass, I'm sorry. I didna mean to upset ye." Euan turned his back on the lads and grasped her shoulders. Peering into her eyes, he rested his forehead against hers. "Wee Georgie will be fine. If ye have had the care of him, the lad kens someone loves him. He'll be there when ye return. And I'll bet he'll have worked hard to make ye proud of him."

Muireall slumped, desperate to collapse into Euan's embrace, put her arms around his neck and cling to him as she'd clung to hope the past month, but they were in full view of the lads—and anyone else in this part of the bailey. Instead, she stiffened her spine and stepped back. "I pray ye are right," she said. "But now ye ken why I must go back as quickly as possible."

Euan sighed and let her go. "I do, lass, more than ye can imagine."

CHAPTER 11

*W*hen Muireall answered her door the next morning, she was surprised to find Annie Rose standing there. "Good morning, Lady Brodie," she greeted her, suddenly nervous. What was the laird's wife doing at her door?

"Annie will do."

Very well, she wanted to be informal. "Lady Annie."

Annie laughed. "Just call me Annie. Please," she answered, opening her hands. "Lady Brodie, even Lady Annie, makes me sound eighty years old!"

"Ye are no' that!" Embarrassed, Muireall stepped back. "Very well, Annie, would ye like to come in?"

"Actually, I came to ask if ye and Ella would like to go riding with me."

Riding! "I…we never…" But she wanted to…oh how she did!

"Ye dinna ken how to ride?" Annie's wide-eyed expression communicated shock.

Muireall shook her head. "Neither of us do."

"Well, then we'll have to remedy that right away." She spread her hands. "Ye canna go everywhere in a boat. And wagons are too slow. Ye must learn to ride. 'Tis one of my most favorite things to do."

Her blush reminded Muireall of Euan telling her while they were still in the cave that his laird was recently married, and gave Muireall the idea what other favorite thing a relatively new bride might like to do.

"We've never needed to go anywhere…so we had nay reason to learn. Only the warriors ride."

Annie shook her head, her jaw clenched. "At Brodie, everyone who wishes to, does."

"What do we need?"

"Boots…I'll find ye some. Trews would be best, but we'll make do. Today, we'll get ye on a lovely, gentle mare and walk about a bit. Perhaps by the time ye go back to Munro, ye'll have learned all ye need to ride… and ride well."

"I hope so. Thank ye."

"Ye wake Ella and meet me in the great hall to break yer fast, and then we'll go, aye? By then, I should have found some boots for ye."

With a grin, Annie left her. Watching her walk away, Muireall smiled. There was something…always positive and cheerful…about Annie Rose. No wonder Iain Brodie had fallen in love with her.

She stepped across the hall and rapped on Ella's door. In moments, Ella appeared, rumpled and with a plaid wrapped over her chemise.

"Did I wake ye?"

"Almost. I heard ye speaking to someone."

"That was Annie, the laird's wife. Ye ken what she's offered. I really want to do this. Perhaps then I can teach Georgie."

Ella nodded. "Aye, then at least he can ride away from his tormentors."

"Put on yer old dress—I dinna think the satin one will suit."

"I'm no' certain if I can…" Ella glanced aside.

"Do ye think ye will get the chance to learn at Munro when ye have no' yet?"

"Nay." She squared her shoulders. "Ye have the right of it. I'll be down soon."

Muireall braided her hair and headed downstairs, excitement making her steps light and quick. She didn't see Annie yet, so she sat with some of the other Brodie lasses. Ella joined them a few minutes later. The lasses entertained them with stories of when they learned to ride, and how Annie was changing their life at Brodie, giving the lasses the chance to learn skills traditionally reserved for the lads. Muireall liked what she heard.

Annie came in a few minutes later. "I left boots for ye at the stable. No sense bringing them in here. Are ye ready?"

Muireall stood. "I am."

Ella popped a last bite of bread in her mouth, chewed and swallowed as she stood. "I am, too."

On the way to the stable, Annie told them about the mounts she'd picked for them. "The stable lads are saddling them. All ye need to do is put on boots and then sit on the horses. We'll get ye comfortable there, then perhaps we'll go for a walk."

"But we're keeping ye from the ride ye wanted to take." Muireall felt she had to object to be polite. And she truly didn't want to keep Annie from doing something she enjoyed.

"I can ride when we're done. 'Tis important to me that ye learn. Every lass should be able to, for yer own protection."

Annie shooed the stable boy out of a stall so Muireall and Ella could change into the boots in privacy. She'd guessed well. They weren't a perfect fit, but close enough. Once Muireall was up on the mare Annie picked for her, her excitement bubbled over. She could do this!

"If only we'd been able to ride before the Rosses took us. We might have ridden away and never been taken," Muireall mused.

Ella looked a bit less enthusiastic once she was on horseback. "Ye might have. I'm no' certain I would have."

Annie chuckled as she mounted and picked up her reins, then theirs. "I'm going to walk ye out of the stable, so ye can become accustomed to a horse's gait. *Dinna fash.* Ye willna fall."

Muireall quickly adapted to her mare's rocking gait. She didn't enjoy the stares they got from the Brodies in the bailey. But in moments, she realized Annie was headed for the keep's gate. Away from the bailey, Muireall relaxed.

Then she noticed Euan watching from the keep's wall walk. She lifted a hand to wave, but felt her balance shift uncertainly, and dropped her hand to the saddle with an oath.

"Are ye steady?" Annie asked.

Muireall nodded, her heart rate slowing. "Aye. I tried to wave to Euan and wobbled. I think he's coming out."

Annie nodded. "Good. He can help ye while I attend to Ella."

Euan caught up with them just outside the gate. "What are ye doing?" He looked first to Annie, then to Muireall. "Do ye ken how to ride?"

Muireall glanced at Annie, then answered for both of them. "I will soon, and I'll thank ye no' to interfere."

Euan whirled to Annie. "What will ye do if one of those nags suddenly bolts?"

"Go after it, of course. But they willna. They're well trained."

"I'm coming with ye," he declared.

Annie smirked. "I thought ye might. We'll be here when ye return."

Muireall wanted to laugh, but Euan's look of disgust made her school her features.

Annie dismounted and kept them busy getting used to how a horse moves at a walk, then handed them the reins and got back on her mare. "Ye seem comfortable enough to hold the reins. Keep walking. If your mount tries to go faster, pull back on the reins. I'll be right with ye if ye need help."

Euan rode up. "So will I," he said, obviously having heard at least Annie's final words.

Annie led off with Ella.

Euan fell in beside Muireall. "How does it feel?"

She shrugged. "Still a bit strange, but getting better."

He reached over and laid his hand on hers and left it there. "Ye dinna have to choke the reins. They willna go anywhere. Hold them loosely and relax."

Muireall grimaced. He'd seen through her nonchalance. She loosened her hold on the strips of leather in her hands and sighed, then glanced at Euan and smiled.

"That's better." He rewarded her with one of his rare grins. "Now look around ye. 'Tis a beauty of a day. The sun is shining, 'tis warmer than usual. Ye are out of the keep and with me. What more could ye want?"

Muireall had to laugh at that.

Euan gave her a wounded pout that quickly dissolved, and he laughed along with her.

Annie twisted in the saddle, glanced back at them and grinned.

Muireall gave her a quick wave, and Annie turned forward again.

"She likes ye, ye ken. Annie doesna teach adults. She starts with the young ones, so they're comfortable with horses and weapons as they grow."

"As ye said, she's…unusual."

"Aye, she is that. But so are ye, lass. Brave and kind, all wrapped in a beautiful bundle."

Muireall blushed. "Have ye been into that strong Brodie ale?"

Euan laughed. "Nay, Muireall. I've nay need of spirits to brighten my mood, no' when I'm with ye."

❧

THAT EVENING, EUAN SAT WITH CALUM, OFF TO THE SIDE by the fire in the great hall, watching some of the clan —and Muireall and Ella Munro—finish their meal at the long tables filling the center of the room. The Munro lasses were the center of attention—especially Ella. And they both seemed to be enjoying themselves. Calum was seething and drinking too much. Euan felt sorry for him. A lass as beautiful as Ella would always garner male attention, even if Calum found a way to marry her. Not a simple or easy task, given what was going on tonight, or the fact that she'd left a betrothed behind at Munro and a husband at Ross. Euan shook his head. He hoped she was worth the trouble Calum would have to suffer through to win her—and to un-snarl all the obligations already heaped on the lass.

As for Muireall—since he'd returned from Ross territory, he had little appetite for food, but his appetite for Muireall had grown enormous. Much like Calum, ale and whisky were the only things he'd found to soothe that hunger.

He'd tried to do as Iain had ordered and be her host and protector while she was here. But he found he couldn't be with her and not want her. Since Ella's arrival, he'd avoided being alone with Muireall for her sake. Riding with her, Ella, and Annie this morning had validated his instinct to keep his distance. He'd enjoyed being with her and teaching her too much. He'd been left hard and hungrier than he could remember ever being, wanting to teach her a very different kind of riding. Longing for Muireall burned in his blood every time he saw her. He feared what he might do if he got her alone.

She'd been threatened, and she'd tolerated more than any lass should in Donas Ross's camp. No matter how much he might need her, for as long as she remained, Brodie was supposed to be her sanctuary.

Yet she was his sanctuary. If only he could find a way to tell her.

Iain was sure to take him to task soon, and he dreaded the confrontation. How could he explain to the Brodie chief the torment he was in?

Iain's marriage to Annie had settled their laird and repaired his skirt-chasing reputation. Would Iain remember what such longing felt like? Since taking over the clan, Iain Brodie never cracked. Nothing ruffled his calm confidence. And his marriage to Annie Rose was as solid and loving as any Euan had ever seen.

Euan didn't expect much sympathy.

Movement at Muireall's table distracted him. Muireall and Ella stood up with two of the other lasses at their table, but instead of going with the others, Muireall headed toward him.

Calum chuckled as Euan tensed. "Here she comes, lad. Are ye going to stay and speak to the lass or head for the hills?"

"The hills are gaining in appeal," Euan told him as he stood.

"Euan, Calum," Muireall called out as she neared, giving Euan no time to escape.

Calum got to his feet, bowed and made his excuses. "I've warmed the chair for ye, lass. Ye and Euan sit and enjoy the fire."

With that, he walked away, a bit unsteady but mobile, probably intent on finding Ella. Euan watched him go with narrowed eyes. Calum would regret leaving him like this. Then he remembered his manners and turned back to Muireall. "I was just leaving. Would ye like to sit by the fire?"

"Nay, Euan. What I would like is to speak with ye. Somewhere private."

Euan's gut clenched. Here was the request he'd been dreading all day. "I dinna think that's a very good idea, lass." He took a step away from her, but she followed.

Her chin lifted. "Are ye afraid of me, then?"

He could not have heard her correctly. "Afraid?" He snorted. "Nay. Why would any man be afraid of a lass?"

"I dinna ken, but ye have been avoiding me. I could only assume ye feared being seen with me. Is yer laird still angry ye brought me here?"

"What?" He waved a hand. "Nay. Iain was never angry about that."

"Then why?"

"He's angry about Donas."

"Why should he care about Donas? Now that he's dead, he canna hurt anyone else. Iain should ken that." She shook her head and pushed a hand aside as if pushing away the topic of Donas Ross. "So, if he is no' angry about bringing me here, then why have ye been avoiding me?"

Euan closed his eyes and huffed out a breath, then took her elbow and led her out of the hall and down a side corridor. Just touching her arm made his hunger for her turn into a great throbbing beast in his blood. "What do ye want, Muireall?"

"I want to ken why, other than this morning, ye have been avoiding me." She whirled to face him, pulling her arm out of his grip. "Is it because I remind ye of what happened? The shipwreck? Yer men?"

Euan's breath froze into a painful lump in his chest

for a moment, the heat of his desire vanquished by the image of James's body at the prow of their stolen skiff. Euan blinked, hard, willing the image away. The pain stayed.

"Euan, I'm so sorry." Muireall laid a hand on his cheek. "I didna mean to hurt ye. But I've been...bereft... without yer company these last few days. Riding with ye only showed me how much."

Euan inhaled. She was standing close. Too close. He could smell her womanly scent and feel the heat radiating from her. Her breath teased across his skin. The throbbing in his blood moved lower.

Before he could stop himself, he took her in his arms and crushed her mouth under his. She tasted like honey. Like salvation. He felt his chest thaw as heat rose from his balls to his belly to his heart. He couldn't stop kissing her, inhaling her scent, murmuring her name. He was hard and starving. She was the only meal he craved.

She kissed him back, once, twice, then pushed him away. "I see," she said, her expression stern.

Maybe he'd drunk too much, because he didn't understand what she thought she saw. But he understood his need to kiss her, so he bent to take her mouth again.

But she put her hand over his lips. "What is this about, Euan?"

He reared back, eyebrows raised. "About? How can ye ask? I thought ye just said ye missed me. I missed ye as well."

"And this is how ye show me? Nay, ye feel guilt over yer men. Ye are trying to take yer anger out on me because ye ken I willna strike back." She lifted her chin. "If it helps ye, I can take it. But Euan, ye canna take the blame for the storm. Can ye no' see that?"

Hot tears had gathered in his eyes while she spoke, making him furious. She'd been correct earlier. He did fear her. Not of being seen with her. He feared hurting her, lashing out at her.

But she apparently had no fear of him.

She stood on tiptoe, leaned in and kissed him, then moved her lips to his cheek to kiss away the salt of a tear that escaped.

Suddenly the floodgates opened. Everything he'd been holding in burst out in one anguished groan. Euan fell against the wall at his back and pulled her tightly to him, his arms locking her in place while her kisses moved over his face. He fought for control without success. When he buried his face in her shoulder, she kissed his ear and threaded her fingers in his hair.

"'Tis going to be well, ye'll see," she cooed, soothing him. "'Twas no' yer fault, love. How could anyone blame ye for the storm or what followed? Ye must no' blame yerself."

"But I do," Euan choked out as he lifted his head and met her gaze, heedless of how his eyes must look. "For all of that, and for not taking ye home right away."

"Ye will take me home when the time is right." She grasped the hand he lifted to her face, curling her fingers around his. "In the meantime, I am content to be where ever ye are." She laid her cheek against his fingers.

Euan's distress turned to hunger again as he released her hand and pulled her more snugly against him.

She rested her head on his shoulder, one arm around his waist and the other above his heart. "*Dinna fash*, Euan," she murmured. "I am here."

Euan held her, every part of his body consumed with awareness of her nearness, her scent, her heat. But somehow, despite his hunger for her, she had calmed him, and with the truth of his need for her out in the open, holding her like this let him breathe easy for the first time since they'd returned to Brodie.

He needed Muireall. How would he be able to take her home and lose her forever?

&

MUIREALL TASTED THE SALT OF EUAN'S TEARS ON HER tongue and ached for him. "Yer anger shows me how deeply ye grieve," she murmured against his skin. "Ye must stop…"

Euan squeezed her as a drowning man would a rope thrown to him in a stormy sea. He groaned into her shoulder. "How can I?"

"Ye and Calum were lucky to have survived. The storm that night was fierce, and the sea wild. Do ye think ye could somehow calm the winds and flatten the waves?" She grabbed his shoulders and held him away from her, searching his face for any sign he would relent. His features betrayed nothing. Yet his breathing had slowed from frantic to more measured. He was coming back from wherever the pain of his imaginings had taken him.

Muireall moved her hands to his face, using her thumbs to dry the damp tracks left behind. "All will be well. Did ye no' tell me that very thing? Do ye think I can believe it if ye do no'? Help me, Euan. Tell me again, all will be well. Ye promised it. And ye will see ye had the right of it if ye will only give yerself some time."

He gave her the slightest tilt of his lips, the barest hint of a smile. "I will try. For ye."

Her heart soared. "And for ye." She nodded. "Good enough. Now walk with me. Take me to the highest reaches of this keep and show me what I might see if I were a bird, free to wander the sky wherever my will took me."

Euan chuckled at that and tipped his head. "Ye will need a cloak."

"I willna. Ye will keep me warm."

He gave her a measured look, as if deciding whether she could withstand the conditions he anticipated, or whether she was offering more than the literal meaning of her words. If he thought she implied more, what would she do? She wanted to comfort him, but beyond that? She didn't know.

"Verra well. Come with me." He took her arm and guided her down another hallway then up a circular stair.

Muireall blessed whatever had given her the impulse to suggest going to the top of the tower to distract Euan. He'd been so strong for so many days, she hadn't realized the utter depth of his remorse over what had happened. Until now. The misery in his eyes and the lonely tear track on his cheek had broken her heart. He'd given no sign he needed anything from her. He'd avoided her. Only when she'd felt his damp cheek press against her neck had she realized she'd been blind to his pain, lost in her own worries.

She trudged up the stairs, feeling guilty and small. She'd been selfish, worrying about Munro and ignoring how returning home without his men affected Euan. Shame nearly overwhelmed her, but his nearness, his heat at her back, kept her going. She'd distracted Euan from his melancholy. She dared not let him see any sign of her distress for fear of bringing it all up again.

"Ye do ken," Euan suddenly said, startling her into missing a step. He caught her before she fell to her knees and pulled her body back against his until she had her feet under her, then released her with a groan. "I'm sorry, lass," he said. His voice sounded strained. She glanced up, but could see only the next turn in the stone steps. How much further to the top? The sooner she got him in to the open air, the sooner they would both feel better.

"I am well," she assured him. "What do I ken?"

"That 'tis dark now. Ye may no' see as much as ye wish."

"Yet the moon will light much of the countryside, I hope."

He was silent for a moment as they continued climbing. "Aye, it should."

At the top floor, a ladder led to a trap door set in the ceiling.

"Are ye certain ye want to go up there?"

Muireall nodded. She'd climbed ladders before. This one should be no different.

"I must go first to open that," he said, indicating the rectangle of wood set above their heads. "So ye will be very careful as ye follow me."

"I will," she replied. "'Tis no' my first ladder."

"Verra well."

Euan climbed quickly, unlatched a lock she hadn't noticed and pushed the trapdoor up and out of the way. Then he glanced down at her and held out a hand. "Come on, then."

Muireall climbed. When she reached the top, Euan was waiting to lift her up onto the rooftop. As he did, the wind caught her hair, ripping it from its loose braid and sending it flying around her head. She got a glimpse of their surroundings and was glad he held her fast. The low wall rimming the flat roof did little to provide a barrier against a fall and nothing to hide the view of the surrounding countryside. Silver moonlight spilled over hills in one direction. And in the other, it frosted wave tips and drew a shining path across the Moray Firth, a bright arrow pointing to Munro. She gasped.

Euan wrapped his arms fully around her and held

her back to his chest. "Aye, 'tis beautiful," he murmured, unaware of what she'd reacted to.

Her chest tightened, and the wind stung her eyes. Still sensitive to Euan's earlier mood, she could not cry. But if ever she'd needed a sign, there it was, writ in silvery runes made of moonlight and waves across the restless surface of the firth. Home lay that way. She stepped out of his arms and moved toward the sea side of the roof, glad the wind blew her hair behind her, out of her eyes.

Euan stayed with her. "The wind off the water smells so clean and fresh," he said, his voice a comforting rumble against her back as his arms went around her again. "Being here is like being on the deck of a ship, wind wild in yer hair and moonlight glinting on the waves."

Muireall lay her hands over his, warm where they touched his skin, cold where the wind raced across their tops. "We're fortunate, 'tis such a clear night. I can see all the way to Munro." The moment the words slipped out, she regretted them.

Euan tensed at her back, released her, then turned her around to face him. Her hair whipped around them both. "I will get ye home, Muireall. I have promised ye. The Brodie has, as well, when he deems it safe for all concerned."

Muireall dropped her gaze to his chest. "I ken it. It was just the streak of moonlight..." Suddenly a tear escaped and dripped, cold and wet, down her cheek.

"Aye, of course. I see it, too." Euan pulled her against him. "I'm sorry, lass. It does seem to make a path...an omen..."

"Aye, but a shining one. Another promise, I think." She lifted her gaze to his.

He brushed her hair back from her face and bent his

head. "If ye will permit, I will seal the promise with a kiss."

Her heart lifted and she took a deep breath. The clean fresh scent of the sea combined with Euan's own gave her comfort. "Aye, I will," she replied and lifted her mouth to his.

He kissed her gently at first, then again more firmly. "I will make as many promises as ye will allow kisses," he told her, then bent to take her mouth again.

Muireall wrapped her arms around his neck and clung to him, soaking up the warmth of his body and the taste of his kiss. "Ye need promise nought else," she whispered against his cheek, "save that ye will kiss me as often as ye can." She stopped herself before she added "for as long as ye can." What would Euan do when she returned to Munro? What would she?

"That's a promise I'm glad to make," Euan told her and took her mouth again, sending her senses soaring like the birds whose view she'd sought to share.

CHAPTER 12

The next afternoon, Euan stood on the rampart of the Brodie keep with Iain and a handful of Brodie warriors by his side. With trepidation, he watched the sail approach. In the last half hour, it had gotten close enough to be plainly seen to be a Ross vessel, headed their way. Which could mean only one thing. The new Ross laird, whether it was Erik or someone else, was coming for the person who'd killed Donas.

But since he and Calum had left nothing of Brodie behind, save the *Tangie*'s wreck, Euan couldn't imagine how they found out. Had they recovered something from the *Tangie* with a Brodie insignia? He didn't recall any such thing being on board.

"They'll be here soon," Iain said, turning from watching the approaching ship to Euan. "I want you, Calum, and the Munro lasses out of sight. You can listen from the laird's lug above the great hall, but ye must keep silent, no matter what is said. Can ye do that?"

"Calum and I will, aye. I canna speak for the lasses, but based on Muireall's actions while we were guests of that lot," Euan answered and gestured toward the sail, now less than a mile offshore, "the lass has sense. I trust she can convince her friend, as well."

"See that she does," Iain ordered and returned his attention to their impending visitors. "They're not coming to propose an alliance. Ye can be certain this visit means trouble of some sort."

"'Tis my fault they have a grievance against us. I should stay to stand with ye against the Ross accusations. Likely they're well aware of Donas's temper and will understand I had nay choice. Iain, I am sorry…"

"Ye did them a favor getting rid of Donas Ross. But the new laird might want the lasses returned…especially the one wed to one of them."

"Ye canna!"

"Nor will I as long as I am no' forced to. She'd best stay hidden and quiet." Iain leaned on the balustrade and studied the ship. "Let's see why they made the trip before we assume the worst." He straightened. "Leave them to me. They're close enough to see us up here, so get ye out of sight. Calum and the lasses as well."

Euan nodded and left Iain with his advisors on the wall. He found Calum in the great hall and sent him upstairs, but spent precious minutes searching for Muireall. He found her and Ella in the ladies' solar, which, he realized, was where he should have looked first. "Come with me," he told them. "We're about to have visitors."

Muireall paled and dropped her needlework into her lap. "No'…"

"Aye, a Ross ship. Iain wants us and Calum out of sight."

Muireall bundled her needlework into the basket beside her chair. Ella had yet to move or speak. Muireall grabbed her hand, startling her into action, then hurried to him. "Let's go then. But where?"

"Somewhere we can follow what's going on but remain unseen." He led them to an upstairs closet that shared a wall with the upper reach of the Great Hall. "This is the laird's lug," he told her when she frowned. "A small portal built into the back wall of the closet will allow us to overhear conversations in the hall."

"Can it be seen from the hall?"

"Nay. A painted border of blocks and grids hides it very well. But we must remain silent in there."

Calum was already inside. "Nothing yet," he reported in a low voice, then spotted Ella and straightened. "Come, lass, sit with me."

Ella nodded and took the narrow chair next to his.

Euan traded a glance with Muireall. "Like as no', they're just being met by Iain's guard and escorted from the bay to the keep."

The wait seemed interminable, but eventually, they heard voices from the great hall, a scramble of noise that went along with the movement of a group of men. Then Iain's voice rang out.

"Gentlemen, to what do we owe the pleasure of this visit?"

"We are no' here for yer pleasure," a man answered.

Euan exchanged glances with Calum, Ella, and Muireall.

Calum shook his head.

Muireall frowned and shrugged, as did Ella.

No one recognized the voice—yet. Perhaps the large, empty hall distorted it. Euan thought one of the lasses would eventually place it.

"Then ye'd best state yer business so ye can be on yer way," Iain replied. His tone was calm, but Euan could imagine the tension in the hall at the Ross's pronouncement.

"We've come to collect the man who killed our laird, Donas Ross, and stole both a Ross skiff and a lass, perhaps two."

Euan frowned and cut his gaze to Muireall, recalling how she'd protested when Donas had said she was one of his. Her fists were clenched, but her lips were pressed together and she remained silent. She met his gaze and nodded. She knew what he'd been afraid of.

Silence reigned for a moment, then a low murmur broke out, likely from Iain's guards.

"Those are serious charges," Iain said, then paused.

Euan could imagine Iain reaching for a way to distract the Ross, and held his breath.

"Why should I believe ye?" Iain continued.

"We have proof," the Ross answered, his tone confident.

Euan and Calum exchanged a frown.

"Proof we'll take to the Earl of Ross. If ye dinna wish to start a clan war ye canna win, ye must turn over yer man. Or men."

The Ross was too confident for Euan's liking. They did have something, then, though he couldn't imagine what. And the Earl of Ross, with many allies, was too powerful to challenge. Brodie would be overrun by their combined forces. Even with the help of Lady Annie's father, James Rose, and other Brodie allies, Euan knew Iain would be reluctant to do battle with the Earl of Ross.

"And who are ye?"

"I am Teague Ross, the laird's emissary."

Both Muireall and Ella gasped and clapped hands over their mouths.

"Teague is our friend Tira's husband," Ella whispered. "He was doing everything he could to join Donas's inner circle."

"So perhaps he's now in Silas's," Muireall added quietly.

Iain's voice silenced any further speculation. "With

accusations of this nature, I'd expect the new laird to bring them, no' his…emissary."

"The new laird has no' yet been chosen. Donas's lady, Silas Ross, leads the clan."

Euan couldn't believe his ears. Silas was as bad as her husband had been. Muireall's slumped shoulders and clenched fists told him as much as her dropped jaw about her disappointment and shock.

"How is Erik allowing Silas to remain in power?" she whispered. "I thought he was poised to take over."

Ella opened her mouth to answer, but Calum held up a hand when Iain's voice reached them.

"In other words, ye are no laird's emissary. Ross is without a chief. By what authority do you come here, then, and threaten clan war?"

Calum smiled a rueful smile.

Euan grimaced in agreement with Calum at the bite in Iain's tone. They'd both been on the receiving end of Iain's ire more than once. Teague Ross was about to discover how uncomfortable that experience could be.

"We have proof…"

"Yer proof means nothing if ye have nay laird."

"Our proof is a Brodie."

Euan clenched his fists and stood. He met Calum's stricken gaze with one of his own.

Muireall clapped a hand over her mouth, stifling a gasp. Ella frowned, her gaze traveling over each of them.

"Who?" Iain's demand rang out, sharp and heart-stopping, like the first crack of thunder in a sudden summer storm.

Who else had survived? Who had they left behind? Recalling how Calum had been treated, Euan's belly roiled until he feared he would be ill. He gritted his teeth and got himself under control. Now was not the time to give in to reproach. He had to pay attention and learn from Iain's questions how they would get back their missing man.

"With some persuasion…" the Ross replied, letting the implication hang in the suddenly chill air, "he admitted to being called Eduard."

Eduard lived! Euan's heart leapt, then shattered with a pain beyond anything he had felt before. He rubbed his chest while the realization echoed again and again in his mind. He had left a man behind. Where had Eduard been while he, and then he and Calum, had searched for the missing men? They'd sailed for miles along the coast before giving up and bringing James's body home. And what about Dugal? Had no one found him? Euan exhaled through pinched nostrils. *Damn it!*

The silence stretched out around them. Euan could picture Iain's forbidding frown, but at this news, white lines would bracket his mouth and every muscle in his body would be tensed with the effort not to strike down Teague Ross where he stood.

Muireall grasped Euan's hand and pulled him back to his seat.

He suspected she knew there was more to come. He might as well hear the rest sitting down.

"Ye came here claiming to have one of my men, and yet ye did not do the courtesy of returning him to his family? How am I to ken the man is who ye say he is? And that he still lives."

"He lives. Or he did when I left to come here."

Euan stood again, determined to join Iain and find out more about Eduard—where he'd been, how they found him, his condition. Those questions and more burned in his chest.

Calum grasped his arm before he could take a step. With narrowed eyes, Calum shook his head.

Euan jerked his arm free and quit the closet, eager

to get downstairs, then slowed as he recalled his promise to Iain.

Calum stayed right on his heels. As soon as he was clear of the door, he closed it carefully, then barked, "Stop right there."

Euan turned to him and spread his hands. "Iain doesna ken all we do about Ross…"

"And Ross doesna ken we are here. If they see yer ugly face, what do ye think will happen?"

Biting down an oath, Euan relented. If the wrong Ross saw him—if Teague Ross was one of the men with Donas that night—they would have their proof in Iain's own hall. Worse, they'd have no more need to keep Eduard alive. Calum's meaning was clear. They must let Iain handle this. He and Calum returned to the closet in time to hear Iain speak.

"Is an innocent captive worth more to Ross than Brodie's regard?" Iain suddenly sounded tired.

"If that innocent captive is worth exchanging for Donas Ross's killer or killers, then aye. Brodie owes Ross a life. We can take Eduard Brodie's, or Donas Ross's killer's. The choice is yers."

"Ye leave me in an impossible situation," Iain objected. "Ye offer nay proof that ye hold any man, much less a Brodie called Eduard, nor any proof a Brodie killed yer chief—if he is indeed dead. Or took a lass…or two…and a skiff. Ye dinna seem to be sure what did or didna happen. So tell me something ye might be sure of. Did ye see one of yer vessels when ye sailed into the bay?"

Euan wanted to applaud as Iain let the silence stretch out. They had not, of course. That skiff was several miles down the coast and well hidden. Too valuable to sail into the firth and sink, the skiff would become a Brodie vessel once a few changes were made to disguise its lines and origin.

Teague Ross's "nay", when it came, was barely audible.

"And have ye seen a lass ye recognize, as ye passed through the village on the way here?"

This nay sounded louder.

"Nor will ye, for the lass ye seek is no' here."

Euan cringed at Iain's fib. True, neither Muireall nor Ella was in the great hall with him, which is what Iain would mean by that statement. True in fact, if not in spirit, which Euan was certain Iain would hold against him later.

"Nor is anyone who might have...*might have...* harmed yer laird." Iain's voice suddenly dripped disdain. "For all I ken, Donas himself sent ye on this fool's errand to stir up trouble among the southern clans. Ye bring daft accusations without any proof. Wild claims of murder and theft, yet here ye dinna find what ye claim was stolen. Did ye think I would simply hand someone over? Out of fear? Of what Silas Ross might do? Or the Earl?"

Iain paused and Euan heard him moving about, his tread heavy and deliberate, moving, he supposed, toward their visitor.

"Ye are lucky," Iain continued, and Euan could picture him standing toe-to-toe with the Ross, "I dinna kill ye where ye stand and send yer body back to Ross in answer to this insulting nonsense. Now get out of my hall while ye still can."

Euan thought Iain was laying it on a bit thick, but given the clatter following his words, his theatrics must have worked. Teague Ross and any men who'd come with him had to be leaving. No one stood up to Iain Brodie in his own hall.

A few minutes later, Iain's voice drifted up to them, calm and steady. "They're gone. Ye lot get down here now."

Euan led the charge. After the scene they'd just overheard, if Iain planned to punish anyone, Euan swore it would be him. Calum was not at fault. Nor, certainly, was Muireall. Or Ella. And if the Rosses did, as Teague Ross claimed, have Eduard—and they must, for how else would they know his name?—Euan was responsible. He'd made the decision to break off the search and sail for home. After finding James's body, he'd had no expectation that any more of his men lived. And had no idea he was leaving Eduard behind to be captured and probably tortured by Silas Ross and her men. The fact that the searchers Iain sent had found nothing, either, was no consolation. He clenched his fists and entered the great hall to face his laird.

BY THE TIME MUIREALL REACHED THE HALL BEHIND Euan and Calum, the two were facing off with their laird. She started to join them, but Euan waved her behind him. Ella paused at the entry, then came to stand beside Muireall.

"The lasses had nay part in this," Euan asserted. "Let them be."

"The lasses," Iain replied, pinning her in place with his steady gaze, "have been in the Ross village, met the people, and seen the fighting force. They have details ye two do no.'"

"Ye are correct," Muireall told him, then stepped up beside Euan, who had stiffened at Iain's words. She appreciated his instinct to protect her and Ella, but his concern was misplaced. Iain was right, and she wanted to help, not hide behind Euan's broad back. "Teague Ross is the man who took Tira Munro...who wed her." She told Iain what she and Ella had told Euan and

Calum in the laird's lug. "He must now be aligned with Silas to have come here."

"Erik would not leave Ross and risk his power base to Silas," Euan observed.

"I dinna understand why Erik has not taken control," Muireall added. Surely Silas did not command loyalty among the men as Erik did.

Euan crossed his arms. "It makes nay sense, but perhaps their elders are bowing to Silas until the matter of Donas's killer is settled."

"'Tis bad for the clan," Iain added. "If Silas has a strong faction on her side, Erik Ross may not have enough of a following to declare himself chief and make it stick."

"I dinna care who leads Ross," Euan announced. "My only interest right now is getting Eduard back."

"I'm calling a War Council this evening. Ye will attend. What ye will no' do is sail for Ross. Not now, not until this is settled. We'll meet with the Brodie elders and arms master to decide how best to retrieve—or negotiate for—Eduard…and avoid a war."

"What about returning us to Munro?" Muireall asked. "We dinna wish to be in the way."

"I'm sorry lass, but I willna. If ye are seen by a Ross, or worse, recaptured, in Brodie company, I'll no' be able to deny our involvement in anything Teague Ross just accused us of." He cut off Euan's objection with a look before Euan could voice it. "We ken ye killed Donas Ross in self-defense. Likely his people ken that, too, even if his widow is too crazed to admit it." He turned back to Muireall. "As long as they hold Eduard, and until we ken who will take power in that clan, nay, ye must stay here."

Muireall pressed her lips together, fighting back a protest.

Seeing that, Iain's expression softened. "I have

promised ye, lass, I will get ye home as soon as we're able. Ye have no' traded one captor for another, though I hope our care of ye has been better than any ye received across the firth. I canna risk what yer discovery would cost Brodie. No' yet."

Muireall's shoulders slumped. She could understand the Brodie chief's position, but it frustrated her, just the same.

"What if we went around the firth, overland?" Calum asked.

Hope surged in Muireall's chest, but Iain quickly squashed it.

"Nay," Iain replied with a frown. "All of ye are confined to the keep until this is resolved." He held up a hand as Euan opened his mouth to argue. "I have spoken. Ross has come here, and they will be sailing this side of the firth as much as they are able, have nay doubt. Just as I have sent boats to sail their side. I'll hear nay more about any of ye leaving Brodie."

Euan's jaw clenched, his lips flattening into a thin line, but he stayed silent, merely giving a curt nod.

His tension told Muireall she wasn't the only one frustrated with the restrictions placed on them. She hoped, after the war council that evening, decisions would be made that would allow her to go home and allow Euan to help retrieve his missing sailor. She knew being denied the chance to correct what he saw as his failure ate at him. Euan had searched as long as he dared, but because of Calum's condition, and with James's body on board, they could not have lingered any longer. She nodded to Euan in sympathy. He glanced at her, then cut his gaze back to Iain.

Calum, too, looked ready to argue, but held his silence.

She gusted out a sigh and turned her face away from Iain. She did not want the chief to see how upset his pronouncement made her. Even though she could see the logic behind it, she still grieved for her family and friends. Did any of them still live? Had Donas, as Euan suspected, lied to her? She could only hope Euan was right.

CHAPTER 13

*E*uan escorted Muireall into Iain's private solar after the evening meal. He felt boxed in by the men already present—gazes had swung to him and Muireall when they entered. And if he felt the press of their scrutiny, Muireall, as the only woman present, must feel it even more. But her expression remained calm. Their only respite came when Calum entered the room with Ella and was treated to the same stares.

Calum settled Ella on Muireall's other side after greeting her and Euan with a nod.

Euan wondered what Muireall thought of the Brodie elders' council. At the moment, he wasn't sure what he thought of them, though he understood Iain's reasons for involving them. He hadn't been laird long enough to have the elders' complete confidence. Many had voted against him, despite his father's wishes that Iain replace him as laird once he was gone. Iain's power base was strong, but not solid, so he was obliged to demonstrate leadership by consulting with so-called older and wiser heads.

The tension in the room was palpable as they waited for Iain to make his entrance. Without a word being spoken, the looks Euan was getting made him feel accused and condemned for bringing so much trouble to Brodie.

Muireall tensed when Iain entered, but Euan noticed Calum nod. Aye, he had the right of it. The elders might want Euan's head, but Iain would keep them focused on solving their larger problems.

Euan waited impatiently while Iain reported the Ross envoy's accusations. Then he called on Muireall and Ella to tell the council what they knew about the shifting power structure at Ross. Finally, it was Euan's turn, to explain what had happened from the shipwreck until he, Muireall, and Calum sailed away from Ross and returned to Brodie.

Finally, Euan finished and Iain took up the discussion. "Our task," he told the elders, "is to rescue Eduard without sacrificing Euan, without Ross ships interdicting Brodie sailings, and without being forced into a war with Ross and the Earl's allies. I'm open to suggestions, gentlemen…and ladies. Speak now."

A clamor erupted.

Muireall flinched at the same time as Calum crossed his arms.

Euan steeled himself to hear condemnation of everything he'd done on that ill-fated voyage.

Finally, one man stood and motioned for silence, then announced, "Despite the envoy's bluster, the Earl of Ross is a weak woman, under attack by the Lord of the Isles, and by Albany. She's unlikely to aid an offshoot of the clan trying to start a war with Brodie."

"Aye," another added, "We have allies as well. Does Silas Ross think she can take on the combined clans south of the firth? She's a fool."

Iain let them talk. His gaze strayed to Euan's and he nodded.

Euan felt a load lift from his shoulders. His hide

would not be flapping from the tower walls this night, figuratively or otherwise.

Iain let them dither for as long as it took a candle to burn down an inch, then called a halt.

"I've heard yer arguments, for and against. The most rational course of action I've heard is one I've already put into motion." His gaze shifted to Muireall, then Ella. "Three Brodies are on the way to Munro to advise them who stole their lasses—and that ye two bide with us for the time being," he added more forcefully.

Muireall surged to her feet. "We could have gone with them!"

"Nay, ye could no'. I will no' risk yer life, lass. I am responsible for ye until we can return ye—safely— home. We dinna ken what my men will find at Munro, nor what greater trouble the Rosses are stirring up on that side of the firth. Until we do, 'tis no' wise for ye to travel." He shifted his gaze to the council's leader, his dismissal of Muireall's sputtered objections plain for all to see. "I hope, as ye do, that we find the Munros un- troubled by their neighbors, for I have asked that the Munros provide a distraction the Rosses canna ignore, by patrolling their border. Perhaps enough of one to allow Erik Ross to displace Silas once and for all." He paused and turned his gaze to Euan. "We will move carefully, taking small measures, so as not to incite Silas Ross into killing Eduard, or sending a force against us. If we are successful in recruiting Munro as- sistance, we will have an easier time retrieving Eduard. But even if Munro declines to get involved, retrieving our man is my first concern. Once he is again among us, we will be in a stronger position to resolve the other matters."

"Then why are the three ye sent to Munro no' going after Eduard, instead?" the council leader asked.

Iain glanced aside. "As I said, I hope for Munro to

provide sufficient distraction. Now, gentlemen, I've heard enough, and I'm certain ye have, as well."

Euan took Muireall's arm and escorted her from the solar.

Calum and Ella followed on their heels.

"Why did we leave?" Muireall asked as Euan hurried her along.

"To avoid getting sucked into a useless, endless discussion," Euan told her. "Iain is up to something. That session was…"

"For appearances, only," Calum supplied.

"Aye. Exactly. Iain has already acted."

"So, will he tell us what else he's planning?" Muireall tugged her arm from Euan's grasp and stopped.

Euan nodded. "I think that last comment was meant for me. Small measures…"

Calum grinned. "*Careful*, small measures. Aye. I wonder what Iain is planning."

"Whatever it is, it canna come soon enough."

❧

EUAN WAS ASLEEP IN HIS CHAMBER WHEN SOMEONE knocked on his door. For one glorious second, he entertained the idea that Muireall waited on the other side, unable to stay away from him. He threw on a shirt and opened the door. Damn, not Muireall. Iain. Euan couldn't contain the sigh of disappointment.

"No' who ye were hoping for?"

Euan grunted and gestured Iain in.

"So were ye dreaming of far-off lands?" he asked and went to stand by the small hearth.

Euan studied his laird. What did he mean by that? "No farther than the other side of the firth," Euan replied, taking a seat on the edge of his bed. "What have ye decided, then?"

Iain frowned and dropped onto Euan's one small chair. "This is where I bow to the inevitable and agree to send ye after Eduard."

Exultation made any last vestiges of sleep flee Euan's body. He leaned forward.

Iain rested his elbows on his knees, then clasped his hands. "Damn it, I dinna want to, but ye have been there, ye ken the village, the layout, the ground."

Euan nodded. All true.

Iain waved a hand. "No one else has a prayer of getting in and out again with Eduard. But," he added and skewered Euan with a glare, "if ye get caught, Ross willna have to kill ye. I'll cut out yer heart myself."

Euan grinned. "That willna happen. Besides, Muireall already has it."

"Tomorrow...later today, that is," Iain said, settling back into the chair and stretching long legs out in front of the hearth, "I'm going to take Annie to visit her da. I'll tell the Rose what we're up against. That means tomorrow night, while we're away, ye must leave." He held up a hand. "I hate having to make it look like ye snuck out to attempt a harebrained rescue. But the Council is not solidly behind any plan we discussed—for hours—after ye left. They trust my leadership abilities on the battlefield. But they're uncertain I ken how best to deal with politics. And I'm trying to avoid all of us ending up on that battlefield. I must be circumspect in going around them. So I depend on ye to succeed."

Euan nodded, understanding. The council seemed determined to make Iain pay for every year of his previously poor reputation, even though most of them had agreed when he assumed leadership of the clan.

Euan was loyal even if they were not. "I have only one condition," Euan told him. "If I dinna return, no matter the reason or what follows, ye must fulfill my promise—and yers—to return Muireall to Munro. Ella, too, if that is what she wishes to do."

"I've never seen ye so taken by a lass, and I should know the signs better than most. I canna forget being involved with dozens before Annie." He chuckled. "She willna let me."

Euan laughed, ruefully, and admitted, "I dinna ken how I feel about a future with Muireall, but I'm drawn to her as no other. I want to be with her every waking moment." He waved a hand at the bed. "Sleeping, too."

"Good. If you want to get back to her so badly, instead of being your usual reckless self, you'll use yer head and be damned careful. Take two men with ye. A small group will have a better chance of getting Eduard out unseen. If ye're very lucky, he'll be unhurt and able to assist with his rescue."

"Aye," Euan said, nodding. "That might do the trick."

Just after sunrise, Muireall and Ella joined the throng in the bailey as Iain, Annie and an escort prepared to leave for Clan Rose. Iain was talking quietly to Kenneth and Euan. Annie had already mounted and from the way her horse Belle was dancing in place, she was eager to be away.

"I hope the Rose will support Brodie," Ella whispered to Muireall.

Muireall shrugged. "He's Annie's father. She says they get along, so I would expect he and Iain will support each other in whatever this trouble becomes."

Kenneth and Euan stepped back and Iain mounted up. "Ready, lass?" he asked Annie with a grin.

Muireall had no doubt he knew his wife well.

"I'll race ye," Annie replied and tapped Belle's sides.

Annie's laughter echoed around the bailey as they bolted through the open Brodie gate.

Iain shook his head and took off after her, leaving their escort to catch up as best they could.

Ella watched them go. "I want a man like that."

She said it so softly, Muireall wasn't sure she meant for anyone to hear, so she simply clasped Ella's shoulder, then turned away. Euan was coming toward them, and so was Calum, who'd joined Euan as Iain tore out of the gate after his wife. Calum was laughing and even Euan had a grin on his face—the first she'd seen all morning.

"There's one ye might consider," Muireall whispered to Ella. "And he's already smitten with ye."

"Calum?" Ella frowned at her.

"Have ye no' noticed?" Though she kept her voice low, Euan must have heard.

"Noticed what?" he asked as he and Calum joined them.

"That my belly's been rumbling since we came out here," she improvised. "Surely 'tis time to break our fast?"

"May we join ye?" Calum asked, his hungry gaze on Ella.

Muireall and Ella exchanged a glance.

"If ye dinna mind, that is," he added.

"We dinna mind," Ella told him and smiled.

Euan watched their brief byplay with interest.

Calum wore his heart on his sling. His interest in Ella had been obvious to Muireall from the beginning. No doubt Euan was well aware, as well. Only Ella had seemed oblivious, but she took men fawning over her as the way the world worked. Nothing unusual.

As those who'd seen Iain and Annie off filed into the great hall and settled at the tables, breakfast became a cheerful, noisy affair. Euan seemed relaxed, even happy, for the first time since the night they'd gone up on the roof. That thought made her think of his kisses, and of how he'd clung to her, breathing her in and tasting her as if starved for only her.

He'd taken the place next to her on the bench and while he actively participated in the table's conversation, his thigh brushed hers often enough for her to know it was deliberate.

Her body responded. She knew she blushed by the heat in her cheeks, but she hoped the others would assume her high color came from laughter, not from Euan's proximity. She could smell him, a satisfying hint of male musk that filled her with longing to see if he tasted as good. And the rumble of his voice vibrated along her nerve endings, making her want to squirm to ease the sudden tightness of her core. She needed... something. She knew not what, but she knew whatever it was, it had to come from Euan. And soon. And she could do something about that.

She dropped her hands into her lap once everyone's attention seemed to be on someone further down the table, then gently, carefully, laid her palm on Euan's thigh.

He froze.

She felt the muscle under her hand tense hard as a rock, then soften slightly as he widened his legs and pushed his thigh tightly against hers.

"Ye are playing with fire, lass," he whispered to her, all the while keeping his gaze down the table and a grin on his face as if his entire focus was there, not on her... or her hand and where it lay.

"Am I?" she breathed and let her hand slide up his leg until she encountered a hardness so hot, even through his trews it nearly singed her skin.

Euan hissed, leaned one elbow on the table and covered his mouth with one fist. With the other, he reached under the table and slid her hand more fully over what she'd found. She glanced aside at him under her lashes. His color had heightened, but that was the only outward sign pressing and sliding her palm over his staff affected him. Under her palm, he stirred and lengthened, growing even hotter.

Suddenly he groaned and lifted her hand away. "I… ye…canna," he told her softly from behind his hand and dropped her hand back in her lap. "No' here."

She nearly asked him *where then?* but managed to press her lips closed. She glanced at Ella, but her attention was on the speaker down the table, as was Calum's. Thank the saints.

What had gotten into her? Touching Euan that way…teasing him…was foolish in the extreme. And unfair, though to be fair, he'd started it by pressing his thigh against hers again and again. Aye, she decided, he'd gotten no more than he deserved.

She felt him take a few deep breaths, then he stood. "If ye will excuse me, I have tasks to take care of."

She nodded and smiled, careful to keep her gaze on his and not to allow it to drop to where her hand had been shortly before.

He left without another word, filling Muireall with a satisfied sense of power. She had gotten to him for a change. She could do it again. Soon. It would have to be soon, if she truly wanted him. She was running out of time to remain at Brodie.

Calum startled her out of her pleasant rumination by standing and making his excuses as well.

As if Euan and then Calum had started something, most of the rest of the table cleared quickly, leaving Muireall and Ella alone.

Ella's gaze followed Calum. "He seems nice," Ella said in answer to Muireall's unspoken question. "But what was going on with ye and Euan?"

Muireall colored and looked away. "Nothing, really."

"Ye are falling for him."

"Aye." Muireall shook her head. "Nay. I canna. Georgie needs me." And she suddenly recalled her father had hinted at an arrangement with Clan Grant. She had no business teasing Euan.

"And Euan needs ye, too. And wants ye, or I miss my guess."

"He may want me, but he doesna need me. He can have any lass who takes his fancy." Suddenly annoyed, Muireall pursed her lips and propped her elbows on the table, steepled her hands and rested her chin on them. She just wasn't sure if she was annoyed with Euan or Ella or herself.

"Listen to yerself. Ye are just trying to escape again. Only this time ye are no' a prisoner." Ella shrugged. "If ye feel what I think ye feel for him, dinna run away. Besides, where did yer escape attempts get ye the last time?"

Muireall shuddered, recalling the sting of the lash. "'Tis no' the same at all!" She slapped the table top with an open hand, then met Ella's gaze and nodded. "And yet, in a way, it is. I see what ye mean. I canna leave my fate to strangers. I must act for myself." she dropped her head into one palm. "Perhaps we should make our own plans to return to Munro."

"Euan doesna seem like a stranger to ye. Anyway, how would we go? Walk the entire way? Steal Brodie horses and ride? Ye might make it. Ye are a better rider than I. But I might no'." She paused and looked up into a corner of the hall. "Oh, we could sail." Then she returned her gaze to Muireall. "Nay, we dinna ken how to sail across the firth. I'm no' of a mind to drown, thank ye."

Muireall clenched her fists. "There must be something we can do."

"Aye. Give Euan time to make good on his promise. Or fall for him and let him fall for ye. Ye might find ye'd rather have the man ye chose in yer bed than return to…what? A choice yer da makes for ye?"

"Georgie…"

"Georgie will be fine, with ye or without ye. He's a smart lad. He's yer brother, is he no'? He'll find a way."

CHAPTER 14

That night, Muireall woke suddenly, startled by…what? Was someone in her chamber? She'd blown out her candle hours ago. Darkness filled every corner. She lay still, breathing softly for a moment, until she realized the sounds she heard came from outside her window.

She threw off the covers, got up and tiptoed across the cold floor to open the shutter and peer out. Below her, a handful of men were preparing horses to ride out. She glanced up and noted the position of the moon's pale sliver. Where could they be going in the middle of the night?

She watched for a few moments, her curiosity unsatisfied, until she spotted Euan among the men. Now she *had* to know. She dressed quickly and threw her warm cloak around her shoulders, then ran down stairs and out into the bailey.

Approaching the men, she quickly spotted Euan's taller form, his back to her as he did something with his mount's saddle. She headed for him. "What's going on?"

Euan whirled, frowning in the gloom. The he nodded as he recognized her, but instead of the smile she expected, the frown returned. "What are ye doing out here at this time of night?"

"I asked ye first." Muireall planted her hands on her hips. "Where are ye going?"

Euan's shoulders dropped and he glanced around at the other men before returning his gaze to her. "Ye'll find out soon enough, so I may as well tell ye. Duncan and Neil are going with me across the firth to free Eduard."

"What? Are ye going to ride all the way?"

"Nay, we'll sail. Angus will keep the horses at an outlying croft so it looks like we did. And the Ross skiff, looking very different than it did only days ago, will get us there."

"Does Iain ken ye're doing this? I thought he bade ye stay."

Euan frowned, then answered. "He doesna. I need to do this while he and Annie are gone to Rose—'tis a chance for her to visit her family, ye ken, so they'll stay a few days."

"And he left no one to keep an eye on ye?"

Euan grinned. "Aye, but they made the mistake of tryin' to outdrink me this evening. They couldna, though they didna ken that until much too late. They're sleeping it off and will likely regret it when they wake...for more than one reason."

"Aye. Iain will have their heads when he finds out," Calum said, coming up behind Muireall.

Surprised, she turned to him with narrowed eyes. "So ye are involved in this as well?"

He shrugged one shoulder, lifting that arm, still in its sling. "As ye can see, I canna go. I'd be in the way. But I'm good with a hammer and pitch."

Muireall sniffed. When he wasn't panting after Ella, Calum must have helped modify the Ross skiff.

"So ye'll stay behind to cover for this fool with his

laird?" Muireall hooked a thumb at Euan, who also shrugged.

"If they fail, 'twill no' matter," Calum said. "They willna return."

"Ah," Euan added with a sly grin, "but if we succeed…"

"Succeed at what?" Muireall challenged, suddenly furious at the mention of Euan not returning. "Getting Eduard out? Or not being seen by a Ross while ye do it?" She wanted to stamp her foot, but knew Euan would think that childish. Instead, she reached out a hand. "I canna stand the thought of ye in Ross hands." When Euan didn't grasp hers, but glanced aside at his mount, her anger returned. "Yer laird refused to send me home to keep ye two—and me—hidden from any Ross eyes. What makes ye think ye can do this without starting the war he fears?"

Euan and Calum exchanged a glance. "I ken what I'm doing, lass," Euan told her. "And I've seen the layout of the Ross village and the surrounding area. I got out before…"

"Ye had to kill Donas to do it!" Muireall objected. "I'm grateful, mind ye, but this time ye risk much more than our three lives. And the risk to ye is much greater."

"I'll be fine. We all will. 'Twill be a simple in and out."

Muireall took a breath. "If so, then take me with ye. They'll expect ye to sail for home. Instead, ye can sail up the Cromarty firth and into Munro." Her hopes soared when, for a moment, Euan seemed to consider it, his head tilted to the side, his gaze flicking to Calum, then back to her.

One of the other men, came over. "We'd best go if we're goin', before ye lot wake up the entire keep." He gave Muireall a long look, then when Euan hitched his chin, the man moved away.

"The mouth of that firth is narrow," Euan answered her, "and bordered on one side by Ross land. We'd be too exposed going in or coming out. Nay, lass, I prefer the wide open lady Moray."

"Do ye?" She hated herself for saying it, but she feared Euan would not come back to her. "She tried to kill ye once, and took one or more of yer men."

A muscle in his jaw jumped, but the tone of his response was even. "She can be a bitch, aye, but she's a bitch I ken better than most. I'm sorry, lass, but ye must remain here, where ye'll be safe."

She crossed her arms. "Safe until all of Ross comes for Brodie."

"I willna let that happen." Euan finished fussing with his saddle and turned to her.

"Then stay here until Iain returns. Until his men return with news from Munro." She put a hand on his arm. "Ye risk too much."

He squeezed her hand. "I started this. I must be the one to finish it."

Muireall's heart leapt into her throat. "Ye may no' be able to do that except by surrendering to Silas."

"That's where ye're wrong, lass. We'll get Eduard out before they ken he's gone. Freeing him will buy Iain time. Silas willna be in control forever."

Muireall jerked her hand out from under his. "She doesna have to be. Yer lifetime will be long enough."

❧

MANY HOURS LATER, EUAN WAS CRAMPED, TIRED AND frustrated. He and his companions had hunkered down in the brush outside the Ross village and stayed quiet all morning. Ross patrols had passed them by twice, providing a few minutes' relief from the tedium. Other than that, all the activity in the village had been normal, everyday comings and goings—and there'd been no sign of Eduard.

"Damn it, I hoped we'd see him by now," Duncan complained. "Ye'd think they'd let him out of wherever they're holding him to *pish*."

"Unless he's in no shape to move about," Neil warned.

A disturbance started near one of the buildings. Euan waved them to silence as voices reached them. In moments, a woman he presumed to be Silas came into view. She had the imperious look of someone used to being obeyed. Her erect posture and stern expression were telling. But the men who surrounded her gave Euan the strongest impression. All but one—the largest man—bent toward her, listening, almost bowing to her. They must be her most loyal backers.

"Ye canna just kill him," Euan heard the largest man say as they got close enough for him to make out the words. "He's worth too much in trade…"

"To the Brodies? They have nothing I want, Erik, except the man who killed my husband."

Erik? Euan perked up. Silas was arguing with the man Muireall had been destined to marry, and who she and Ella thought would take over Ross now Donas was dead. But at the moment, Silas still seemed to be in charge.

"I'd rather send their man's dead body back as a warning," Silas continued. "Followed by Ross warriors to kill them all and burn their holdings to the ground."

Euan pursed his lips. If Silas remained in power, the trouble that kept Iain awake at night could happen. He shifted his weight. It was up to him to prevent that.

Erik folded his arms across his chest and took a wide-legged stance, squared off with Silas. The other men took a step back.

That interested Euan greatly. So Erik did command

respect—or fear—from the other Ross warriors. Yet he was the one arguing for a less bloodthirsty course.

"Yer thirst for vengeance does ye nay credit as a leader, Silas. Ye will bring death and destruction to us all if ye continue on this path."

"This path? This path!" The outrage in her voice was unmistakable. "Ye call avenging my husband a path? I call it my due."

Erik shook his head, then glanced at the men around him and Silas. "I had hoped to give ye a decent interval to grieve before we took up clan business. But ye leave me nay choice, Silas Ross. I call for an election."

His announcement was met with shouts of assent from several of the men gathered around them.

"Ye hear them." He turned to face the men and raised his voice, not giving Silas time to respond. "Gather the clan. We must put this to a vote. Silas will force us into a conflict we have no business undertaking."

Euan could see the argument had drawn more of the clan, and the crowd was growing by ones and twos. The men pushed forward, but the women had gathered, too, standing toward the back or to the side of the two contenders for Ross leadership, well out of the way, he noted, if fighting broke out.

"The time has come for new leadership," Erik continued, turning slowly to address the growing crowd from one side to the other. "We'll get no backing from the Earl, given the pressure from the Lord of the Isles and Duke of Albany."

Euan was happy to hear that. As long as these men thought they'd be fighting alone, they'd be slow to take up a battle. Where was Silas? She'd melted into the crowd. A shaft of dread speared down Euan's spine to his gut. Was she positioning herself to attack Erik? Or taking advantage of the distraction Erik had caused to kill Eduard and present his body to the clan as a sign of her resolve?

Frustration tightened Euan's muscles. If that was what she meant to do, there was nothing he could do about it. The three of them could not enter the Ross camp without joining Eduard as Ross prisoners.

"If Brodie calls on its allies, they will destroy us." Erik continues speaking to the crowd, unaware his rival had gone…where?

There she was! Euan finally spotted her, surrounded by a wall of her men. She had only stepped back into the protection of her supporters. Then she stepped toward Erik and called out, "He's wrong." She spread her arms wide, encompassing the men of the clan. "No one can defeat the warriors of clan Ross!"

That pronouncement also got a cheer, loud and long. Euan's heart sank. If Silas could whip them into a fighting frenzy, not only would Erik lose, Eduard would be in even greater danger.

"Spoken like a lass." Erik's voice rang out above the noise. "A lass with no training and no experience fighting for her own life or the life of her clan."

Silas scowled and took a step toward Erik. "Ye think a woman canna lead?"

Erik looked down at her, his expression mournful. "I think ye are mad with grief, lass." That quieted the crowd. "And while I grieve with ye…"

"Ha! Ye lie. Ye have wanted to be chief for years, but Donas was too strong for ye," Silas scoffed, red-faced. "Now ye think the way is clear for ye to take over. Ye are wrong again!"

With a wave of her hand, her phalanx of guards parted, and two men walked forward, supporting Eduard between them. The crowd went still.

Euan sucked in a breath and waved for his companions to keep silent as they shifted beside him, preparing to rise. They could not charge into the Ross village and rescue Eduard in the middle of an angry mob.

"We canna just sit here," Duncan hissed.

"We do nothing, damn it," Euan told him, "except sit here and watch. If they dinna kill him in front of us, we'll get him out after dark."

"But..."

"Go in there now and we'll wind up just like him, no help to him or ourselves. Now *wheesht*, and pay attention to where they take him."

Eduard slumped between his captors, conscious, but forcing them to bear his weight. Good man! Bruises marred his face and arms, so Euan had no reason to think they did not also decorate his torso and legs. He'd been beaten, but seemed otherwise unharmed.

From the frowns directed at Silas, Euan could hope Erik was on the way to winning this battle. The rest of the clan did not appear to be eager to shed Eduard's blood, or to approve the way he'd been treated up to now.

Then Silas pulled a dirk and laid it against Eduard's throat. Euan's blood ran cold, and he had to force himself to remain in place. The optimism he'd felt just a moment ago evaporated into even greater fear for his friend. Beside him, Duncan and Neil tensed.

"What are ye doing, Silas?" Erik barked.

She pressed the blade's edge against Eduard's skin. A thin line of red appeared along it. "Ye may no' have the bollocks to avenge Donas, but I do!"

"Ye fool!" Erik shouted and lunged. He knocked her arm away from Eduard's throat, then grabbed for the knife in her hand.

She twisted around Eduard and went for Erik with an unearthly howl.

Erik was right. Silas had to be out of her mind to

attack a seasoned warrior like Erik. He was nearly twice her height and easily double her weight—all of it muscle. Euan couldn't see everything that happened, but as long as Eduard remained standing and Erik prevailed, Euan didn't care.

Erik got a hand on her wrist and turned the knife away from his chest. But then she gripped his wrist and pulled, forcing him to balance against her weight. He fended her off, his expression betraying determination. She was craftier than Euan gave her credit for. Perhaps because she knew Erik did not wish to hurt her, she had a small advantage. She had no such compunction about hurting Eduard or Erik. He kept forcing her back, but she charged again and again while he shouted at her to stop, for her men to hold her before she got hurt. No one moved. In the end, it was Silas who lay bleeding, the dirk protruding from her abdomen.

"Is she dead?" Neil whispered.

Euan shook his head. No one was moving to help her, so he assumed she was. Erik looked stunned, and Euan was certain the man had tried to turn his blows to disable her, not to kill her. Something had gone terribly wrong.

In the confusion, Euan noticed Eduard's guards, distracted by the fight, had released him. "Run, ye fool," Euan urged him silently.

At that moment, Eduard made a break for the trees, but he didn't get far. The Ross guards caught him and, at Erik's signal, returned him to the cottage Silas had marched him from. Euan nodded. He had him now. After dark, they'd free him. In the meantime, Euan was satisfied Erik had other problems to deal with. Chances were, they wouldn't beat Eduard again before the Brodies could get to him.

CHAPTER 15

*M*uireall fretted all day. Once Iain and Annie returned from Rose, should she tell Iain where Euan had gone? If she spoke up, Iain might feel the need to send more Brodies into danger to go after him. But if she kept silent, Euan might not get the help he needed if he was in trouble. She couldn't decide the right thing to do. She paced in her chamber, wearing a track across the cold stone floor as she walked back and forth, debating with herself.

She wasn't the only one left in the keep aware of where he and two others had gone. Calum knew as well. And Euan would not appreciate either of them telling Iain before he got back with Eduard. Euan would want to face his laird with the evidence of his success. If he came back without Eduard, Iain would flay him. Nay, she didn't think Iain would really do that, but he'd be furious. And what if Euan didn't come back at all…she sank onto her bed and dropped her face into her hands. What would she do if he did not come back?

Needing some fresh air, she left her chamber, intending to go outside. But she ran into Annie crossing the great hall.

"Ye are back!" Muireall exclaimed before she could stop herself. She knew she must sound, as well as look, guilty of something, but seeing Annie startled her.

"Aye. Iain as well. Ye look as though ye have seen a ghost. Is something amiss?"

Muireall shook her head. "Nay. No' really. At least I dinna think so. I hope no'." God, she was babbling.

Annie propped her hands on her hips and peered at her as if she was a bug in the oat flour. "I believe I ken what is fretting ye so. Come with me."

"What? Where?"

Annie grabbed her arm and pulled her along to Iain's solar.

Seeing Iain at his worktable, Muireall dug in her heels. "Nay, Annie. There's nay need to disturb the laird," she protested, but Annie wouldn't let her go.

"Ye'd best explain to this lass what's going on," Annie announced to her husband. "She's worn herself to a frazzle in the two days we've been gone—though our absence has little to do with her state, I'll wager. 'Tis Euan's absence that worries her."

Muireall gasped. How could Annie know that?

Iain slid his gaze from his wife, who'd gotten the beginnings of a smile from him until she started talking, to Muireall. One eyebrow went up. "I dinna think that's necessary, my love."

"I do. If ye willna tell her, I'll tell her myself."

"Tell me what? Is Euan well? Dear God, he's no' dead, is he?" Her eyes welled, making her want to turn and run. But Annie still had a tight grip on her arm.

"Iain..." Annie's tone brooked no dissent.

Muireall squeezed her eyes shut and heard Iain sigh, then the scrape of his chair as he stood up.

"Come here, lass. Sit by the fire. Euan is well. As far as I ken, that is."

Muireall opened her eyes to see Iain standing by a

chair next to the hearth, his hand open, palm toward her, inviting her to sit. She moved to the chair he indicated and sat.

Annie took the seat next to her, leaving Iain on his feet.

He paced a step or two, then turned back and nodded. "I'm worried, too, but I couldna leave Eduard a prisoner at Ross. Euan was…is…the best hope to get him back. I willna go into the politics behind it. Suffice to say I couldna send him openly. But he's been there, seen the area and the Ross village. He knows how to get in and how to get out. So I sent him. Also because he's Euan. He's responsible, determined, and despite causing chaos, always lands on his feet."

Muireall liked that Iain put his trust, and maybe, if she correctly understood what he very carefully wasn't saying, his lairdship, in Euan's hands. But he was worried, though. Like she was. She glanced at Annie, who nodded and smiled. Of course Annie knew all about it. And now Euan's leaving in the middle of the night made sense. "So ye havena heard whether he…"

"We willna ken until his skiff returns. With Eduard, or no'. I dinna like waiting, either, but 'tis what we must do." He stopped pacing beside Annie. He laid a hand on her shoulder and squeezed. She placed her hand over his, an unmistakable gesture of support.

"Thank ye for telling me," Muireall finally managed to say.

"And ye'll tell no one, aye?"

"Of course no'. I'm very good at keeping secrets."

Iain and Annie exchanged a glance, then Annie stood. "That's that, then."

"Only…" Muireall hesitated, then plunged ahead. "Have the men ye sent to Munro returned?"

Iain glanced at Annie, his expression bleak, and

Muireall's heart froze to ice in her chest. She started shivering and crossed her arms.

"They have no'. No' yet."

"Ye fear something happened to them." Muireall felt it in her bones.

"I always have that fear, any time I send men out on a mission. But lass, there are many reasons for their delay. The best is that they are enjoying Munro hospitality and will be back soon."

"And the worst?"

Iain pursed his lips, and Muireall immediately pictured the wreck of the *Tangie*. They could be lost in the firth, like some of Euan's crew. Because of her. "*Ach, nay…*"

"*Dinna fash*, lass. If they are no' returned to us tomorrow, I'll send another boat."

"And risk more men on the firth?"

"The firth is no' the greatest danger."

"Ross ships, then."

"Possibly, but no' likely. More likely is they've drunk too much Munro ale and will sail back tomorrow."

Annie spoke up then. "'Twould be just like them."

"Aye. Ye lasses go on and let me think. I have to plan for several contingencies. Though they're no' all bad, they all end with me telling the council what we've done. That will be a difficult meeting."

Annie gave him a sympathetic kiss on the cheek, then she and Muireall left the solar.

"Well, what shall we do now to cheer ye up? Aye, of course. Ye havena tried archery yet. Let's go. I want to work off some worries, too."

Muireall readily agreed, though the meeting with Iain had depressed her. Still, it was one more skill she might be able to teach Georgie before he had to compete with the other lads. And now that she didn't carry the burden of Euan's errand alone, she could enjoy Annie's company. She found herself becoming more infatuated with Annie's spirit—and independence—with every meeting between them. Annie let nothing stand in her way. She either went through it or if that failed, around it.

Muireall told herself she had a touch of that same spirit. She had tried—twice—to escape Donas Ross. With Euan's help, the third time had worked.

If she could learn to take care of herself as Annie did, she could teach Georgie to stand up for himself and give him some skills that might gain him respect from the other lads. And she might never need to wed, though that was cold comfort when what she really wanted was Euan—if he was still alive—to offer for her.

Annie interrupted her thoughts as they reached the archery practice area. "Tell me about Munro," she suggested, "while I set us up."

Muireall obliged, watching Annie gather arrows from the straw bales used as targets. "The Munro is currently without a wife," she began, thinking Annie meant her father more than her clan. "He lost his last one in childbirth eight years ago."

"I'm so sorry," Annie replied and picked up several bows the lads had left behind, standing them on end and using her weight to test their flex.

Muireall took that as encouragement to continue. "He leans toward supporting Domhnall of Islay. The Lord of the Isles, ye ken."

"Aye, we do."

"More politically practical, I suppose ye'd say, than Albany, given so many other clans nearby look to the west."

"What about Ross?" Annie decided on a bow and selected an arrow.

Muireall snorted. "We have longstanding relationships with various septs of Ross throughout their territory—some good, some nay. Taking Ella, Tira, and me will not help resolve that. Though with Donas out of the way, Erik may be able to mend relations." If any of the Munros were left. She still didn't know for sure. Why hadn't her father, even if he didn't know who took the women, send word out to neighboring clans. The resounding silence troubled her—more than she dared show.

Annie pulled and let fly. The arrow thunked into the center of the bullseye drawn on the farthest bale.

"Oh...I'll never be able to do that."

"Of course ye will. I'm going to teach ye."

Annie had her test the pull of several bows until they found one that satisfied Annie, if not Muireall. All of them felt strange and awkward in her hands. She had seen how the younger lads struggled to nock an arrow and often dropped them rather than letting them fly. She'd be so embarrassed if she couldn't do better.

With Annie's help, her first attempt fell short, but at least she didn't drop it. Annie asked about her family while getting her properly positioned again.

Muireall revealed that her father lived, as well as two brothers. She didn't want to give anyone at Brodie any more information than that—it might get back to Euan.

"Take a deep breath as ye pull, then let it out slowly and pause. Then let go," Annie coached her. From then on, her arrows reached the first row of straw bales. Some even embedded themselves, though many went wide of the mark.

All too soon, it started to get dark and Muireall's hand tired.

Annie called a halt. They sat on the target bales, enjoying the gloaming and talking.

"It must have been terrifying, thinking ye were

going to drown trying to make it around the headland," Annie said.

"Honestly, I dinna have time to be too scared before I passed out. Euan pulled me out of the water. Then, for a while, I was afraid of him. How could I know what he would do? But eventually, he admitted who he was and so did I. From then on, we worked together to escape."

"That's our Euan. He's a good man. Brave, smart, strong, though Iain is right to be concerned. He's also reckless at times. But ye dinna wish to hear that, do ye?"

Muireall couldn't argue about Euan's good points. "If he's so wonderful, why is Iain so irritated with him, and why is he no' married?"

Annie gave her a long look. "Interested, are ye?" She laughed. "He's gotten in trouble before, acting before thinking. He and Iain...go back years. Iain is not that much older than Euan."

"Do ye ken what he was like as a lad?"

"No' really. Iain has said Euan's responsible streak may be why he's no' yet wed. He has kissed a few lasses, but nothing like Iain in his day. Euan's always been more focused on making himself better—bigger, stronger, a better fisherman, a better fighter, and so on. I dinna ken what drives him, but that doesna leave him much time for the lasses."

Muireall was happy to hear he hadn't bedded every skirt he'd ever been offered.

"I will say I've never seen him so devoted to a lass as he appears to be to ye, though 'tis true I havena known him very long."

"He feels obligated to me. Because he saved my life. I've tried to tell him he need not be, but he's also stubborn."

Annie laughed. "Aye, that's our Euan." She stood. "Come away and let me show off a bit."

Muireall stood and went back where they'd left the bows and arrows.

Annie picked up the bow she favored and fired an arrow into a near target. Then split it with another arrow.

Muireall gasped.

"'Tis nothing," Annie told her. Watch this." She took aim at the arrow she'd left in the far target's bullseye, pulled and let fly. Before Muireall knew what happened, that arrow was split as well, Annie's latest shot vibrating at its center. "That's enough. The fletcher will have my head if I ruin any more. But thanks for letting me show off a wee. I dinna get to do that very often. 'Tis no' good for the lads to be intimidated—or outshot—by a mere lass." She gave a hearty laugh, and Muireall joined her. "'Tis getting too dark to see, anyway," Annie continued. "Let's go get some supper."

AT SUNSET, ROSS MEN GATHERED AGAIN IN THE OPEN space in the center of the small village. Euan perked up. Something was about to happen.

Erik joined the group and they formed an arc before him. He looked tired, but his voice was strong when he announced, "Silas still lives." He paused and his gaze traveled the arc, making contact with every man there. "But ye ken what her loss has done to her mind. She threw herself on my blade."

Euan and the men with him traded glances. They hadn't seen, and had wondered how Erik had come to stab her when he so obviously tried not to harm her.

"She is no' fit to lead this clan," Erik continued. "So I ask ye, will ye have her—if she lives—or me? Ye ken who I am, what I've done and what I stand for. I call for a vote. Who is with me?"

A low rumble filled the air as the men reacted to Erik's announcement. First one fist shot up, then another and another, along with a chorus of *ayes*. In moments, it was over. Erik was the new Ross laird. Euan breathed a sigh of relief. Muireall had related her encounters with Erik and believed that despite his temper, he could be a thoughtful man. Euan expected, if it came to it, Iain could treat with a laird who deliberated before he acted. Even better, Erik saw the value of their hostage. Eduard's life would no longer be threatened. But accidents happened. And even though the vote had gone to Erik, Silas's supporters could still wreak havoc and force Erik's hand by killing Eduard.

Euan had to free Eduard tonight.

Among the discussions going on after the vote, Euan heard one man say, "Brodie did us a favor, getting rid of Donas."

Erik shrugged off that remark. "We are still owed recompense," he answered, "if no' a life. We'll see how they respond to get their man back."

Euan frowned at that. Brodie could not afford much compensation. Once they freed Eduard and got him home, they'd have to figure out a solution both Brodie and the new Ross would accept.

CHAPTER 16

$\mathcal{B}$y midnight, the Ross village had gone still and silent, the clan settled down for the night after hours of celebrating, including drinking casks of ale and whisky. Euan expected they'd be out for hours and hard to wake even then.

Mindful of wandering patrols, Euan and his men rose from their concealment and spent a few minutes stretching cramped muscles.

Euan left them to watch his back and signal if they spotted trouble coming. He moved silent as a wildcat to the cottage where Eduard was held. A guard slept across the doorway. Euan sent him deeper into slumber with a quick blow to the head using the hilt of his dirk. Rising, he lifted the latch and slowly pushed open the door.

Eduard lay on a pallet on the floor, alone save for the unconscious guard at his door. Euan crouched and shook his shoulder, then quickly clamped a hand over his mouth to stifle a shout.

Eduard's eyes popped open.

Euan felt his jaw lift and flex as he drew in air, then he recognized Euan and nodded. Euan removed his hand and helped him stand.

"It took ye long enough," Eduard groused, then grabbed Euan in a bear hug.

Euan hugged him back, disconcerted by his thinness. "They didna feed ye?"

"Partly from the wreck and being on my own without food for a few days. But it was also one of the ways that she-devil tried to break me," Eduard admitted.

"Let's get ye out of here and gone. We'll feed ye on the firth."

Eduard nodded and followed Euan to the door. Euan looked out. Nothing moved, and his men had not signaled with an owl's hoot to warn of trouble coming. He stepped over the guard and helped Eduard do the same, then silently pulled the door closed and latched it. With luck, no one would miss Eduard until well after the sun came up and they were nearly home.

They made the trip back to the hidden skiff quietly, delayed only by one patrol that never knew they were there but passed within ten heart-stopping feet of where they'd paused when they heard voices. Euan had held them frozen in place for long minutes after to make sure the patrol was truly gone and would not hear them when they moved.

Even the sail across the firth seemed favored by the lady of the firth, with a following wind and calm sea. They beached the boat at sunrise and entered the Brodie keep before any but Cook and her helpers were up.

"This man needs a good meal before we can send him home to his wife," Euan announced as they entered her domain. Cook had her back to them and whirled about with a shriek, then lay a hand on her ample bosom and smiled. "Ye scairt me half to death!" she exclaimed, then came forward to embrace Eduard. "But ye found my lost man, bless ye."

Eduard rolled his eyes at Euan.

"They didna feed him," Euan informed her. She stepped back and studied Eduard.

"I see that. Ye've lost a stone, I'd hazard. More than is good for ye." She pointed to her work table. "Sit, and I'll see ye fed."

"Thank ye," Eduard told her as he obeyed. "The food the lads brought with them didna last long."

"*Dinna fash*, I ken what ye like." She gave him a saucy wink.

Euan nearly choked.

Cook bustled about and started laying things in front of Eduard. Bread, cheese and ale appeared first, then apples, honey and a whole salted fish. "That should get ye started," she told him.

Eduard chuckled around a mouth full of bread and honey and nodded.

"I'll leave ye to it, then," Euan said. "'Tis time I told Iain of yer return. I dinna think he'll mind being awakened for this news."

"No' so fast, laddie," Cook told him. "Ye are here. Ye will eat with Eduard before ye go anywhere." She crossed her arms, a heavy wooden spoon in one fist.

Euan knew when he was beaten. Besides, he was hungry. He sat.

An hour later, full to bursting, he left Eduard in his wife's care, made his way to the door of the laird's chambers and knocked.

In moments, Iain opened the door wearing his shirt and nothing else. "What's amiss? Ah, 'tis ye. Did ye get him?"

"Aye."

"Were ye seen?"

"Nay."

"Good. Bring Eduard and the two who went with ye to my solar in another hour. Muireall and Ella, too."

Euan nodded.

Without another word, Iain shut the door.

Euan breathed a sigh of relief. Still alive, still breathing. Iain had dismissed him so quickly, chances were he'd interrupted Iain and Annie. His timing couldn't have been better, with Iain eager to get back to his bride.

But when they met later? He shuddered and went to round up his two companions and waken Muireall. She'd want a few minutes to get presentable before meeting with the laird. He returned to the kitchen last, wanting to give Eduard time to warm himself in the kitchen and eat his fill.

Eduard pushed his platter away as Euan entered. "I canna eat another bite," he announced. "Thank ye, love. I think I'll live now."

"I should hope so. Ye put away enough for two men, ye did." She favored him with a broad grin. "It does my heart good to see ye home and hale, husband."

"Iain wants us," Euan informed him with a nod to Cook.

Eduard stood. "Then we'd best go, aye?"

Cook shooed them out of her domain.

Euan could hear the rumble of voices as they neared Iain's solar. He paused at the door and grimaced at Eduard. The Council was in there, too.

Iain stood when they entered, went to Eduard and embraced him. "'Tis good to have ye back."

"'Tis good to be back," Eduard replied with a rueful grin. "Thanks for sending a rescue party."

Iain looked chagrined and returned to his worktable. "As to that..." he started and pinned Euan with a steely glare. "This particular rescue party had no' been authorized to make the trip."

Euan did his level best to look guilty. Better the Council punish him than Iain.

"What?" Eduard paled and abruptly sat in the nearest chair. "Silas Ross was about to kill me."

"We didna actually save him," Euan broke in. "Erik Ross did that." Before the council started demanding a war, best they know the new Ross leader was not cut from the same cloth as his predecessor.

Iain raised an eyebrow and settled back in his chair. "Go on."

"There was an argument, as ye might imagine. Then a scuffle. Erik Ross made every effort to keep from harming Silas. When it was done, she was bleeding. Somewhere in the course of the fight, she stabbed herself with her own dirk. A few hours later, Erik forced a vote and took over as chief. Ross is his now. If he can hold it. Silas still has men…if she lives."

"As does Erik," Eduard interjected. "More than she has, I think. Or had. They'll watch his back."

"We can hope. 'Tis my belief he'll be a better leader than Donas or Silas," Euan agreed.

"And did he happen to mention his position on the small matter of the death of Donas Ross?" Iain slapped a hand on his table, snapping their attention back to him.

"Aye. That we owe compensation…"

Iain winced.

"If no' a life…" Eduard added. "Though Erik seemed less bent on revenge than the widow. He mentioned wondering how we'd respond once we got…me…back."

"And now that we no longer have to trade for him…" Euan began, but Iain cut him off.

"Erik will face pressure from his clan, and no' just Silas's men. He'll have to prove his strength and leadership. What better way than by taking on Brodie?"

Euan knew Iain well enough to know he'd thought about that before sending Euan across the firth. Getting Eduard back had been more important. "We overheard discussion about that," Euan offered. "They know we have allies, and they dinna expect the Earl to come to their aid. So they'll be reluctant to start something that will go against them."

Muireall and Ella had entered a few moments before and sat to the side, while the discussion went on, watching with more than a passing interest.

"I may have a solution that will satisfy Erik Ross," Muireall said when the discussion hit a lull.

Iain's head whipped around, and he stared at her as if he'd forgotten she was in the room.

"Indeed?"

If anyone other than Iain had used that tone, Euan would have flattened him for speaking to Muireall with such disbelief and dismissal. But Iain had a right—and a responsibility. They'd caused this problem and risked compounding it by the trip to rescue Eduard. Iain held the safety and future prosperity of Brodie in his hands. He had to question anything from an outsider that affected his duty to the clan. He would distrust anything that seemed too pat, too easy.

❧

MUIREALL FORCED HERSELF TO HER FEET AS EVERY GAZE in the room swung to her. She could do this. She could stand before the Brodie laird and council and offer them a way to avoid war. She owed it to them, for Euan's rescue of her. And she didn't think Erik would mind if she betrayed his confidence for this.

She took a breath. "I ken who Erik wants to marry —and it wasna me. If ye ken the right people and can stomach a bit of matchmaking, ye may be able to arrange a trade that will satisfy Erik. A life, not a death, to build relations with Ross."

Most of the council started grumbling and

turned away. Aye, it was a woman's solution, an appeal to Erik's heart. But none of these men had seen Erik's face, the day he'd told her he'd never marry her. The frustration and sadness and longing in his eyes and in his voice when he named Fiona Rose. If Iain would take her seriously, her suggestion might get them out of the trap the storm had led them into.

She lifted her chin and locked gazes with Iain. His expression was solemn, but she could sense the sharp intelligence behind his midnight eyes. For a moment, his gaze left her and connected with Euan, but she barely had time to breathe before it returned to her, skewering her in place.

"Who?"

"Excuse me?"

"Who is the lass ye say Erik Ross wants to wed?"

"Her name is Fiona. Fiona Rose."

"Rose?" Iain looked dumbstruck. She could almost hear his mind work as he shuffled through the possibilities, the different courses of action—and their consequences. Then he gestured to the man nearest the door. "Fetch my wife, if ye would."

Muireall watched the man go with a frown. Of course, Iain's wife might ken the lass. Annie was a Rose before she married the Brodie laird.

The rumble of conversation in the room grew louder as they waited. Finally, one of the men spoke above the noise. "I say we fight. They tried to kill our shipwreck survivors, and held Eduard hostage."

Apparently, his comment emboldened another man to speak up. "Matchmaking? Pah! We'll look like weaklings."

"Aye," another agreed. "Better we go down fighting than arranging marriages for our enemies."

Muireall crossed her arms, waiting for some reaction from Iain, but he just let them talk. She wondered why, until another man spoke up.

"So ye dinna mind seeing yer sons killed, is that what we're saying? Or yer wives…well, there's a lass in the room so I willna say it. But ye ken fine what comes of war with another clan, and how the lasses suffer. We're better to avoid it if we can."

The door opened after that comment. Annie Brodie came in and scanned the room. Her eyebrows went up in surprise when she spotted Muireall and Ella among the men. Then she found her husband and smiled. "Ye sent for me?"

Iain held out a hand to her. She moved to him as he answered. "Aye. We've had an interesting bit of news. It seems the solution to our problem with Ross may be love, no' war."

"Well, that is refreshing."

A few of the council chuckled.

"So, why do you need me?"

"Do ye ken a lass named Fiona Rose?"

"Aye, of course. What has she to do with…"

"Muireall tells us Erik Ross wishes to wed the lass. If we could arrange the match for him, it might give us a way to build good will with the new Ross chief and avoid hostilities."

Annie's shoulders had slumped while Iain spoke. She glanced at Muireall, then turned back to her husband and shook her head. "Unless something has changed since we returned from Rose, Fiona is still betrothed to a MacBean. Surely someone would have mentioned if that had changed."

"So we fight," the man who'd earlier called for battle spoke into the sudden silence. "Doing aught else was a daft idea to begin with."

Iain pressed his lips together. "Are ye sure, Annie?"

"Aye. I'm sorry."

"Is it a love match?" Ella spoke up.

Annie shook her head. "Nay, I dinna believe so. It was arranged years ago to strengthen the ties between Rose and MacBean. As far as I ken, the two were betrothed as children and have never met since."

"Perhaps..." Muireall said, then covered her mouth with her fingers.

"Go on," Iain invited.

She glanced at Euan, who nodded his encouragement.

"Perhaps if ye were to intercede with the Rose...on Erik Ross's behalf. If something else can be worked out...some other match for the MacBean lad..."

"'Tis worth a try," Euan said, his voice surprising her. He'd stayed quiet up to this point. "Many of the Rosses are glad Donas and Silas are out of power. Erik seems more level-headed..."

"If ye do this for him, it would go a long way," Ella said, finally joining the conversation.

"My father will no' break a betrothal agreement," Annie said.

"No' without a very good reason," Iain amended. "Which this is. Rose would be drawn into any clan war Ross starts." Iain turned his gaze to Muireall. "Did Erik say he's met this Fiona, and whether she returns his interest?"

"He did. In Inverness, he said, before I *arrived*." She pursed her lips, then continued. "He intended to defy Donas to wed her. Now that Donas is no longer in charge, it willna take him long to offer for her."

Iain and Annie exchanged a glance.

"Well...it appears I'll see my da again sooner than I expected," Annie announced.

"And if ye return us to Munro, Ella and I can tell them Tira is fine, aye?"

"Ye could, but 'tis still a bad idea, lass. Until we ken what has happened to them...or hasna."

Her heart sank. Iain had appeared interested and impressed by the help she offered. But taking her home was one suggestion too many, it seemed.

"Send the lass home," one of the men interjected. "She can do more good there than here."

"And if it comes to a fight with Ross, she'll be safely out of harm's way," Euan added.

Annie's gaze shifted from her to Iain, who shrugged.

Muireall didn't know how to interpret his shrug, but apparently Annie did.

"'Tis the right thing to do," she told her husband. "As soon as our lads return, if the news is good, let the lass return home. She needs to see all is well there."

"She needs to stay out of Ross hands." Iain answered.

"I can get them there safely," Euan said, standing.

Muireall wanted to hug him.

"At the dark of the moon," he continued, "in the skiff with the dark sails—the very one we just used to retrieve Eduard—they'll never see us, even if one of their ships passes right by us."

"And if they do, they'll kill ye and anyone with ye. Or keep the lasses and do worse."

"No worse than was already done to me," Ella's voice rang out. Muireall squeezed her hand, shocked that she would lay claim in public to how she was treated.

"Maybe now that Erik is chief, they'll lose interest in raiding, whether for brides or anything else." Euan lifted his chin. "I can do it. Ye ken I can."

Iain glanced aside at Annie, then back to the council members. "Ye are all for this fool stunt?"

A few nodded, a few said, "Nay."

"Very well. We have a week until the new moon.

Annie, in the meantime, I'll send Kenneth with ye to Rose. Ye must do yer best to talk yer father into this scheme." He held up a hand as the warmonger in the council started to object. "I'll smooth things over with the MacBean. If all goes well, by the time ye lasses can leave, we'll ken whether we have a chance of making this work—or no'."

Muireall couldn't believe it. A week! If the news was good, she was going home in a week.

❧

EUAN KNEW, DESPITE HOW RELUCTANT HE'D SOUNDED, once Brodie fishing boats had sailed the firth and returned unmolested, Iain would agree to send Muireall home. They had only Silas's envoy's word that Ross wanted to even the score. Erik had other priorities. So far, everything had stayed quiet.

But swaying the Rose to wed Fiona to Erik was good insurance. None of them knew what kind of pressure Erik was under from Silas's men. A goodwill gesture might well prevent a war.

The only part of this he didn't like was sending Muireall home. He'd promised, and she needed to know her people were unharmed. He understood that. But he was coming to realize taking her to make sure her people were unharmed was different than leaving her behind and sailing away.

He walked out of the meeting with her, then pulled her aside and allowed the rest to pass by.

"Ye ken I will take ye home," he told her once they were alone in the hallway, "but it doesna mean I want to any longer, or that ye have to remain. Return with me, lass."

Her eyes went wide.

"Ye just said I'd be safer on Munro land."

"Perhaps. But war with Ross is just as likely at Munro as it is here. And Munro is easier for Ross to raid, as ye ken fine."

She crossed her arms and shuddered. "Ye dinna have to remind me."

Euan took her hand. "I hate the thought of losing ye, lass. Since I hauled ye out of the firth, I've been responsible for ye." He hesitated, not sure how to tell her what he was feeling. "How will I care for ye if I am here, and ye are there?" For a moment, he thought a shadow passed over her eyes, then she smiled.

"That's the way if it, Euan. I'm glad ye saved me, but that does mean ye must protect me for the rest of our lives. Someday, I'll have a husband to do that."

If only he were more sure of himself—and of her. He wanted her. Beyond that, he didn't know what he felt. He cared for her, but did that mean he should ask her now for her hand? Or would it be kinder to let her return to a life she knew, to people she loved, and court her from afar? It wouldn't be easy, but it could be done.

On the other hand, when he met her father, he could offer to marry her. The thought had a certain attraction, but it wasn't fair. Her family would be emotional about getting her back. She would need time at home without the pressure to marry right away. Nay, she wasn't ready to wed. Nor did he think he was. He let go of her hand.

She looked down at hers as if seeing it for the first time.

Or perhaps looking for signs of warmth left behind by his hand. He still felt her warmth in his.

"I care for ye, too, ye ken," she added. "And I will miss ye. But I miss my family. And Georgie. I have obligations there. Ye must understand."

Aye, Georgie. And obligations. Those he did understand, all too well. Still, ridiculous as it was, if he didn't know better, he'd think his feelings were hurt. He thought she cared for him—deeply. But she didn't—not more than she cared for a wee lad, and not enough to want to stay.

Well, he had a week until the dark of the moon. He'd use that time to woo Muireall and win her. Then they'd do something about wee Georgie together.

CHAPTER 17

The Brodies Iain sent to Munro returned that afternoon. And the news was exactly what Muireall had hoped for. Her father had been overjoyed to hear the lasses were alive and well. He and his men had searched for weeks. But with no bodies, and no other clans nearby claiming to have stolen Munro brides, eventually he had to assume the lasses had drowned, their bodies washed out into the *firth* or carried off by animals. That last made Muireall shudder. Her poor da. Not knowing must have tormented him so—as well as the other lasses' families. Even if she couldn't return home yet, she was glad Iain had given her clan some good news.

As Iain had suggested, his men had been delayed by Munro hospitality, but also by convincing Muireall's father not to strike back at Ross in retaliation for stealing the lasses and for the suffering their unexplained disappearance had cause. Since the man responsible was dead, the Munro had agreed simply to patrol their border with Ross against more raiding parties. Euan said Munro's forbearance should help Erik Ross consolidate his hold on his clan.

As opposed to his earlier distance that had made

Muireall think he'd been avoiding her last week, since he'd returned from Ross with Eduard, everywhere she turned, Euan appeared. One time, he'd be across the room and would merely catch her eye and smile. The next, he'd sit with her at supper and regale the table with the tale of Eduard's rescue or laugh over some clan gossip. She felt like a deer being stalked, the hunter seeing her first from a distance, then moving ever closer, in tighter and tighter circles, until he had her.

She preferred Euan's attention to his earlier avoidance. She liked that he was back to acting responsible for her, caring for her, spending time with her. She just wondered where it was leading.

In a few days, he would sail her home. Ella, too, had decided to go, at least to see what sort of reception she would get there. If Dermott would not honor their betrothal, she could come back to Brodie. Calum had made his interest clear to everyone else, if not to Ella. And in any case, Muireall was starting to see reasons why Ella would prefer Calum over Dermott. Calum was a much better man. Plus, she would be welcome here, and able to make a new home for herself away from all that had happened to her over the last month. Nothing Muireall had suffered at Donas Ross's hands, even the lash, could compare to that.

Her own future might be in question, too. She did not think she would face the same censure as Ella at Munro, so she could stay there if she wished. But Euan would be here, far across the firth at Brodie. Would he offer for her, and try to bring her back once she had a chance to visit her family? If he did, could she leave Georgie? Well, there was no sense in worrying about all that now. She'd learn where things stood when she returned to Munro.

In the meantime, Euan was everywhere, and she liked it.

She was on her way to join Annie for a riding lesson when Euan intercepted her.

"I'll go with ye," he said when she divulged her destination.

"That's no' necessary. Annie and I will be fine."

"Nonetheless, I'll ride with ye."

Annie grinned when she saw Muireall enter with Euan. "Do ye need a lesson, then?" she teased him.

"Nay, but ye need an escort if ye're planning to leave the keep. And I ken ye are."

"*Ye* are, and Muireall has made enough progress to ride with ye, as long as ye dinna try to race."

"Ye are no' coming?" Muireall faced her, wide-eyed. She wasn't at all sure that riding out alone with Euan was a good idea.

"Nay, I have some things to do for Iain. So Euan, take good care of our lass, will ye?"

He smirked. "I will."

Annie gave him a wink and left them.

"I..." Muireall started to object, but Euan cut her off.

"Up ye go, lass." Annie had already saddled Muireall's usual mount. Euan helped her up, then quickly readied his horse.

Before Muireall knew what had happened, they were riding, side-by-side, out the gate and across the meadow behind the Brodie keep. It was a rare sunny and warm winter day. Muireall had ridden enough by now to enjoy the breeze and the effort of riding. The sun on her face was an unexpected pleasure. And, she had to admit, to herself at least, so was the man riding beside her.

"Where to?" she asked.

"Have ye ever seen a ghost?"

Muireall's skin prickled. "A ghost? Nay! Nor would I wish to."

"No' a real one. I'll take ye to the wee glen. In it is an ancient stone ye must see."

"Only a stone?"

"Aye. Only a stone. A ghost of the past, left behind."

She nodded, intrigued. "Very well. Is it far?"

He grinned and shook his head. "Nay. Only on the far side of those trees."

After what seemed like miles, they broke out of the green shade of the pine forest into a small glen. Off to one side, a grey rectangular stone stood sentinel over the clearing. Euan led her to it, and they dismounted.

It was smaller than Muireall first thought. Half her height, or a bit more. It looked as if someone had scraped badly spaced lines up one side, then decorated the face of it with loops and what might be crude drawings of some creature. The stone was weathered enough she couldn't tell. "What is this?" she asked as she walked around to see the back and other side.

"No one kens for certain. Left by some of the Pechs as a signpost for others, perhaps."

"This stone wasna hewn by Pictish fairies," Muireall objected.

Euan grinned. "How would ye ken? 'Tis very old."

Muireall ran a finger across the top of the stone, where moss made a green carpet. "They'd be too wee to stand it in place as it is."

"Aye, well, ye might have a point." He moved behind her, took her hand and traced her fingers over the lines running down the side. "Some say this is writing, though I canna see it."

"Mayhap some has worn away." Muireall could scarce concentrate on the stone before her. Euan's fingers caressed her hand while his body heated her back and sent coils of wanting spiraling through her. She'd been alone with him before, but something about this glen made her feel they were the only two people in the world. Anything they did here would be lost in time, just like this stone. She turned in Euan's arms to face him, then brought her gaze up to his.

She'd once thought his eyes were sea green, when he'd first saved her from drowning. Here, they were as deeply green as the moss on the ancient stone, or the grass beneath their feet in summer. Framed by the russet of his eyebrows, they were as dark and mysterious as the rock at her back.

He gave her no more time to study him, but leaned in and brushed his lips across hers, then again, softly, leaving her no doubt he would demand more.

She met him, kiss for kiss, touch for touch. When she parted her lips, his tongue invaded her mouth and she tangled hers with his, then sucked as she tunneled her fingers in his hair.

Euan moaned and pulled her closer, his arms like the warmest furs that had ever comforted her, then steel bands, telling her without words he would never let her go. Muireall caressed his face, wishing the simmer in her blood could go on forever. When he cupped her breast, instinct drove her to arch against him.

"Muireall," he breathed. "Ye are perfect. So beautiful, in my eyes and in my hands. Do ye have any notion what ye have done to me?"

"What?" she got out before his mouth claimed hers. When he let her breathe again, she asked again. "What have I done to ye?"

It was his turn to hold her still and study her. His eyes moved lovingly over her face and throat, down her body and back up again. "I want ye lass, but more than that, I want ye with me. When I wake each morn, I wonder where ye are. When I close my eyes at night, I wish ye were beside me. Somehow, ye have become as necessary to me as the blood in my veins. When we are away from each other, I feel as though I'm missing a part of my body. My heart."

"Euan, I dinna ken what to say." Her heart beat as fast as a galloping horse, and she needed Euan's strength to remain on her feet.

"Let me love ye, lass." He paused when her breath caught. "Nay, I willna take ye. No' until I can wed ye, if ye'll have me, but there is so much more I can show ye."

"Then show me, Euan. In this magical place, I want to learn."

He laid her on the sweet moss beside the ancient stone and quickly unlaced the bodice of her dress. He moved it aside while his lips, teeth and tongue traced a path from her mouth down her throat to her chest. The heat of his mouth penetrated her shift as if it wasn't there. But even that thin fabric was more than Muireall wanted between her skin and Euan's mouth. She untied the neckline and smiled when he pulled it away, then gasped when his lips closed over her nipple and sucked. A bolt of pleasure arced from her breast to the peak of her thighs, hazing her mind with sensations she'd never experienced before. He pulled her to sitting and kissed his way across her shoulder, making her pulse dance, then twisted her to reach the nape of her neck.

Muireall knew the moment Euan saw what had been done to her. He froze, his lips still on her skin, but she knew his eyes must be wide and his brow furrowed. Then he lifted his head and moved around her, pulling her dress down to her waist.

"Who did this to ye?"

She fought for calm, knowing the truth would only add to the burdens Euan carried, but she had no believable lie at the ready. Women were rarely lashed, and only for the worst offenses, none of which she wanted him to think she'd committed.

"Donas Ross." The words sounded as if they came

from someone else's throat, so softly did she utter them they seemed to echo from miles away.

Then Euan pulled her up to her knees, turned her to face him and held her shoulders, his gaze fastened to her eyes. Though her breasts were bared, he never glanced down. "Why? How could he do this to ye?"

"I ran away. I tried to…"

Euan's face reddened. His eyes narrowed before he released her and scrubbed his hands over his face.

She pulled her shift up and tied it, then reached for her dress, intent on covering herself. Suddenly, she felt too exposed, as if Donas Ross was standing nearby, leering at her.

"I wish he still lived so I could kill him again," Euan ground out, then lowered his hands. "No lass should ever feel the stripe of the lash on her body." He reached out to help her pull the dress up to her shoulders.

She appreciated that he knew the mention of Donas Ross had broken the lovely spell of the wee glen for her. His sensitivity endeared him to her as much as his fury on her behalf.

"Had I known then what he had done, he wouldha died much more slowly. In as much agony as I could inflict, for the harm he did ye."

Muireall clenched her hands. "'Twas my own fault, for not getting away. For getting caught. The first time, he merely confined me for three days without food. This," she said and hooked a thumb over her shoulder, "he did after my second attempt."

Euan shook his head. "He was a cruel, evil bastard. What he did to ye makes me wonder what he did to other lasses in his care."

Muireall choked, then laughed. "His care. No' how I would describe it."

Euan pursed his lips, looking sheepish. "Nor I, truly." He caressed her face with a gentle hand. "I would gladly have taken the lashes for ye. I'm sorry ye suffered as ye did."

She leaned into his hand and sighed. She'd feel contented if only they were not talking about Donas Ross's perfidy. "I'm sorry, too. Though some good did come of it." She lifted her gaze to his. "I met ye."

"Aye, and I met ye."

"I ken it doesna make up for what happened."

"Dinna compare the two, lass. Ye are a blessing unlooked for, but greatly treasured. Ye ken I want ye...I want ye to stay with me."

She straightened away from him and studied her hands.

He sighed. "'Twas the wrong thing to say. And I ken yer reasons for going home. For Georgie. But ye canna deny what is between us. I want to make ye happy, Muireall. I want ye to be my wife."

She knew what she wanted to say. She wanted him, too. A future as his bride would be more than she'd ever hoped for. But her life, her obligations, were at Munro and at her father's discretion. Euan's were at Brodie. And after he'd told her while they were still trapped in the cave, what he did *not* want in a bride, she feared he'd change his mind once he got her home. She could not agree until he knew everything about her. When he took her home, he would see for himself and decide.

She stood and began straightening her clothes. Euan got to his feet and moved to her, doing up the lacings he'd loosened, careful not to touch her any more than necessary to tighten them.

After a moment, he spoke again. "Ye dinna have to answer me now, Muireall. There are things we must take care of, before either of us can be free to wed. But I want ye to ken," he tied the last knot and took her face in his large hands, his gaze boring into hers, "ye have my heart. 'Tis up to ye what ye do with it."

His image suddenly blurred. "I dinna see how the future we hope for can ever be," she choked out. "But ye have my heart, as well."

"We will find a way, lass. We must. If it takes time, so be it, but I'd have ye to wife today if I could."

He could. She knew he could. They'd only need to pronounce the words, to pledge their troth to each other. Here, before the ancient stone, would be a fine place. Then finish what they'd started, and let him take what he'd refused to take from her. Her maidenhead. Her innocence. Then it would be done.

Part of her yearned for it. For Euan. The need so strong she shook with it. The hand she lifted quivered, and her thoughts tumbled like the dry leaves blown across the glen by the rising winter wind. 'Twould be easy to do. As easy as loving Euan. They'd return to his clan married, she his, and he hers. But he didn't know everything about her. And the truth he didn't know might change his mind and close his heart to her forever.

❧

EUAN WATCHED TINY CHANGES IN EXPRESSION FLIT across Muireall's face. Her love for him shone in her eyes, but her face betrayed hope, then sorrow, then emotions he could not name. The hand she lifted toward him trembled with the strength of her feelings.

He dropped to his knees and took her hands in his, yet her body still quaked. "I love ye, Muireall. No matter what happens, no matter what ye decide, that will never change. I will love ye with every day of my life, and my last breath I'll use to say yer name."

"Euan...ye canna make such promises."

"I can, lass, and I do. There is no more solemn, sacred place on Brodie land, save the kirk, to make such vows, than by this ancient stone. I make them here, to ye. So ye will ken, when ye are ready, that I will be waiting for ye. I will still want ye. I will still love and protect ye."

"Some men would simply take what they want, and force me to wed."

Euan's heart sank. "I am no' Donas Ross, nor even Erik Ross, to bind ye to me with hurt and anger—and fear. Ye ken me better than that."

She gave him a small, sad smile. "Aye, I do ken ye better than that. If only…"

"If only what, love?"

She sighed. "If only our lives were simpler. If only… well, they are no'. As much as we might wish for this, our lives are on opposite sides of the firth."

Euan refused to give up. "Perhaps for now, but not forever."

Muireall's chin trembled and fresh tears coursed down her cheeks.

Euan stood and pulled her into his arms. He let her cry against his shoulder until she calmed, knowing she cried for more than what they'd declared today. She'd been so strong, he expected she had a month's worth of tears to shed. Tears she could use to release the fear, the anger and pain of her capture and confinement, and of what Donas Ross, that bastard, had done to her. He was certain she hadn't told him all. He only knew she'd been whipped because she couldn't deny the scars on her back. What other scars did she bear that the eye could not see?

There must be other things holding her back. She loved him. She could not deny her feelings for him, nor her desire for him. And he loved her and wanted to wed her. To love her for all their lives.

Was there something at Munro more binding than that? The lad, Georgie? Surely someone would care for wee Georgie until he was grown. When they got to Munro, Euan would see to it. He knew better than most what the lad was going through. He would meet the lad and find a suitable place to foster him among the Munro families. Then Muireall would be free of that burden, and she could be his.

Two days later, Muireall folded the last shift and laid it beside the old faded plaid Annie had given her. She'd need its warmth for the crossing, so she would take it. Annie had tried to give her a new Brodie plaid, but Muireall had refused it. She was not a Brodie and besides, it was new. Someone here could get years of use out of it. Just not her. She'd laid the dresses she'd been given on the bed as neatly as she could. She couldn't in good conscience take them, either. She'd appreciated every one of them. They'd kept her warm and dry and presentable to Euan's clan, but they were loans.

Euan's clan. Not hers. Though it could be hers. Euan wanted it to be. He wanted her. He'd made that plain enough, in word and in deed, his promises heartfelt. Just the thought of his kisses set her tingling. The memory of his arms around her made her hug herself, but it wasn't the same. Nothing was the same as Euan.

She didn't want to leave him. But she was getting her wish at last. Or was she?

Aye, she'd been away from Georgie too long.

A knock interrupted her thoughts and she laid aside

the corner of the plaid. She opened the door to find Ella.

"Are ye taking the dresses?" Ella asked without preamble.

"Nay. I'm taking naught but what I must wear to be decent and warm."

"Then I must leave behind the yellow dress?" Ella's face fell.

"'Tis up to ye. I dinna think anyone will begrudge ye the enjoyment of it."

Ella stepped into the room and took in what Muireall had laid out. "But ye think they'll begrudge ye these?" she asked, waving a hand at the dresses draped across Muireall's bed.

"Nay. Some other lass might need them, be she a Brodie or a visitor like me. I have dresses at Munro."

"As do I. But nought like the..."

"Take it," Annie said, entering the room. She looked about and frowned. "And ye, Muireall, ye ken ye are welcome to these."

"I do and I thank ye for the use of them, for yer hospitality. Ye took me...us...in and have no' begrudged us a thing. Even more, ye taught us to ride, taught me archery. I canna thank ye enough for making us welcome."

"Aye, I feel the same," Ella added.

"'Twas little enough. Ye helped Euan and Calum return to us. Brodie canna repay ye for that."

"And Munro will be equally in Brodie's debt for returning us home," Muireall said. "So we're even."

"And ye are welcome at Brodie any time, for as long as ye wish. Ye ken that, right?"

Muireall nodded. "I do." She glanced at Ella. "We do."

"I'll let ye finish, then. Godspeed to both of ye. I hope to see ye again someday soon. Perhaps ye and..."

She paused and glanced aside, then continued, "Well, I'll miss ye."

"We'll miss ye, too, more than ye ken." Annie hugged Ella, then turned to her.

"I willna make a demand, but ye ken Euan feels strongly about ye. Listen to the man, please?"

Muireall nodded, unable to reply, and Annie left them. She closed the door, turned back to Ella, and found her voice. "Are we making the right decision? Am I?"

"Ye ask me? I'm confused enough for both of us. At least ye dinna have a betrothed at home and a husband at a rival clan."

Muireall tried to laugh, but couldn't manage it around the lump in her throat. "Nay, praise the saints in Heaven. But we'll sort out what to do about ye, never fear." She crossed to the window and pretended to look out. All she could see was Euan's face as he declared his love for her. "'Tis about Euan I canna decide. He and I...well, never mind." She forced a smile and turned back to Ella. "We'll be across the firth and home before we ken it. In a few days, all this uncertainty will be behind us."

"But what if we fall into Ross hands again? They could take us on the firth, or once we land near Munro."

Ella's stricken expression brought Muireall up short. She'd thought Ella would jump all over what she'd started to say about her and Euan and demand she finish the sentence. She stopped because suddenly, she didn't want to share with anyone, not even Ella, what she and Euan had done and said at the ancient stone.

Instead, Ella hadn't even noticed Muireall's hesitation. Ella had to be feeling worse than she did, now that everyone knew what had happened to her at Ross. Her prospects for finding a well-placed husband at Munro were far worse than Muireall's. Muireall took a breath and forced a smile. "Well, then, we both must do what we can to get on with our lives, aye?"

Ella nodded. "If only I knew where to start."

"Ye did that when ye took yerself down to that beach, lass, and trusted the Brodies on that boat. Ye decided to change yer fate, and ye did everything ye could about it. Ye are stronger than ye ken."

That seemed to cheer Ella up a bit. She straightened and a hint of a smile played around the corners of her mouth. "I did, aye. I did. I am."

"Of course ye are. I wouldna say it if it were no' true."

Then she wrapped her arms around her middle. "But what if Thomas comes back for me?"

"He canna ken where ye are. Ye simply disappeared. Ye couldha drowned in the firth. And if he thought ye sought to escape overland back to Munro, he'd never think a lass could survive the journey, especially no' on foot. Nay, he may have looked for ye near the Ross village, but in a few days' time, he'd have assumed ye are dead."

"Good," Ella said, nodding. "That's good." Then her face fell. "But I'm no' truly divorced from him. And if he decides to raid Munro for another wife, he'll see me. Mayhap I should stay here."

Muireall took her hands. "Euan willna let that happen. We'll be safe, and soon we'll be home, and then Da willna let it happen. They're keeping watch against Ross raiders. And we can count on help from Brodie. And perhaps clan Rose. Erik Ross is smarter than Donas was. He will not want to involve them."

Ella brightened and tightened her grip on Muireall's hand. "If we're allied with Brodie, ye will see Euan again. Ye could ask yer da to arrange a match. Perhaps

Euan would consider marriage if the idea came from yer da...and his laird."

Or if her father had arranged a match for her with Grant, her dream of a future with Euan would fall apart...the weight of that possibility was more than she could bear at the moment.

Ella frowned. "If ye are truly in his heart, and I think ye must be, he will."

"I dinna ken if he will after he finds out who I really am...he is no' fond of the idea."

"What if ye asked Annie for her help? Perhaps she can suggest just such a match—with ye."

"Nay. That would make me pathetic. I must wait. If Euan wants me, perhaps he'll want me enough for his heart to return him to me once he kens. If no'..." she shrugged. "Nay, I willna force him. He must offer for me."

EVEN THOUGH SHE'D BEEN TOLD BY THE BRODIES WHO'D already been here that her people were still alive and no Ross raid had troubled them—other than the one that took her, Ella and Tira—Muireall still nearly swooned with relief when she, Ella, Euan and Calum arrived at Munro. Her father, Hugh, met them at the door of the keep.

"I hardly dared believe it," he said, wrapping her in his massive arms. "Ye are alive!" He held her away from him and studied her. "Are ye well?"

Moisture filmed his eyes, surprising her. She couldn't recall ever seeing her father cry. Those as-yet-unshed tears made her regret even more the time she'd been forced to spend away from home. His emotion warmed her, even though she knew the subtext of his question. She was thankful she could give an honest answer. "Aye." She nodded. "I am well…and whole," she added in a softer voice. "I wasna harmed." Not in the way he meant.

"That's good, then." He dropped a fatherly kiss on her forehead, then set her away from him and looked up.

Muireall took his cue. "I am honored to present Euan Brodie. And Calum Brodie."

"I hear I owe ye thanks for saving my daughter," her father said, before she could finish the introduction.

"And Euan, this is my father," she finished, speaking on the heels of her father's announcement. She hesitated, knowing she should have told Euan sooner, in private. Here, he would have no time to absorb or accept what she was about to reveal. She should have told him in private, but she was a coward, afraid the truth would turn Euan's heart away from her. She'd delayed until she had no choice. She looked at the ground as she said the words, "Laird Munro and Baron of Foulis," then forced her gaze back up to Euan's face.

Euan's expression remained neutral, betraying nothing. He inclined his head to her father. "I was pleased to be of service, milord. I'm honored to meet ye."

Muireall started, surprised when he didn't react. In the cave, he'd been quite clear about his disdain for laird's daughters, which is why she'd never dared tell him. Now that the truth was out, he had no reaction? What had worried her so?

"Muireall never told me her father was Laird Munro," he continued calmly.

Muireall quailed inside but kept her chin up. He was angry. She was sure of it.

Her father glanced at her and frowned.

She was certain from the heat climbing up her neck that she was quickly turning red.

"Aye, well, anonymity is sometimes the best protection," he said.

Euan gave her a long look. "How is it neither of the other lasses gave ye away at Ross? 'Twould seem it would have improved their lot with that clan to betray ye."

Muireall shook her head. "The only one I feared was Tira. Ella would never betray me. But it seems even Tira treated me with honor."

And Euan would not have touched her or told her he loved her had he known who her father was.

"Good thing," Euan remarked, then cleared his throat. "I beg yer pardon, Laird Munro."

Her father laughed. "Ye have nay need to beg mine. Or my daughter's, I'll wager. Come inside. Let's talk further over some ale."

After Calum excused himself, likely to find Ella, Muireall preceded them, wishing she could see Euan's expression, but he followed her father. Was he angry she'd never told him who she really was? He'd once said he would never marry the daughter of a laird. Yet he'd spent weeks caring for her and at the Pecht stone, had sworn his undying love. Did his oath truly bind him when she had lied to him? By omission, aye, but lied nonetheless. If the reverse were true and he'd failed to tell her he was the son of a laird, she'd be angry, too.

As soon as they entered the hall, Muireall heard Georgie calling her, making her forget her worries over Euan. "Muireall! Muireall, ye're back!" He ran to her so fast she feared he would not be able to stop and would knock her over, but she managed to stay upright as he barreled into her. "It has been so long. Where were ye?"

"Georgie, *wheesht*. Let me introduce ye to someone. This is Euan Brodie. He's a...friend of mine."

Euan cut an unreadable glance her way, then smiled at Georgie.

She didn't miss her father's eyebrows lift. He must have read something in her tone, something she was not yet ready to admit, or to discuss with him. Euan's reticence upset her.

Euan knelt to be on eye level with the freckled lad and offered his broad hand. The large bandages that replaced the wrappings she'd torn from her shift had themselves been replaced by a few small strips on the deepest wounds that were still healing.

Georgie looked at her, uncertain.

She nodded, so Georgie put his much smaller hand in Euan's. "Good day, sir," he offered.

Euan widened his smile. "Good day to ye, too, my man. Muireall has told me many things about Munro, but mostly she spoke about ye. Ye have nay idea how much she's missed ye. I'm pleased to meet the man she cares so much about."

Muireall loved the way Georgie's chest swelled and he stood taller at the Brodie warrior's complements. "Thank ye, sir. But I dinna ken anything about ye."

"Well, then, let us allow Muireall some time with her father. Ye and I will go over there by the hearth and get acquainted, aye?"

Georgie looked to her for permission, his expression beseeching. Euan had already won him over.

He'd won her over, too, despite her concern about what he was feeling toward her right now. No matter what, Euan's attention seemed to lend her brother confidence, and she could see the envious glances of some other lads in the hall. Euan's attention would lend Georgie some popularity, as well.

"Well, go on with ye," she chided. "Euan is full of stories ye have never heard. I'm sure he can tell ye a few while Da and I talk."

Georgie flashed a grin and led Euan to a seat by the hearth.

Muireall watched them go, heart filling with love for the wee lad and admiration for the man beside him.

"So that's how it is, aye?" Her father's voice startled her and she glanced aside at him then to the floor.

"How what is?"

"Dinna try to fool me, lass. I've kenned ye since yer first breath. I see the way ye look at Euan Brodie. Does he return yer regard?"

"Aye, he does." At least he did. And now? She turned away and walked with her father toward his private solar. "But his life is at Brodie. Mine is here." She would not diminish him in her father's eyes by relating the disdain he'd expressed in the cave for laird's daughters. She couldn't tell yet whether, now he knew about her, that disdain crowded out the feelings they'd shared at the Pecht stone.

Her father didn't answer until they were in private—the door closed between them and the ears in the hall. He sat by the hearth and gestured her to the opposite chair.

"What do ye want, lass? Though I wouldna like to lose ye to Brodie so soon after I got ye back, ye ken I've had my eye on an alliance with Grant. Ye'll no' be here forever. Aye, Georgie will miss ye, but the lad must grow up. The last month has been hard, but…well, I want ye to be happy. Ye must have been through so much. Ye deserve something of peace and happiness. If Euan Brodie is the man who gives ye that, then perhaps we can come to an agreement."

"Nay, da. Georgie must come first. I'm the only mother he's ever kenned. He's too young for me to just walk away from him."

"Ye coddle him."

Her father's suddenly gruff tone hurt and angered her, yet she suspected he was trying to make it easier for her to decide. "I dinna. Ye havena seen how the other lads treat him."

He shrugged. "All boys fight—it toughens them."

"No' the way Georgie has had to. They dinna treat him in front of ye the way they do when ye are no' present. He's small for his age, so he's an easy target, despite being yer son. He may only be the spare, but if anything were to happen to Archie, he'd be laird and Baron some day. He canna grow up fearing the very lads who'll become his clansmen, his warriors, his advisors..."

Her father held up a hand. "I dinna see what ye describe, but it may be as ye say." He pursed his lips and looked aside. "Verra well. We'll give it some time. Ye will come to me if ye change yer mind."

She nodded. "Of course."

He stood and opened his arms.

She went into his embrace and hugged him back.

"'Tis good to have ye home, lass. I canna tell ye how heartsick I was when ye disappeared. Ella and Tira, too. We searched and searched. The whole clan..." His voice broke and he hugged her harder, then let her go. "What happened to ye at Ross?"

She stepped back. "Tira is still with Ross, married to a man called Teague—happily, it seems. Ella..." She paused, reluctant to relate what had happened to Ella, but knowing her father must be told. "Ella was forced to marry a man called Thomas. She said he treated her well enough, but after Euan rescued me, she no longer wanted to stay at Ross." She resumed her seat and gestured for her father to do the same, then told him the whole story, from Euan saving her from drowning, killing Donas to protect her and let them get away, then sailing young James's body home to Brodie. She left out what Donas had done to her, and her humiliation after she left Euan in the cave. He'd find out about the stripes on her back soon enough from the maids. She just wasn't ready to admit to them, fearing he'd gather the clan and ride on Ross the next minute. Let him get past the emotion of her homecoming. She'd tell him once things had settled down, once he knew the man who'd taken a whip to her back was already dead.

In the meantime, he wanted to know about Euan. "He's a good man, Da. Responsible. Honorable. Stubborn." She laughed. "I could go on, but ye get the idea. I do love him, but I have obligations here, and he has the same at Brodie. 'Tis no' our time. Perhaps someday, when Georgie is older. Bigger and stronger, too."

Her father nodded distractedly as he stared into the fire.

She could see he needed time to think about what she'd just told him. "Speaking of Georgie...I'd best go rescue Euan."

Her father's gaze returned to her and he smiled. "Aye, ye had. I expect Georgie will have talked him dry by now."

She stood and kissed his cheek. "I'm glad to be home, Da. Ye canna ken how much I missed ye, and everyone here."

When she returned to the great hall, Euan and Georgie were where she'd last seen them. At the moment, Georgie was talking, more animatedly than she'd ever seen before. She smiled and watched for a moment, until Euan saw her and beckoned her with a wave of one big hand.

"This lad will make a great bard someday," he told her, standing and putting a comradely hand on Georgie's shoulder.

Thank God he hadn't ruffled his hair. But nay, Euan was too sensitive to the lad's precarious confidence to treat him as a wee child.

"He'll be that, or anything else he wishes to be, when

the time comes," she agreed. "Now, if ye two men have done, I'd like to borrow Euan. Do ye mind, Georgie?"

Her half-brother gave her a manly nod. "Ye may."

She thanked him as seriously as he'd given her permission, though they both knew none was required. Then she walked Euan out into the bailey.

"Thank ye for what ye just did for Georgie. I canna remember a time when he looked or sounded so confident. And the other lads watching will treat him with more respect, having seen the respect ye gave him."

"He is yer brother, aye?"

"Half. And his mother died in childbirth. I've raised him..."

"*Ach*, now I understand. And he's the heir?"

"Nay. Archie is. He's due back from fostering soon. Then he'll join Da's warriors. Georgie hopes never to be laird, of course. If he's very lucky, he never will be."

CHAPTER 19

In only a few days, it seemed to Muireall that Euan got over the unwelcome surprise of her parentage and warmed to her again. Georgie monopolized as much of his time as he could, but Euan still managed to seek her out. She hoped Euan's magic with Georgie would continue to work. Other lads had been friendlier and more inclusive, a major change from the way they'd treated him before he'd spent that time with Euan in the great hall.

She felt sorry for Calum, who spent as much time with Ella as she would allow, but she gave him precious little. With her reputation in tatters, she could not welcome male company. Muireall spent as much time with Ella as she could, but Georgie clung to her and when free of him, she wanted to be with Euan.

Muireall and Euan returned from riding in time for the midday meal. "I'll help ye with my mount," she offered, but Euan waved her aside.

"Dinna fash, love. I can do both in the time 'twill take ye to do one." He wrapped an arm around her and pulled her in for a kiss that held much less heat than the kisses they'd shared away from the keep. "If ye like," he added when they broke apart, "send Georgie to help me. Then ye will have at least a few minutes to yerself."

"Thank ye, I will. He doesna let me out of his sight unless 'tis to be with ye," Muireall responded and ran a hand down his cheek. "By the time I get cleaned up, 'twill be time to eat, so dinna let him slow ye too much."

"Nothing will slow me from coming to ye." Euan grinned and turned her toward the door, then pushed her away with a pat on her rump. "So go on with ye, and send him out."

Muireall crossed the bailey still wearing the contented smile she always seemed to have in Euan's presence, when she heard horses approaching.

Thomas Ross rode in with a dozen men.

She didn't stop to think. She just ran for the door of the keep. In the great hall, she saw Ella climbing the stairs to the upper level. "Ella," she shouted. "Get out of sight! Fast!" She ran to Ella and pushed her up the last few steps and into the upper hall.

"Have ye gone barmy?" Ella objected, pushing her away.

"Thomas is here with a dozen men. Ye have to hide. Somewhere no one will look for ye."

"Oh, God, nay…where? Where can I hide?"

"On the roof," Muireall told her after a flash of memory put her on the Brodie roof with Euan in the moonlight. "Everyone kens ye dinna like heights. They'll never look for ye there."

"I canna!"

"Ye must. Thomas has to be here for ye. Why else would he come?"

Ella wrung her hands.

"Look, I'll go up with ye. If ye stay seated behind the low wall, no one will see ye, and ye willna be able to see beyond it. And ye'll be able to hear when they leave."

She pushed Ella toward the closet with the ladder to the roof. "We must go now!"

Ella finally moved and Muireall breathed a sigh of relief. She could hear voices down in the great hall, but they all still sounded like Munro men. They'd probably just heard about the Ross's arrival. She started up the ladder, Ella right below her. The trap door to the roof was heavier than she expected. Euan had opened his so easily. But she got it open, though she was certain the entire keep heard the thunk when it fell onto the roof above. But she didn't stop. She climbed out, then on hands and knees, reached for Ella.

But Ella had stopped halfway up the ladder.

"Come on, Ella. Ye can do it!"

"Nay, I canna."

"Would ye rather go back to Ross with Thomas?"

Ella's former betrothed had made it clear he would not honor their marriage contract. She'd been ruined, as he put it, by being forced to marry Thomas Ross. Muireall's heart broke for her. Now that Dermott had made the reason for his refusal publicly and abundantly clear, Muireall couldn't even look at him without wanting to scratch out his eyes. But when Ella saw him, all Muireall saw in her was sadness, not anger. She'd given up. But Muireall couldn't let her give up where Thomas Ross was concerned. Even if she had to frighten her in to moving.

Ella's eyes widened and tears glinted. She pulled herself up two more rungs, then paused again.

Muireall heard male voices moving closer. They were louder than before. "Ella, come on!" she hissed. "Someone is coming upstairs. They'll be looking for ye."

Ella shook her head. "I canna. I'm already too high. I canna get down, either."

"Oh, Christ. Can ye close the door with yer foot?

No' all the way. Just enough that they canna see in there?"

Ella shook her head. Her knuckles were white.

Muireall could see she couldn't let go. "Damn it," she muttered and swung her legs back onto the ladder.

Ella whimpered as the ladder shifted under Muireall's weight.

"Dinna move," she told Ella.

"I canna."

"I'm going to climb down and close the door. Just hang on."

Ella nodded. The rest of her was frozen.

Muireall worked her way down far enough to swing around to the low side of the ladder. The sound of cloth tearing made her wince. She twisted her head, trying to see what ripped. *Ach, nay*, she'd caught her shoulder and torn a long rent across the back of her gown. She could feel a cold draft from her shoulder to her spine. Well, she'd have to deal with that later. She found enough toe and footholds to get down the side opposite where Ella clung, whimpering as the ladder shifted with each move Muireall made. Once down to the floor, she grabbed the edge of the door and swung it closed until only a crack remained open. She exhaled and turned back to Ella. How was she going to get her to climb the rest of the way to the roof?

The door swung open at her back.

Muireall froze, then turned.

Her father stood there, a knowing smirk on his face that quickly turned to outrage.

"What is that?" he bellowed, charging into the confined space, grabbing her arm and pulling her out into the torchlit hallway.

Muireall quailed. He could not miss the stripes on her back nor what they meant.

"Who did this?"

When she didn't answer, he grabbed her other arm and pulled her around to face him. "Who, daughter? Who hurt ye?"

Muireall sighed. There was no hope of avoiding this. "Donas Ross."

Ella surprised her by coming to stand with her. How had she gotten herself down the ladder? Muireall took her hand, acknowledging the courage it had taken Ella to come to her defense.

Muireall's father looked from her to Ella and back again. "All of ye?"

Ella shook her head.

"Just me," Muireall admitted. "Punishment for trying several times to escape and return home before..."

"Before she was taken as Tira was, and I, as well" Ella answered for her. "And now that man is here, demanding ye return his *wife* to him. Ye ken I dinna wish to go."

The Munro released his grip on Muireall's arms and stepped back, his expression bleak.

❧

A FROZEN HUSH FELL OVER THE GATHERING AS THE Munro led Ella into the great hall, one big hand wrapped around her arm. Muireall followed, teeth clenched, furious that her father would consider betraying her friend.

In the silence, Thomas's voice rang clearly to the rafters, demanding to see his wife. "Where is Ella Munro Ross?" he roared. His back was to them.

"Ye mean the lass ye stole?" The Munro's response was louder and even more heated.

Thomas whirled and frowned when he spotted them.

"Along with my daughter, lashed by Donas Ross like a common criminal. Yet ye, another Ross, dares to step foot in my hall, bellowing demands? I should kill ye where ye stand."

"Nay, Da!" Muireall gasped. That would only make things worse—for Munro and for Brodie. Ella remained silent, and that worried Muireall. Ella knew what was at stake, and what could happen if Thomas died here. Muireall thought Ella had at least some feelings for Thomas, enough not to want to see him killed.

"Donas Ross is dead," Thomas spat. "Someone took yer revenge for ye." His gaze cut to Euan, who'd appeared out of the crowd and come to stand at Muireall's other side. Calum, as usual, at his side.

Muireall's father released Ella's arm.

Rather than running, which Muireall thought she might do, Ella stepped away from him and approached Thomas.

Muireall moved up to stand beside her father, as stiff with anxiety for Ella as Ella had been on the ladder just minutes before. But she'd somehow gathered her courage and gotten down from it. Muireall hoped her courage would last through the confrontation with Thomas Ross.

Her father fairly vibrated—whether with anger over what Donas had done to her or Ella's situation, she didn't know. Perhaps both.

"I heard ye were here." Thomas didn't greet Ella. His first words to her were clearly an accusation.

Ella lifted her chin. "I dinna ken how ye heard, but it matters not. Here I am, and here I will stay."

Muireall wanted to cheer at the brave front Ella put up, facing a big warrior like Thomas. She would not have to face him alone, however. The Munro and several of his men moved to flank the couple. But they didn't interfere with the business of a husband and wife.

Euan took her father's place at her side, deceptively still except for the muscle jumping in his jaw. She could see he wanted to act, but in her father's hall, it was not his place to do so. Not without invitation.

"Ye are my wife." Thomas continued speaking to Ella as if Munro men did not surround them. "Like it or nay. Now that I ken ye live, I've come to take ye home."

"I willna. I divorce ye."

"Well, I dinna divorce ye. Ye are mine, and ye will come with me or there will be trouble...more trouble... between Ross and Munro."

The tears running down Ella's face hurt Muireall's heart. "How can ye?" she demanded. "Ye ken I dinna want ye, or a life at Ross."

"We are wed. 'Tis that simple," Thomas replied. Without taking his gaze from Ella, he added, "Laird Munro, ye ken what must be done here. Do ye risk clan war and deny me my right to this woman, or do ye send my wife home to Ross with me?"

"To be treated as my daughter was?"

Muireall clenched her hands. Could her father talk him out of taking Ella?

Thomas looked affronted. "Nay! Donas is dead. Erik Ross is chief. He is a fearsome warrior, but he will no' allow any woman to be treated as Donas did yer lass, no matter the cause."

"No' even Silas?" Euan's voice startled everyone, and gazes turned to him, then back to Thomas.

"Silas died of a wound—a self-inflicted wound. I suppose she couldna bear to be separated from her murdered husband."

To Muireall's relief, Euan frowned but didn't argue the point, though it unnerved her to hear Thomas say *murdered.* Euan had fought bravely and won, but only because Donas forced him to. She recalled the tale Euan had told of Silas's attack on Erik and how distraught Erik had seemed at her injury. Perhaps at least Thomas's words about Erik were true, and things would be very different at Ross now that Erik was in charge.

"I'm sorry, lass," the Munro said, at last, to Ella. "I must respect the rights of a husband to claim his wife. Go with him." Then he turned his gaze to Thomas. "Munro will visit from time to time to see that Ella is treated well. Ye will welcome my men, or there will be trouble between Munro and Ross, and I will no' regret that. But ye will."

Muireall gasped and Ella choked out, "Nay!" then broke into sobs as Thomas nodded, grasped Ella's arm and led her away. Everyone in the hall remained silent and frozen in place until they were gone. Then a low rumble punctuated by angry shouts filled the hall.

"Wheesht!" The Munro's voice broke through the noise.

Muireall collapsed onto a bench Euan led her to and waited for the hall to settle. Calum joined them, his fists clenched, his skin red, fury glinting in his eyes.

"'Tis done, and Ella's husband has claimed her. But Munro will send men to ensure her well-being. We can do nay more, as ye ken fine, without risking a war that will burn its way around the entire firth. If—and only if—it is proven that Ella is mistreated, or both she and Thomas agree to divorce, will Munro act. Until such a time, I'll hear nay more about this." With those final words, he left the hall.

Muireall, sick to her stomach, looked to Euan. "I canna believe he let her go."

Euan shook his head, helpless fury written in his eyes as his gaze stayed pinned to where Thomas had disappeared with Ella. "He had nay choice, lass." His tone was milder than the rage pouring off him, evident in the set of his shoulders and his clenched fists. "Ella kens what's at stake or she would have fought Thomas. Instead, she went with him." He tightened his clenched fists, then opened them and nodded. "She's a braw lass."

"I dinna like it," Calum interjected. "We shouldha done something to save her."

"None of us like it," Euan replied. "Least of all Ella, but she did as her laird—and her husband—bade her do."

"What choice did she have?" Muireall demanded. "Her own laird gave her away."

"None, really. Nor did yer da." He turned and took Muireall's hand. Heat poured off him, confirming the fury she'd seen in his bearing. "That makes her no less braw. I do believe Thomas will make certain she stays safe and well." He sighed, as if releasing some of his anger. "He kens what's at stake, too."

❧

DESPITE THE ASSURANCES HE'D GIVEN MUIREALL AND Calum earlier, Euan was still furious about the circumstances of Ella's departure. He'd seen Muireall settled, then hauled Calum outside for some swordplay to work off the anger burning through both of them. Calum left when they finished, but Euan stayed to watch over some of the younger lads as they practiced. Finally, he decided it was time for an ale and headed through the bailey toward the entrance to the keep.

"Leave me be!" A young lad's voice drew Euan around the corner of the Munro tannery. He stopped, dismayed by the scene before him. Georgie had his back to the adjacent wash house. Laundry hanging on lines between the buildings screened him from view by anyone in the main part of the bailey. But this little back corner was perfect for what the three lads surrounding him had in mind.

"Ye runt," one of them taunted. "We've got ye now."

Georgie made a break for it, trying to run through them, but one of them tripped him and he went down hard. Euan stepped forward as they started kicking him, but Georgie grabbed one lad's leg and pulled him down, too.

He fell over Georgie, some protection from his friends' boots until he reared up and starting punching Georgie in the head.

Georgie rolled to his side and his arms flew up, protecting his eyes and ears, but that left his belly exposed.

Euan roared. "Get off him." He surged forward and grabbed the two lads on their feet, held one of their arms in one massive hand, and picked up the other lad by the scruff of his neck and let him dangle from his shirt, feet kicking.

Georgie rolled to his feet, breathing hard, nose bloodied.

Euan was certain he would be painfully bruised. "Get ye to the healer right away," Euan told him. "She can treat what needs treating. Then get in the loch—the cold will help the bruises."

Georgie nodded and went on his way.

Euan set the third lad on his feet but wasn't fool enough to let go. He slammed all three against the wall where they'd trapped Georgie. "Names," he demanded.

"Killer," one announced.

"Bone-breaker," said another.

"Cock s—" the third started.

"Shut it," Euan growled. "Since ye think 'tis a game to beat up wee lads, and since ye lack the honor to admit who ye are, let's see if the Munro recognizes the cowards who attacked his son, aye?"

Two of the boys suddenly deflated, but the third lifted his chin. "He willna do anything to us. We be the future of this clan."

"No' if I kill ye first." Euan jerked all three beside him and marched them out into the bailey, trailing shirts and pants some poor lass would have to wash again. "If ye three are the future, this clan is in trouble," Euan muttered and dragged them to the keep. At the door, he faced a quandary. He couldn't let any of them go to free a hand and open it. He shook the lad in his left hand. "Open the door."

"I dinna wish to."

"Open it, or I'll throw ye through it."

"Ye canna. The door is too thick."

Euan swung his arm back as if readying to throw. The lad in his hand fell back with it.

"I'll do it," the lad announced and reached for the handle.

Someone else opened the door at that moment and tried to step outside, but Euan and his charges blocked the way.

"Excuse us," Euan said mildly as the lads struggled to break free of his hold. "Could ye tell me where the Munro is?"

The man pointed toward the laird's solar without a word, then stepped back.

Euan entered with his three charges and marched them through the great hall, accompanied by the titters of the serving lasses working there. All three lads turned red. Good. Euan wouldn't hurt them, despite what he threatened, but he wasn't above embarrassing them to their toes.

When they reached the door of the laird's solar, Euan nodded to the third lad and the lad opened the door without Euan having to say a word. He tossed all three into the room, stepped in and closed the door behind him. With his back to it, the three were not going anywhere.

"What's this?" The Munro stood and took in the defiant expressions on the lad's faces.

"I caught these three..."

"How dare ye?" The Munro rounded on Euan. "Tossing Munro lads into my solar as if they are common..."

"Thugs?" Euan interrupted, knowing the Munro was still seething over having to let Ella go with Thomas Ross. "A cowardly mob, beating up a younger, smaller—lone—lad?"

"What?" The Munro turned back to the three. They took to studying the floor.

Though they'd been caught at the worst possible time, given their laird's frustration and fury, Euan had no sympathy for them. "I caught them beating Georgie. They cornered him behind the tannery. I sent him to the healer."

The Munro looked stunned. "Is he..."

"He'll be fine. He fought bravely, but these three against a smaller lad—'twas no' a fair fight."

"We're just trying to toughen him up," the mouthy lad spoke up. "He willna face just one opponent on the field of battle."

"But he'll be bigger and stronger and *trained* when he does," Euan snarled. "Ye lot have dishonored yourselves today, and from what I understand, ye have done so many times before I caught ye just now."

Another of the lads snorted and spat at Euan.

He must have forgotten the Munro was in the room. Muireall and Georgie's father came from behind his worktable and grabbed the lad by the ear.

"All of ye will spend the next year mucking out the stables and keeping the bailey clean." He shook the lad by the ear, then let go and moved to the next. "If I see one steaming pile of shit in the yard, ye will wear it for the next week." Then he moved to the leader of the trio. "And if any of ye touch another wean—lad or lass or beast—I'll throw ye in the dungeon for a month, covered in horse shit, and let the rats show ye what it feels like to be tormented." Then he stepped back and clenched his fists. "As tempted as I am to give ye a taste of yer own medicine, I willna stoop to yer level. But if I see a scratch, a bruise, an unhappy expression, on any bairn in this clan—ever again—I will blame ye, and ye will suffer the consequences. Now get out. Ye have work to do."

The three filed past Euan, but the leader couldn't resist one last smirk. Euan's hand whipped out and caught him around the neck, firmly but more gently than he deserved. "Dinna mistake yer laird, lad. And dinna mistake me. Whatever ye get from him, I'll give ye'll twice over. And unlike him, I have no compunction against beating ye senseless. So mind yerself. Oh, and fair warning. Sometimes those wee lads grow into the largest and strongest of men." Then he moved his hand to the middle of the lad's back and shoved him toward his friends.

In his haste to get away, the lad tripped over his own feet and sprawled full-length on the floor.

"'Tis just a taste," Euan added as the lad picked himself up and glanced around, eyes wide, then hastened out of the solar.

"'Tis the first time I've seen that ruffian look scared," the Munro announced with a satisfied smirk. "Thank ye for bringing them here and not just giving them what they gave Georgie." He returned to his seat and collapsed into it with a sigh.

"Of course. 'Twas no' my place to punish them. 'Twas their laird's, though I was no' above scaring them a bit."

"Muireall has tried to tell me what was going on—many times, but I thought she exaggerated. Lasses and their soft feelings, ye ken. I shouldha listened. If a warrior such as ye thought the lads went too far, then I have to believe it."

"Ye can believe it. And though I was tempted, I didna hurt any of them. Despite my threats, I'll leave any future punishment up to ye. I willna be here to see to it."

"Oh, they'll be punished. They're too proud by far—two are sons of my tacksman. The mouthy one is the blacksmith's lad. Cleaning up after the horses is just what they need. Georgie needs toughening, but in training. No' by the likes of those three."

Euan nodded. "But once I leave, the bullies will still find ways to torment him. The trouble isna over, it has just gone underground even deeper."

The Munro nodded as if coming to a decision, then spoke. "Would ye consider taking the boy under yer wing by fostering him at Brodie? Along with the Brodies who were here earlier and spoke so highly of ye, my daughter tells me ye are a man of morals, courage, and skill. Ye'd make a fine example for the boy to follow." He gestured with one open hand. "Get him away from those three and any more like them. At Brodie, he can grow and train as a lad ought. And his presence will have the added benefit of strengthening the ties between our clans."

Euan didn't want to refuse. The opportunity was good on several levels. But he still had a concern. "And if Ross still wishes to take revenge for Donas?"

"Then every clan around the firth will be drawn into the fight. He'll be no safer here than at Brodie. Less, if those lads think they can still get away with bullying him."

Euan nodded. "I see yer point." And he knew all too well how easily that could happen.

The Munro hesitated, then added "I see another motive as well. It will also make my daughter more inclined to join ye at Brodie, aye? With her charge also there?"

Euan grinned. "Ye are a wise man, indeed."

"Then think on it. But ye must decide before ye must leave."

CHAPTER 20

Muireall entered her father's solar, expecting to find him alone. The lad he'd sent as messenger told her he'd summoned her for a private meeting. Yet there stood Euan and Georgie. Euan looked pensive, but Georgie looked positively radiant—except for the new bruises decorating his face.

"What happened?" she demanded, moving to her younger brother and studying his features. He was so dear to her it hurt her, too, when the bigger lads beat him. If she was bigger and stronger, she'd put a stop to it—make sure those lads found out how it felt to be smaller and weaker and outnumbered. So far her father had refused to believe her, saying young boys fought and got banged up all the time. He didn't see it as anything unusual or worrisome. Every time it happened, she wanted to scream, but she feared if she gave full vent to her frustration, her father would send Georgie away rather than dealing with the troublemakers. She couldn't bear to lose him.

Georgie opened his mouth to answer, but Euan spoke first. "I came upon three lads beating him, and brought the proof to yer laird."

"Three?" She turned, aghast, to her father, who shrugged.

"They willna be a problem any longer."

That was supposed to be an apology? Muireall's eyes narrowed. "After all the times I've told ye, only *now* ye believe, and only because Euan tells ye?"

"And because he dragged the three who were doing it into my presence. *Dinna fash.* They're getting well acquainted with horse…droppings…as we speak."

Muireall fought to control the mounting pyre of outrage threatening to burst from her. She'd fought for so long to protect her brother, and had been met with her father's indifference and platitudes. Now that he'd seen the proof Euan offered, that was the best punishment he could think of? "Shoveling out stalls is supposed to teach them a lesson?" She couldn't believe her ears. She thought he finally understood the seriousness of the threat to his youngest son. "Those lads deserved time in stocks…or the lash." She choked on the last word.

Euan cut a sharp glance to her, then to her father.

She shook her head. She didn't want hers mentioned in front of Georgie. She was no longer in danger. Georgie was.

"Well, as to that, I have agreed to consider a different course of action." Her father fidgeted for a moment, then caught her gaze and spoke. "I'm thinking of fostering Georgie at Brodie. If the Brodie agrees, he'll be trained and live there for seven years."

Muireall's knees went weak.

Euan moved quickly to put a chair behind her, then took her elbow and lowered her into it.

She shook off his hand. "Nay…" Suddenly she couldn't get her breath. Something was squeezing her chest and a rock had lodged in her throat.

"'Tis for the best, daughter, and well ye ken it. But

dinna fash. If he doesna thrive there, the Brodie will send the lad home. And ye may visit him, of course."

She turned, blinking back tears, to Georgie, who came and hugged her. The smile he'd worn when she entered had been replaced by an expression too solemn for one so young. "I wish to go, Muireall," he told her. "Euan will train me to fight. And he says someday, I may be as big as he is. He's going to help me grow like he did."

Like he did? What did that mean? Euan's gaze was on the floor, but his cheeks and nose were unusually pink. "What does he mean, Euan?"

He lifted his gaze to her and shrugged. "I was once like Georgie, the smallest lad the others picked on. I surprised the hell out of them when I returned from fostering. Bigger and stronger than the lot. I ken what Georgie has been through. I want to help him."

Muireall wiped her eyes. Was there no end to the good and noble things Euan was willing to do for her and for her clan? Yet, she could not bear to lose Georgie this way. She'd just gotten back to him, and he'd been so overjoyed she was home...but her feelings didn't matter. Sending him with Euan was the best thing they could do for him. She gave him a tremulous smile, then turned her gaze to her father and nodded.

"Well then, now that's settled, lad, ye should go make sure ye are packed and ready. Go on with ye, now."

"Ye are leaving today?" she asked Euan.

Georgie gave Muireall another hug, then clasped hands with Euan. When he did the same with his father, Muriel was certain her heart would break. Her young lad would go away and come back nearly grown. Nay, she didn't know how she would bear it, but she must find a way.

"Aye, 'tis time." His gaze bored into her.

She knew he was asking, without words, whether she was ready to go with him. She wasn't! How could he expect her to leave home so quickly? Her world and everything real to her had been stolen by Ross raiders. By Donas Ross's punishment marking her back. She hadn't yet found the lass she used to be, the responsible one, the caretaker, the laird's eldest. She was home, but she didn't yet recognize herself in it. She'd lost who she was, even to the man now staring at her, waiting for her to say something, to nod. She wanted to, but she couldn't.

"Is that all we need to discuss?"

Muireall lifted her gaze to her father's in surprise, but he wasn't looking at her. His question had been directed at Euan.

Euan pursed his lips then shook his head, all while keeping his gaze fixed on her. "Aye, that's all...for now."

Her father expected Euan would also ask for her hand. Yet he'd just failed to do so. She wanted to clamp a hand over her mouth to hold back a cry of despair, but instead she held herself stiff and silent, her gaze on the hearth, rather than on the two men. What about their promises at the ancient stone? Had he forsworn them so easily? She needed time at home, but not forever. She needed Euan, too.

Her father waited a beat, then nodded. "Thank ye for yer care this day of my son. Godspeed back to Brodie."

Muireall should be going back with him, too, but she'd failed to nod, to tell him she was ready, so he didn't offer for her. After all that had passed between them, she didn't know why. She'd thought he would agree to be betrothed. She thought she'd have some time. Instead, she had no choice but to watch him take Georgie away. She knew it was for Georgie's own good, but losing both of them at once slew her.

She forced herself to her feet and followed Euan out of the laird's solar and across the great hall. When he stepped outside, she came out behind him. "Are ye going to leave without Georgie?" She glanced around, expecting to see him.

"Nay. I told him earlier to meet me here. What do ye really want to ask me?"

He was too perceptive by far. Muireall looked around her, taking in the keep, the people, the sights she thought she might never see again. She took a breath and turned to Euan. "Ye have brought me home. 'Twas the last obligation ye felt ye had to discharge after the shipwreck."

Euan paled, then colored, but she didn't let his reaction to her reminder about the *Tangie* and what followed stop her. "But 'tis no' the last promise ye made to me. How can ye just leave?" She would not beg him to stay. She was the daughter of a laird. She would *not*.

"I must, as well ye ken."

"Why?"

His gaze shifted to the sky above the keep's walls and he studied for several endless moments. Muireall held her breath, not sure what she wanted to hear him say. Finally, he dropped his gaze to her face and gave her a lopsided smile that nearly broke her heart.

"I've done what I promised, lass, and carried ye home, where ye need to be. 'Tis time for me to go. I must do what ye said ye wished for, what I promised, and leave ye here...unless ye have changed yer mind?"

Muireall swallowed and wrapped her arms around her middle. She wanted them around Euan, but she could not do that, not here. Not now. "So suddenly? We've barely arrived. Why must ye return to Brodie so soon? I never dreamed ye would take my brother with ye." Muireall did her best to put her heart in her eyes, if not in her words. She'd lost Ella. She wasn't ready to lose Georgie. She'd just gotten back to him. Or for Euan to leave. He'd been such a big part of her life since that fateful day on the beach. How would she go on without him?

"Ye dinna need me." He ran the back of a curled finger down her cheek.

"I do," she protested. Normally, his touch would have heated her skin, but she'd gone too cold to give rise to those kinds of feelings.

"Ye have yer clan, yer friends, yer family...yer home. Wee Georgie will be safe and well cared for. That is everything ye said ye wanted. I'm happy for ye, lass. I am."

He didn't look happy. He looked like he was putting a brave face over the heartache he really felt. Or was she just hoping for that? "I do need ye. More than ye ken." Everyone she cared about was deserting her, taken away or leaving by their own will, despite how she'd fought to get back to them.

"Ye are just sad to see me go. Once my sail is out of sight, ye will forget all about me."

"Nay, never. If only ye could give me some time..."

"My clan needs me, too. Iain does. I canna stay and turn my back on them..."

"Yet 'tis my place to turn my back on mine," Muireall answered, tensing with irritation at his statement. How could she get angry with him, now of all times? But why was a woman always the one to leave her home and family? A man could do the same, if he wished, couldn't he?

But nay, Georgie must go, and Euan must take him. To keep the lad safe.

She pressed her lips together and gazed aside at the keep around them. The water was too far away to see. She needed to be home! After a month living in fear and pain at Ross and after more time at Brodie, she needed to feel normal, to be in a place she knew like her own skin, seeing people she'd grown up with, family she loved. Yet weren't Georgie and Euan family to her, too? It wasn't fair. She felt as trapped as she'd been in that cove. Only this time, Euan refused to rescue her.

It was her fault he hadn't offered for her when her father gave him the chance.

Georgie came out then, a bundle in his arms—all his worldly possessions.

She ruffled his hair, then lifted her gaze to Euan's face. He was frowning at her. "Go, then, if ye must," she told him, being as brave as she could for Georgie's sake. "It is as ye say. I will be fine. All that I longed for is here. Save this wee man." Georgie ducked out from under her fingers.

Euan's eyes widened and his head tipped back as if she'd struck him. "All?" He clamped his lips shut as if he hadn't meant for the word to slip out, and his expression hardened. "Send for me if ye ever change yer mind, Muireall. Until then, I wish ye well."

She couldn't respond. Her throat closed up, choking off anything she might have said to make him go back to her father to claim her hand, then take her with him as his wife. She could only look at him, trying to memorize every dear feature, every line on his sun-bronzed skin, every lock of his russet hair. His eyes, now the green of impure glass. His lips. She sucked in a breath. "Kiss me goodbye," she managed to whisper.

Euan studied her for a moment, as if he, too, was trying to commit her face to memory. "I dinna think so," he said.

Agony filled her chest as her heart shattered into a thousand pieces. He would deny her even that last bit of comfort.

"'Twould hurt too much," he said softly, then turned

away and collected Georgie, who'd wandered off while they talked. In moments, Euan, with Georgie at his side, walked through the gate. Out of her life.

The lad turned back and waved. Euan did not.

Muireall shivered and wrapped her arms around herself, but found no warmth. She might never be warm again. At least she would be spared watching Euan's sail disappear over the horizon. Still, she stood, stiff as the high timber walls around her, staring, long after they disappeared, tears she'd fought to deny in Euan's presence finally running freely down her cheeks.

EUAN HAD BEEN GONE ONLY HOURS, BUT MUIREALL missed him more than she ever dreamed possible. Now that she knew her clan and her younger brother were safe, she realized the home she'd yearned so strongly to return to while a captive of the Ross clan and while a guest at Brodie had lost its appeal. She'd romanticized the day-to-day and now the reality didn't…couldn't… match her homesick longings. Nor could she find herself here. The lass she'd been was gone forever. She'd never be whole away from Euan. He held her heart.

Euan was gone, and with him, all her illusions.

Riding seemed to be her only solace, though it did not give her the solitude she craved. Her father insisted two Munro warriors follow as her escort. She spent the time attempting to practice what Annie had taught her, but her unhappy thoughts kept her from focusing as she should. Finally, she shrugged and wrapped her arms around her middle, accidentally jerking the reins. Her mount reacted with an annoyed whinny and a twitch of its ears. Embarrassed, Muireall patted its neck and glanced at the men following her.

Her escort kept their distance. She hoped they hadn't noticed.

She'd expected a homecoming of a different sort, a happier sort. Yet, as it was, some of the clan eyed her with suspicion. They did not believe she'd remained untouched.

She belonged with Euan. Why oh why hadn't she been satisfied when the men Iain had sent returned to tell her all was well, and that her clan now knew she was safe and cared for. But no, she had to see for herself. Once she'd seen the reality of Donas Ross's lies, she should have realized there was nothing for her here. She should have begged Euan to stay, or to take her back with him. But she'd been unable to think and barely able to speak. It had happened too fast, too suddenly.

She knew her father would broach with Iain the subject of a marriage alliance, since he had handed his youngest son over to Euan for safe-keeping and training. Yet she couldn't ask. Euan had the chance while speaking to her father and had not offered for her. And even though Euan had told her to send for him if she changed her mind, begging for him to return so quickly would be disgraceful.

She would be hard pressed to find a man willing to risk taking her to wife, but it didn't matter. She wanted only Euan.

Yet he'd refused to kiss her as he left. His final words still cleaved her chest like the blade of a claymore. *'Twould hurt too much.* He cared. Just not enough to see through her hesitation, claim her, and make her his.

If only he knew he'd taken her heart with him to the other side of the Moray firth.

❧

Muireall didn't wonder at the summons from her father the next day. He often called for her when he wanted to talk through an idea or find out what was going on in the clan that others would not tell him. But when she entered his solar, one look at his expression told her this would not be a typical discussion between them.

The Munro stood behind his work table, fists planted on the surface, mouth set in a grim line.

Muireall suddenly felt seven years old again and wondered what she'd done wrong this time.

"Take a seat if ye will, daughter."

Without a word, she sat and folded her hands in her lap.

"I ken this news may no' be welcome, but an opportunity has presented itself and I believe it is a good one."

Muireall's heart dropped into her belly. Surely he couldn't mean what she greatly feared he was leading up to. She kept silent and reacted only with a frown.

Her father straightened at that and crossed his arms. "I've received a query from Dubh Gordon," he said and paused as if waiting for her to say or do something.

Normally she might have stormed out of his solar at the mention of the Gordons. But the last month and more had not been normal. She didn't want to hear the rest, but knew she must.

"Go on."

"'Tis as ye might suspect, a betrothal proposal. He's asking for yer hand, lass."

"A Gordon. Ye ken how I feel about them after a Gordon cousin withdrew his offer for my hand three years ago when he found a lass more to his liking."

"I do."

"Do ye think this Gordon kens what happened...

with the Rosses…?"

"Nay, and he'll have to be told, else his first look at yer back will mean trouble for ye and Munro. And Ross, most likely. As hard as we've worked to settle things with Ross, I dinna wish to start a war with Gordon."

"Aye, after his clansman embarrassed me as he did, we'd have no reason to promise damaged goods to another Gordon in retribution." She didn't bother to hide her sarcasm with a polite tone.

Her father sighed. "Ye are no' damaged goods, Muireall."

"Nay? Euan did no' offer for me when ye gave him the chance."

"I felt certain he would do so before he left for Brodie. But he didna, so that still leaves the matter of finding ye a good husband. And making a good alliance for Munro."

Muireall got to her feet. "Aye, *there's* the thing ye're after."

"Dinna scold me, daughter. Ye ken I must. 'Tis my responsibility as laird."

"And mine as the laird's daughter." She took a few steps toward the door, then reconsidered. Without Euan, what choice did she have? "So tell me about this Dubh Gordon."

"He's chief of a sept to the east."

"Practically a lowlander, is that what ye're telling me? What, is he toothless but rich? Or still a lad in wean's breeks?"

"Neither. He's older than Euan, younger than I."

"That's a pretty wide range, Da. Erik Ross is sounding better and better."

"I can arrange that if that is what ye wish."

"Nay, ye canna. Erik will wed Fiona Rose, or the peace the Brodie brokered with Rose and MacBean will fall apart. And if Munro gets into it, we'll just complicate an already precarious balance."

Her father lifted his hands in the age-old gesture of surrender. "What would ye have me do, daughter?"

"Tell him nay. Tell him to tell all Gordons with designs on a Munro lass to look elsewhere. I'll no' have him."

"Ye must marry someone."

"Must I? The one I want doesna want me enough to ask my father for my hand." Despairing beyond words, she left the solar and stalked out to the bailey, determined to work off the emotion clogging her throat. She had only herself to blame for why Euan hadn't offered for her. It was her fault, after all. She had done such a thorough job of convincing him she needed to be at Munro that he couldn't conceive of taking her away from the home she'd longed for. Not to mention she'd kept from him who she really was. Perhaps if he'd had time to accept her station, things would have gone differently.

Archery practice was underway in the yard. Perfect. She picked up and tested several bows, then lined up with the rest of the lads and picked her target. shocking the lads and the arms master, who started her way. But she quickly demonstrated her prowess, hitting the center of her target again and again in quick succession. He stopped in his tracks, mouth as agape as those of the rest of his trainees. Calmer, Muireall nodded to him, set her bow aside and walked sedately back into the keep. Once the door closed behind her, she clenched her fists and fought back a shout of triumph. Thank ye, Annie! She understood why Annie had wanted to show off a bit before they went inside that evening. It felt so good.

She missed Euan, but she could make a life without him. Georgie needed him more.

CHAPTER 21

$\mathcal{E}$uan sat with Calum and Eduard by the hearth in the great hall after most of the rest of the clan had left for their beds. He'd been drinking steadily since the evening meal ended, but it wasn't helping. Nothing did. He couldn't stand it any longer. He missed Muireall with everything in him. A handful of days had reduced him to moping about the keep, snarling at anyone who came near, then drinking himself to sleep at night.

Fortunately, Annie had taken charge of Georgie. Seeing him only reminded Euan of Muireall, and that hurt more than he could bear.

"I'm tired of carrying yer miserable arse up those steps," Eduard complained with a sideways glance at Calum. "If he didna have a busted wing, I'd let *him* do it."

"But ye see I canna," Calum groused. "And Eduard shouldna. Ye have to stop this." He kicked at Euan's outstretched leg with one booted foot. "Ye've gone barmy since leaving the lass with her kin. 'Tis no' so far. Go see her. Hell, offer for her. If she's in a state anything like the one ye're in, she'll be so glad to see ye, she'll accept before she comes to her senses."

The idea had its appeal. Euan lifted his glass and sniffed. Whisky fumes filled his nose and made him cough. He set the glass aside, suddenly disgusted with it. He turned his head to his shoulder and inhaled. Ale and stale sweat. Disgusted with himself, he finally heard what Calum and Eduard had been telling him since he left Muireall behind. He'd grieved long enough. Time to make a decision. He could see only two paths—get on with his life without her or go after Muireall and make her his.

He stood, surprising both his companions. "Sod off," he told them. "I'm going to bed. I'll go after her in the morning."

The next morning, Euan awoke with a clear head, Calum's words still ringing in his ears. His friend was right. Going to Muireall, asking for her hand was the only solution to the *dreich* mood he'd been in since he left her at Munro. He threw off the covers and dressed quickly.

He found Iain and Annie breaking their fast in the laird's solar, documents on the table between them. Annie noticed him first.

"Euan, good morrow to ye."

"What is it?" Iain asked, not unkindly. "I'm ready for a distraction from these tallies of the catch and the harvest." He glanced at Annie. "We've enough to get us through the rest of the winter, and to have a small Candlemas feast. Talk to Cook and see what she can do."

Annie stood. "I will." She gathered up the parchments and patted Euan on the arm on her way out.

"So," Iain said, leaning back in his chair, "this is the earliest I've seen ye since ye returned from Munro. Has the whisky finally lost its appeal?"

"It has," Euan agreed. "But no' the lass. I need to go back. To fetch her. Marry her. With yer permission."

Iain studied him, then nodded. "Ye have it. Muireall is a braw lass. Ye could do much worse."

"I hope I willna have to. I told her to send for me if she changed her mind about staying at Munro. She hasna done so, but perhaps she needs some encouragement." Euan smiled for what seemed like the first time in days. The first he recalled, anyway. "I'll take Calum and a few others with me. With luck, we'll be back with her before ye ken we've gone."

"See to it, or we'll come looking for ye."

"There's another thing…"

"Aye?" Iain cocked an eyebrow.

Euan knew he was surprised he hadn't gotten out as quickly as Iain said 'aye.' "Now Georgie is here, ye havena changed yer mind about fostering him, have ye? The Munro will want a report." He pursed his lips. "I ken I havena looked after him as I should…but Muireall might be much more willing to agree if Georgie remains here. She was so determined to get back to him at Munro, I was surprised to walk away with him so easily. Still, he'll grow and get stronger away from the lads who were tormenting him. If he's anything like I was, he'll surprise the hell out of them in a few years. I look forward to seeing that."

"I'd forgotten what a runt ye were as a lad. It took ye a while to grow into yerself."

"It did. I was small for my age until I had thirteen summers, then I grew so fast my bones hurt all the time. That or it was the training auld Dougal put us through." Euan paused, sadness filling him. The man's son, Dougal Og was still missing from the *Tangie*. Euan could only think he'd drowned. "At any rate, ye ken how I was teased until I started getting too big and too strong for the other lads to take on. I get the impression the treatment Georgie has gotten has been worse. Muireall will be relieved to have him away from there until he grows. The Munro agrees, of course, or he would be there now."

"It seems an equitable solution to several problems —and desires. I agree."

Euan nodded, flashed a grin and got out as fast as he could. He didn't want to give Iain time to reconsider.

WITH IAIN'S BLESSING IN HAND, EUAN MADE USE OF THE tub and donned clean clothes. Then he, Calum and a few others took a boat across the Moray firth and into the Cromarty to Munro. He had to get Muireall back if he had to crawl from the seashore to her door to do it. The hike to the Munro village seemed to take forever, but when they arrived, Euan had no doubt the trip was worth it.

Muireall saw him as they entered the keep. She ran to him. His heart clenched in his chest as she fell into his arms. "Marry me, lass," he murmured, lacking the wit to even greet her. He had to get those words out first. "I canna live without ye. These last days have been torture worse than anything Donas Ross could have devised. I missed ye more than I ever thought possible to miss anyone," he added.

"And I missed ye, Euan Brodie. I've been so lonely without ye. Without ye, it took me only hours to realize there's nothing here for me anymore, nothing more important than ye."

"I ken I refused to kiss ye before I left Brodie. Would ye..."

"Aye, I would," she interrupted him.

Euan obliged and quickly lost himself in the feel of her lips, the scent of her skin and breath, the warmth of her body under his hands.

Calum came up and clapped Euan on the back,

breaking them apart. "I see it didna take you long to find the lass," he teased. "'Tis good to see ye again, Muireall. This poor sod has been wretched without ye."

"*Wheesht*," Euan warned.

"I've been miserable without him, too," Muireall said, moving her gaze from Calum to Euan and running her fingertips down the side of his face. "I'm glad ye have come," she added, then turned back to Calum.

But Calum wasn't looking at Muireall. Euan followed the direction of his gaze but saw nothing remarkable.

Calum turned to Muireall. "Ella has not returned?"

Muireall grimaced and Euan's belly clenched. "I'm sorry."

Calum's fists clenched and he stalked away, back toward their boat.

"Mostly, I'm sorry for him," Muireall told Euan.

"No' yer fault, lass. Better he hear it right away than get his hopes up."

"I think she was very much at sea—she didna miss Thomas, but I dinna believe she felt like she fit in at home anymore, either. Perhaps now that Erik is in charge at Ross, Thomas will turn out to be what—or who—she needs."

Euan cocked an eyebrow. "Like I am what—and who—ye need?"

"Aye, Euan, that ye are." She laid a hand over his heart. "I never shouldha doubted it."

"I've more good news, but I must talk to yer da first."

"Aye? Well, let me take ye to him, then."

❧

A DAY LATER, MUIREALL DIDN'T KNOW SHE COULD BE SO happy. Though she was marrying during Candlemas, the memory of Silas's taunt the morning Muireall had been forced to strip and bathe in front of the entire clan had no power to upset her. A fire burned brightly in the great hall's hearth. Boughs of fir draped the mantle above it, interspersed with mistletoe from the surrounding forest, the only decoration available this deep in winter.

She and Euan stood in front of the hearth, she in her best dress, Euan in finery borrowed from a Munro near his size. Hand in hand, they faced each other, her clan forming a large semi-circle surrounding them. Hearing Euan pledge before them to love and honor her all the days…and nights…of their lives thrilled her as much as when he'd said the same at the ancient stone on Brodie land. She pledged the same to him. They kissed and it was done.

They were married in the old way. A wedding in the kirk would have to wait until they returned to Brodie, when its priest was in residence. Calum had returned without explaining where he'd been overnight, and stood with him, though an air of gloom hung around him.

"If only Georgie and Ella were here to celebrate with us," Muireall murmured.

Euan did not give her time to dwell on her friend's future. He pulled her to him and kissed her soundly again. More cheers erupted from the gathered crowd. Muireall laughed at the good-natured teasing, then pulled Euan forward to their seats of honor at the high table. Euan would take the laird's seat and she the chair reserved for the laird's wife, empty these long years since Georgie's birth. She'd warned Euan the feast could not start until they were in place, so he cooperated and came with her, only tugging her back into his arms for another kiss three times as they crossed the hall, then again before they took their seats.

At that, everyone else found a place and the servers carried out platters and trenchers and plates of food. Muireall sampled fish and venison and several varieties of fowl, cheeses, apples, bread spread with honey, wine and mead until she could take no more.

Finally, she leaned over to Euan and whispered in his ear, "Meet me on the beach."

His eyebrows arced in surprise. "'Tis a long walk on a cold night..."

She just smiled and left him to escape whenever he could. The wedding feast had been underway for hours and while Euan felt obligated to speak to every person and drink each toast to their happiness, Muireall had eaten and drunk more than enough. She'd been surrounded by a wall of conversation, music, and noise longer than she could stand. She needed the breath of air she'd find next to the firth as much as she needed Euan there with her.

She knew the gathered crowd would assume she'd gone to Euan's chamber to prepare for his arrival. Instead, she went to hers, put on her cloak and gathered up her spare plaid, a sheet and a woolen blanket from her bed. For a moment, she eyed the furs piled at its foot, knowing they'd provide warmth the blankets could not. But they'd be too heavy to carry, and they'd be too hard to clean if they got caked with sand or seawater.

She took a back stairway out of the keep to avoid the wedding feast. When she stepped outside, the chill took her breath for a moment, but she carried on, waving to the lone sentry as she passed out of the gate. He'd think her mad, and Euan even madder when he followed, but she didn't care. They would have years to make love in their chamber. Not so long ago, Euan had saved her from the waves. Tonight, she wanted him to claim her by them, as well.

Her burden had started to feel heavy by the time she reached the shore. She spread the plaid in a sandy spot, then lay the sheet over it. She wanted to carry proof of her innocence back to her clan. The sheet would do for that. Wrapped in her cloak, she draped the blanket over her as well and sat, watching the stars fall in the clear, cold winter sky.

Sooner than she expected, Euan arrived.

"Did ye run the whole way, then?" she asked with a smile and shared the blanket, letting him pull her back against his chest then wrap it around both of them.

He nodded, breathing hard for a moment, then heaved a great sigh. "I dinna think I'd be able to escape yer clan, but claiming the need to get rid of some ale did the trick. No one stopped me when I left the hall."

Muireall laughed and enjoyed the answering rumble of Euan's chuckle at her back.

"Ye have been watching the stars, I see."

"And the waves, as well. Did ye ken they glow in the darkness?" She turned her head to gaze up at him. "Aye, of course ye did."

"They seem to catch the faintest glimmer, be it starlight or a sliver of moon. One thing I've learned from Iain over the years…did ye ken he draws?" he began, "is that there is much in the world of great beauty." He kissed her temple. "Though none greater than my wife."

She tucked her head under his chin and pressed against him, considering. She'd always thought Ella the most beautiful, and still others more than she herself. But if Euan thought her a great beauty, who was she to gainsay him? "Thank ye, husband. Ye please me greatly as well."

"*Ach*, lass, I havena begun to please ye," he growled and shifted out from behind her. He lay her back on the sheet and stretched out beside her, then covered them both. "Though ye have picked a challenging spot...but I ken why ye have."

"Because of how ye saved me. It seems only fitting that ye..."

He gestured at the waves rolling onto the beach below them. "Make ye mine by them as well?" He nodded and cupped her cheek, then bent to kiss her. "That does seem fitting," he added when they came up for air.

She waved a hand, indicating the area around them. "'Tis almost as if we were alone in the cove again—only without the fear of drowning."

"Without the whole of clan Ross after us, either," he teased. "I like this beach much better." He let his hand trail down her throat. "I'll do my best to make certain we both enjoy what we do here."

She placed her hand over his and drew it down over her breast. "I ken what is to happen. I'm glad it will be with ye."

"As am I, love." He bent to take her lips again and whispered, "As am I."

Euan's hand slipped inside her cloak and warmed her through her dress, making her nipple bead and fire race from her breast to her core.

He trailed kisses down her throat and onto her chest, pulling down the neckline of her shift to lick and nuzzle even lower.

Her body softened as strange sensations raced to her fingers and toes, then back to the spot Euan's mouth covered. His warmth heated her skin, but went deeper, melting her muscles, her bones, leaving her pliant and empty. She needed him, needed his touch, his kiss, everywhere. What insanity had made her think this cold beach was a good idea?

"I would have yer first time be somewhere ye could be more comfortable, lass," he murmured as he reached for her skirts and smoothed them upwards. "But if this is what ye wish…"

"We have time for comfort later, husband," she told him. Her heart swelled over his concern for her. He'd done nothing but care for her since he'd pulled her from the waves. She should have known her choice of location for their tryst would disconcert him. "Ye ken my reasons…"

"I do. And I will do all I can to keep ye safe and warm…"

"As ye have since I met ye. Yer touch sets me ablaze, my love. I need nay more than that."

"Very well," he told her with a smile that lit her heart.

In a moment, she felt his hand on the skin of her thigh. She might have expected his fingers to be cold, but they were as warm as the rest of his body, now next to hers, his leg over hers, trapping her limbs, yet protecting them from the chilly wind leaking under the blanket by their feet.

"Ye are my beautiful bride," he told her as his hand slipped up her leg to the juncture of her thighs.

Muireall gasped as he feathered the curls he found there, then slipped his fingers into her private folds. She'd never felt a sensation so exquisite, or that made her ache so, hollow and empty and begging for Euan to fill her. She'd dreamed of this day forever, it seemed, and now it was happening, she never wanted it to end. Her body responded as he explored, making her moan and writhe under his hand until the stars over her head fell behind her eyelids. She arched on a long moan, then relaxed into Euan's arms, murmuring his name.

"Ye are ready for me, lass, with barely a touch. Such a treasure…"

He lifted up onto his hands and knees above her, nearly losing the blanket to the wind.

She grabbed it, draped it back over him, and tucked in the sides, pleased to find the wind had blown his kilt up with it, baring his lower body. She ran her hands over his backside and reveled in the flex of muscles underneath her palms. "Unlike yours, my hands are cold…" she apologized.

"Think nothing of it," he told her. "And dinna stop what ye're doing." He lowered himself between her thighs. "I will go as slowly as I can, but ye once said ye ken how it goes between a man and a woman."

"Aye, and that the first time can be painful. I'm ready."

He chuckled. "I ken ye are."

Something nudged between her legs. Something very hot, very firm. "Oh!" she said on an inhale. "That had best be ye and no' some creature of the sand."

He laughed at that, and she was surprised to find she could as well, despite the anxiety coiling in her belly.

"Ye ken it is. Now we begin…" He thrust, breaching her defenses only a little. She tensed, then relaxed into the unfamiliar but pleasant fullness. "'Tis no' so bad," she told him, warming.

"A bit more then," he said and filled her further.

Something twinged.

"I'm there, lass. The next bit will sting."

She nodded and he thrust through, filling her completely, then holding still while she sucked in one breath after another, fighting to make the pain subside. When, after a few breaths, it did, she wrapped her arms around his neck and kissed him. "Now I am yers, and none can say nay."

"That ye are, love, my wife. Mine, forever."

His words were sweet, but his voice sounded strained.

"Am I hurting ye?"

He chuckled at that, too. "Nay, but I want to move in ye. To bring ye pleasure after the pain. Are ye ready?"

She nodded, unsure.

He withdrew almost all of the way, then slid back inside. "Are ye well?"

"A little sore, but no' much. Try again."

He obliged, starting slowly, then building in speed and intensity. Her body responded, surprising her when the pain faded and pleasure began to take its place. It built and built with each of Euan's thrusts until she only knew Euan's voice, his scent, and the heat and size of his body where they joined together. Gone were the waves, the wind, the cold. Her world consisted of Euan and the pleasure he brought her, until she could take no more and crested the wave of sensation he'd built. In moments, he, too, dived over, calling her name and filling her with wet heat as he thrust harder and deeper. Then he slowed, and stopped, breathing hard, sharing her breath, kissing her with a mindless abandon she could not have imagined before this night.

He collapsed onto her for a moment, then rolled to the side, pulled her against him and tucked the blanket firmly around her body and his. "Are ye well, lass?"

She draped a leg over his side and caressed his backside with her foot. "More than I ever kenned I could be, husband," she told him, then lifted her lips to his. "I'm with ye, after all."

❦

EUAN COULDN'T BELIEVE HOW OPEN AND GIVING AND willing and eager Muireall had been in his arms. She was everything he'd never dared dream for in a wife and lover. "Next time will be better," he promised, holding her close. "And warmer."

Her chuckle vibrated against his chest.

"Aye. In hindsight, this does seem to have been a daft idea."

"Nay, lass. 'Twas memorable. Something we'll be able to tell our grandchildren someday."

She stiffened for a moment, then relaxed and chuckled again. "What a thought to have now! Yet, we could..."

"Aye, we could. 'Tis possible, but no' likely. So if ye'd like to try again, let's gather all this up," he said and grabbed a handful of blanket, "and return to yer chamber. There, I can love ye as ye deserve to be loved. Slowly, gently, and at length. By a roaring blaze."

Muireall grinned and stretched her arms above her head, then rolled atop him. "I dinna ken whether I can walk so far," she said, then kissed him soundly. "No' yet, anyway."

CHAPTER 22

The next evening, Muireall was deep in conversation with Euan when the rumble of voices in the great hall changed. She glanced up but saw nothing amiss. Folk were eating their supper as usual. No one had come running from the kitchen. But the rumble was getting louder. That left only the door into the keep, behind her.

She suddenly realized the expression on Euan's face had changed. He was staring behind her, surprise and consternation drawing down his brow over widened eyes. She twisted around in her seat, then jumped to her feet. "Ella!"

Euan put a hand on her arm, holding her in place. "And Thomas. Something is wrong."

Thomas stood behind Ella, arms planted on his waist, frowning. "Ye are home. Look around ye. Everyone is fine. So tell me how long we must stay here for ye to get better."

Muireall blanched. Ella looked pale and thin and sad. Her heart broke for her friend. What had Thomas done to her?

The Munro stood, eating knife in hand, and called out, "Thomas Ross, what are ye doing here now, and what have ye done to yer wife. I warned ye to care for her."

"I heard ye." Thomas's retort was sharper than the blade in the Munro's hand. "And I tried to do as ye bid. But she was determined to return here." He cut his gaze to the Munro. "So I brought her." He turned back to Ella and his voice softened. "I feared for her life, so I brought her."

This whole time, Ella stood, frozen, staring across the great hall as if she'd never seen it before.

With a disgusted growl, the Munro left his place and made his way nearer the couple. Muireall joined him. Euan stayed by her.

"What has happened to ye, lass?" Hugh Munro's voice was gentler than Muireall had ever heard it, and his expression, as he studied Ella, sorrowful.

Ella still didn't speak, so Thomas spoke for her. He moved beside her and faced her.

"I kenned ye wanted to come home. Ye were sickening, not eating. I canna keep ye if ye are so set against being married to me. I have brought ye home as ye demanded, hoping yer laird can talk some sense into ye."

The Munro opened his mouth to speak, but Ella beat him to it.

"I'm sorry, Thomas, but nay. Ye stole me from my home and forced me to marry against my will. I...tried. To save our clans from war, I went with ye. But I will never agree to go back with ye again."

Thomas studied her for a long moment.

Muireall wondered what he was waiting for. Looking for. As he'd proven the last time he was here, he had every right to throw Ella over his shoulder and carry her out of the hall and back to Ross, no matter what she said. Muireall wanted to go to her friend, to stand with her, if not between her and Thomas.

But Euan knew her too well. He grasped her arm and held her in place.

Muireall narrowed her eyes at him, but kept her mouth shut.

The Munro remained silent, too.

Muireall expected he hoped the quarreling spouses would find a way to make amends without him. He would have to side with Thomas Ross, as he'd had to when he first took Ella away more than a week ago. Only Ella could save herself from this horrible situation, and only if she could convince Thomas to agree to let her go. Muireall doubted Ella expected any help from the Munro.

Thomas's voice pulled Muireall's attention away from glaring at her Da.

"Very well, then, Ella Munro, as long as ye dinna carry my child..."

She shook her head, embarrassment coloring her face as she clenched her fists. "I dinna. Ye ken I am bleeding."

"Then to save yer life, ye give me nay choice. I must give ye what ye want. I divorce ye, Ella Munro Ross."

Gasps echoed around the hall and to the rafters, but they didn't divert Thomas Ross's attention from Ella.

Ella pressed her lips together, then took a deep breath. "And I divorce ye, Thomas Ross."

Without saying anything else, Thomas studied her for another long moment. Then he turned to the Munro and spotted Euan and Calum beside him. His eyebrows lifted, but he kept his composure. "Ye will want to ken, Erik has gone to Rose to marry and collect Fiona Rose. We hear the MacBean once betrothed to her will now wed another Rose lass."

"That will do," the Munro responded.

Thomas nodded to him. "Ye will have no more

trouble on yer border with Ross. Nor," he added, with a frown at Euan, "will Brodie. The Ross laird has said so."

With that, he turned and left the keep.

Euan's gaze stayed on the door to the bailey, his eyebrows lifted in surprise.

Muireall could guess what he was thinking. Their plan worked and the crisis was over for now.

Through the open door, Muireall could hear Thomas calling to his men to mount up and go. She rushed forward and embraced Ella. "Ye are free!" She exhaled the breath she'd held since Ella had stood up to Thomas.

Ella stepped out of Muireall's embrace. "I am mortified that he did this...in this way."

"But ye must be relieved he will no longer pursue ye."

"I am relieved, aye. But I dinna ken what to do now." She glanced around at the faces surrounding her, most showing their surprise with raised eyebrows or dropped jaws. "I'm not sure I belong here anymore, either." With a cry, she made her way to the stairs and disappeared up them.

Muireall felt sorry for the lass, but had no idea what to do for her. As her friend, she would have to think of something, to be sure. Then she noticed the expression on Calum's face. He'd frozen when Thomas and Ella entered, but he'd perked up since she was freed.

"What are ye thinking?" Euan asked him.

"I'm thinking we canna leave for Brodie just yet. I need some time to woo that lass."

&

THE FOLLOWING DAY, MUIREALL GATHERED WHAT SHE would need of her belongings for the next few days, while Euan met with her father to make arrangements to carry the rest of her belongings to Brodie. Despite the fact that Ella still broke down and cried every few minutes, Muireall was thrilled for her. She might be exhausted and ill, but she was free of Thomas Ross, free of the Ross clan altogether. Ella went with her, down the stairs to the great hall, Ella helping her carry her bundles.

She couldn't fail to note the pleased expression on Calum's face as he approached them, Euan at his side.

"Are ye well, lass," he asked Ella.

She gave him an uncertain smile. "I will be."

"Why no' take a walk with me, then?" He held out his arm.

Shocked, Muireall looked from him to Euan, who nodded. So Euan had no concerns about Calum pursuing her friend? She thought back over her time at Brodie and how Calum had behaved, then nodded back. Nay, neither did she.

"But…" Ella objected, "ye were leaving for Brodie."

Muireall suddenly knew what she could do for her friend. "Aye," she said, "we were. We are. Why no' come to Brodie with us, as my companion? Some time away from Munro will do ye good."

Calum beamed at her. "Indeed. Ye must."

Ella looked from Calum to Muireall to Euan, then nodded. "Very well. Give me a few minutes to gather my things, and we'll go."

Euan took Muireall's hand. "There now, all will be well."

In a few minutes, Ella was back, a small bundle in her hands.

Euan took the Munro's arm. "We'll take good care of the lasses, sir. Georgie, too," he promised. Then he took Muireall's hand and led them out of the village, on the way to their boat and their future, across the firth.

EPILOGUE

"**C**an ye believe it? Annie's with child!" Muireall plopped down at the table in the great hall next to Ella, broke off a hunk of oatbread, and took a bite.

"'Tis taken her long enough," Ella remarked while Muireall chewed. "Aye, I heard the news this morning during the sewing circle. Which ye missed…again. I rarely see ye, and I'm supposed to be yer lady companion. Out riding?"

"Aye. Then archery practice with the younger lasses. Annie wants me to take over for her in a few months until after the baby comes. I still have a lot to learn before then."

"Ye must be thrilled. Since we returned to Brodie, ye've done little else—except closet yerself away with that handsome husband of yers. Are ye certain ye're no' expecting, too?"

"Nay, thank the saints. I'm too busy for that." A young cat jumped onto Muireall's lap. She smoothed its fur then scratched behind its ears. She couldn't believe everyone she cared about, everyone she loved, had returned to her. Even the kitten escape artist young Janie had asked her to fetch that first day she'd arrived at Brodie. It now followed her everywhere she went in the

274

village and keep. She and Euan were happily married. Calum was slowly finding his way through to Ella. Georgie was with her. Euan cared for and trained him as a young lad ought to be—with a firm but loving hand. She couldn't believe she once thought staying at Munro was the only way she could be happy.

"And she's having too much fun." Euan came up beside her and threw a leg over the bench, plucked the cat from her lap and set it on the floor, then settled at her back.

Muireall silently blessed him for saving her from having to explain to Ella that she wasn't avoiding her. Ella was spending a lot of time with Calum, and seemed happy for the first time since they'd been taken from Munro by Ross warriors. Muireall wanted to encourage that happiness. One good way was to make herself scarce so Ella had plenty of time to spend with Calum. She hoped one day they would be together. She was careful not to make an issue of it, which might make Ella avoid him.

"Ella," he greeted her friend. "Annie's news 'tis no' the only thing to set tongues wagging about this day."

Muireall turned to face him. "What could be more important than a Brodie heir on the way?"

"The Brodie heir Iain named until a Brodie heir is born. Kenneth, of course. That choice has surprised no one. If the wean's a lad, and God forbid something happens to Iain before the lad is old enough, Kenneth will hold the chieftainship for him and train the lad."

"What does that mean?" Ella asked.

"It makes Kenneth officially second in command to Iain, which leaves the position of arms master open." Euan grinned. "Iain just named a new one to replace him."

"Who?" Muireall asked, but from the expression on Euan's face, she was pretty sure she knew the answer.

"Me."

She threw her arms around his neck. "Oh, Euan, that's wonderful. Ye are perfect for it!"

"Aye. I have a wife who's doing her best to learn the job as well."

While Ella laughed, Muireall sat back with a snort and fixed her husband with a steely stare. "Dinna tell me now ye have the job, ye are going to object to training the lasses. I'll no' stand for it. Annie willna, either."

Euan held up both hands. "Nay, nay. Of course no'. Ye will keep training the wee lasses. When they get older, any who want to continue will train with the lads. The competition will do them all good."

"Euan! That's brilliant. But, *ach*, the Council will..."

"Do nothing. Iain, Kenneth and I are in complete accord. Annie and ye have demonstrated the value very well. Ye have won, lass."

Muireall glanced at Ella and grinned, then turned back to Euan. "Only the first of many..."

Euan kissed her, then leaned an elbow on the table. "We have reasons. Iain thinks trouble is coming. More archers, including the lasses, could make the difference in protecting the keep."

"But...I thought things were settled with Ross."

"Aye, they are. Erik Ross is no' the problem. We've long known we're caught twixt Domnhall of the Isles to the west and Albany in the south. Iain supported Annie's radical ideas with the Council for that very reason. In truth, he's been readying Brodie since he took over. And with James Rose, they've been building alliances with other clans. 'Tis one reason what happened with Ross—with ye—was so important to him. We couldna have an enemy so close by. Nor could Munro." He sat up and took Muireall's hand. "Whatever happens, Brodie willna stand alone."

READ THE NEXT BOOK IN THE SERIES

HIS HIGHLAND LOVE

A Love Denied

Kenneth Brodie offered for young Mary Catherine Rose but her father declined, then a year later accepted an offer from another clan. Furious at hearing Cat would be married soon to someone else, Kenneth fled to France and drowned his disappointment in wine, women and war.

A Love Lost

Two years after her father demanded they wait until Cat was older, she doesn't understand why Kenneth hasn't returned for her. Broken-hearted, Cat spurns yet another betrothal her father arranges and runs away to her cousin in St. Andrews, vowing never to marry.

A Love Worth Fighting For

By the time Kenneth returns home, trouble is brewing in Scotland. Sent to St. Andrews as hostage for his clan to the Regent, Kenneth resents being exiled—until he encounters his lost love, Cat Rose. When war breaks out, they must escape. And even though he betrayed her with more than one mademoiselle, he's the only man Cat trusts to get her home to the Highlands. Can she forgive his past and renew the love they once shared?

Keep reading for a sneak peek…

Catherine's crestfallen expression nearly swayed Kenneth from his purpose, but her safety was more important than how much he wanted her.

"What are ye doing here? Is yer husband with ye?" He kept his tone neutral, as though his question was only meant to be polite conversation, not a veiled expression of yearning from a man who hadn't seen her in much too long.

"My...? Nay, I am no' wed. I never have been, though Da has tried often enough. I came here to avoid his latest attempt."

The upwelling of joy in Kenneth's chest nearly overwhelmed him. He fought the urge to reach for her. "I heard ye were betrothed to a Makintosh."

"Among others. Da has tried three times to find an alliance with a husband I will accept." She crossed her arms and glanced around as if making sure they were alone. "The only husband I want...I ever wanted...is ye. So why did ye no' come for me? We had an agree—"

"Childish fancy," he said, cutting her off before her words could wound him any worse.

She blinked and took a step back.

She'd waited for him, fought her father to honor her

promise to him and his to her. All the while, he'd been fighting in France and bedding every willing mademoiselle who crossed his path. He swallowed, hard. He was not even worthy of her regard, much less her love.

"Ye thought any of that was serious?" The words burned his tongue. It hurt to speak the lie nearly as much as it probably hurt her to hear it. But Kenneth could not let her get involved with him again, not while he languished in Albany's care, and given his past, not ever. So he twisted the knife. "Ye were a wee lassie, and I no' much more grown."

Her lips thinned and a muscle in her jaw jumped. "And we are so much older now, aye? Or are ye so much more experienced that a lass like me can no longer satisfy ye…?"

Ach, Cat. Still spitting and hissing and going after what she wanted. She made him proud, and terrified him. He lifted his chin, but forced back the smile that threatened to undo every bit of distance he'd just fought to put between them.

"Aye, ye have the right of it," he answered, hating the way she seemed to shrink as his words penetrated. He softened his tone. "Heed me. Ye must no' be seen with me. I'm no' here because I wish to be. So flee, Cat. And dinna speak to me, or of me, again." She stiffened and opened her mouth to argue, so he forced past his lips the lie he feared he would always regret. "Yer da will do what is best for ye." He waved a hand as if pushing her away. "I never will."

Click Here to Buy His Highland Love

ACKNOWLEDGMENTS

When I decided to write and self-publish a new Highland historical series, there were several people whose support I absolutely had to have to make the series a success. My heartfelt thanks go out to my editor, Maureen Sevilla, my cover artist, Tamra Westberry, my Beta readers, Lisa Benton-Short and Laura Stephens, and last but never least, my husband, Laird Peter. Book One is done! On to the next!

ABOUT THE AUTHOR

Willa Blair is an award-wining Amazon and Barnes & Noble #1 bestselling author of Scottish historical, light paranormal and contemporary romance filled with men in kilts, psi talents, and plenty of spice. Her books have won numerous accolades, including the Marlene, the Merritt, National Readers' Choice Award Finalist, Reader's Crown finalist, InD'Tale Magazine's RONE Award Honorable Mention, and NightOwl Reviews Top Picks. She loves scouting new settings for books, and thinks being an author is the best job she's ever had.

Willa loves hearing from readers!
Contact her:
www.willablair.com
authorwillablair@gmail.com

Sign up for my Newsletter
Find links to the rest of my books

www.ingramcontent.com/pod-product-compliance
Lightning Source LLC
Chambersburg PA
CBHW010736130726
47899CB00015B/3278